READER'S DIGEST

Dead Good Read

READER'S DIGEST

Dead Good Read

21 Classic Tales of Mystery & Horror

THE READER'S DIGEST ASSOCIATION, INC.
PLEASANTVILLE, NEW YORK/MONTREAL

A READER'S DIGEST BOOK

Designed and edited by Eaglemoss Publications Ltd.

READER'S DIGEST PROJECT STAFF

Project Editor: Susan Randol
Senior Designer: Carol Nehring
Editorial Manager: Christine R. Guido

READER'S DIGEST ILLUSTRATED REFERENCE BOOKS

Editor-in-Chief: Christopher Cavanaugh
Art Director: Joan Mazzeo
Director, Trade Publishing: Christopher T. Reggio
Senior Design Director, Trade: Elizabeth L. Tunnicliffe

Library of Congress Cataloging in Publication Data

Dead good read : classic tales of mystery and horror.
p. cm.
Retellings of more than twenty classic horror tales from before the early twentieth century by such authors as Oscar Wilde, Mary Shelley, and Edgar Allan Poe.
ISBN 0-7621-0347-7
1. Horror tales. 2. Children's stories. [1. Horror stories. 2. Short stories.]

PZ5 .D323 2001
[Fic]—dc21

2001019228

Printed in Singapore.

1 3 5 7 9 10 8 6 4 2

Foreword

Classic tales of horror have frightened readers for generations, and they are no less terrifying now in a new millennium. Many of the best-known stories are familiar not just from books, but from movies and television as well, and some will probably not be so well known even though their authors are. Curl up and prepare to be scared as you read on ...

Contents

Introduction

Many of the most famous writers of the nineteenth century wrote scary stories, which have become classics of their kind. Popular authors like Charles Dickens and Robert Louis Stevenson loved weaving frightening, but moral, tales for their legions of readers, while Oscar Wilde put a characteristic amusing twist into his most famous ghost story, THE CANTERVILLE GHOST.

Mary Shelley wrote the classic story FRANKENSTEIN in 1818 and laid the foundations for the writers who came after her to tell tales of dread and horror with style and imagination. The best known stories, from DRACULA and THE PHANTOM OF THE OPERA to A CHRISTMAS CAROL and THE PIT AND THE PENDULUM, are included in this collection, together with some of the lesser known such as THE VIOLET CAR by E. Nesbit and THE OPEN DOOR by Charlotte Riddell.

These stories, all published by the early years of the twentieth century, give the reader a look into a vanished world—and a tingle up and down the spine.

Wolverden Tower

Retold from a story by Grant Allen

Maisie Llewelyn, a beautiful, dark-haired Welsh girl of 20, was on a train on her way to Kent. She was visiting Wolverden Hall, a magnificent manor house owned by her wealthy friends Colonel and Mrs. West. She sat thinking about the wonderful Christmas party the Wests had organized. Actors from London had been invited to take part in the tableaux that would form part of the evening's entertainment. Mrs. West met her at the station in a carriage, and soon they were rattling up the drive to the ivy-covered mansion.

"I hope you don't mind, you will be sleeping in a ground-floor room in the new wing," said Mrs. West as they went in. "The house is absolutely full for the weekend."

Maisie was delighted when she saw her lavishly decorated room and noticed the sturdy shutters on the windows which made her feel quite safe. She walked over to a tall window and admired the view. The village church was inside the grounds of Wolverden Hall, and Maisie was struck by the whiteness of its tower. As she and Mrs. West strolled out to the terrace and on toward the gate into the churchyard, Mrs. West explained that the church was very old. It had been built on the ruins of a Saxon place of worship. Her husband, she said, had recently had the tower rebuilt, which was why the stonework was so white.

The two women crossed the churchyard and went into the porch. An old lady was sitting on a bench there, muttering to herself. She didn't get up when she saw Mrs. West, but when she spotted Maisie her eyes lit up as if she recognized her. The old woman's stare made Maisie feel uncomfortable, so she turned and started to talk to her companion.

"This church is lovely," she remarked, "but it's a pity about the tower–it looks out of place."

"I'm afraid we had to rebuild it," replied Mrs. West. "It was in a dangerous condition."

"Lies! Lies! Lies!" mumbled the old woman from her bench. "It would never have fallen, for Wolverden Tower was protected thrice with the souls of maidens against attacks by Man or the Devil."

"Come on," whispered Mrs. West to Maisie, "we'll leave her to her rantings."

But Maisie did not seem to hear her and stood listening to the old woman, whose voice had risen to a high, quavering sing-song.

"It was protected at the foundations against earthquake and ruin," she chanted. "It was protected in the middle against storm and battle. It was protected at the top against thunder and lightning."

When she had finished this little speech, the woman got up and shuffled out of the porch. She pointed a skinny hand at the tower and called out, "That's what the rhyme says, see:

A thousand years the tower shall stand
Till ill assailed by evil hand.

Then she glanced back at Maisie with a hungry look, walked across the churchyard to a large stone burial vault, and sat down on a seat at the entrance.

Maisie shivered. "Who is she?" she asked Mrs. West.

"Her name is Bessie. The servants are afraid of her—they think she's a witch. But really she's just a pauper. She knows a lot of dreadful stories about Wolverden Church though, and she comes here almost every day. We offered her money and a house in Surrey if she would leave Wolverden, but she says she must stay with the bodies of her dead. She does frighten me sometimes, I must admit."

As Maisie and Mrs. West crossed the churchyard back to Wolverden Hall, they passed the vault. Maisie could see that Bessie now had her face pressed to the door and seemed to be whispering at it. They hurried back, and Maisie was glad to return to her comfortable room, where she changed into a simple white satin dress for dinner. She was much admired by the other guests, and a handsome Oxford student sat beside her as they waited for the tableaux to start.

A number of the guests, and several actors, took up their positions on a specially built platform for the first tableau, which

Underlined words are explained in **WORD POWER**.

was called *Jephthah's Daughter*. Dressed in various shades of gray and white, they re-created the moment described in the Bible when the daughter of Jephthah, accompanied by her maids, leaves her father's house. Her fate is to spend two months on a mountain before being offered as a sacrifice to God.

Maisie thought this was too sad a scene for such a happy occasion, but soon someone started to play the piano and entertain the audience with songs until the next tableau was ready. This showed a scene from the Greek story of Iphigenia, a beautiful young girl who was offered as a sacrifice by her father Agamemnon to the goddess Artemis. The dignified father stood beside the pyre, his eyes turned away from his terrified daughter, who was held by stern guards. Behind her stood a semicircle of maidens, dressed in flowing white gowns.

Maisie was immediately struck by the beauty of two graceful girls whose robes didn't seem to be Greek.

"Look at those two striking girls on the right," she said to her companion. "Don't they look beautiful?"

The student stroked his moustache and said, "Well... um... I have to say I wouldn't exactly call them beautiful. And I don't like the way they've done their hair—they look too modern."

"Oh, no, I don't mean those two," answered Maisie. "I mean the two beyond them."

The student stared at her in amazement. "I can't see..." he began, still studying Maisie's face, but then he stopped.

Maisie didn't seem to notice and asked him to explain the story. The student raced through the events of the Greek myth, then hurriedly excused himself, saying he had to find his cousin.

Maisie watched as the tableau broke up and some of the players, who were not needed for the next one, came down from the platform and joined the other guests. The two striking girls headed straight for Maisie and sat down, one on each side of her. They immediately started to talk to her, and she found them charming. They both seemed to know Wolverden extremely well.

The conversation was interrupted by the sound of the piano once more, and a soprano started to sing a well-known Scottish ballad called *Proud Maisie*. Maisie hated this song, particularly the second verse:

Tell me, thou bonny bird
When shall I marry me?
When six braw gentlemen
Kirkward shall carry ye.

When she heard these words, the color drained from her face and she felt faint. As the singer stopped, the taller of the two girls, Yolande, said to Maisie, "Don't you like that song?"

"I'm afraid I hate it. Those horrid words 'When six braw gentlemen

THE FACTS

Charles Grant Blairfindie Allen (1848-1899), known as Grant Allen, was born in Canada but educated in England. As an adult, he ran a college in Jamaica for some years, then in 1876 moved to England for good. He wrote works about science and religion, and was also the author of many stories about the supernatural. Among these was the collection Twelve Tales, from which *Wolverden Tower* is taken.

kirkward shall carry ye' haunt me. I wish I had never been called Maisie!"

"Perhaps it is sad," replied Yolande, "but it's natural to die. Why are you attached to a world of misery? People with eyes such as yours—and mine—can look into the future and ought not to shrink from death. For death is only a gate, a gate to life in its fullest beauty. It is written over the door, *Mors Janua Vitae*—Death is the Gate to Life."

Maisie's head was spinning. She thought she had seen those Latin words somewhere around Wolverden Hall. It seemed that Yolande had, too. "What door?" she asked nervously.

"The door to the vault in the churchyard."

Now she remembered. "How dreadful," she whispered, half to herself.

WORD POWER

tableaux—dramatic scenes acted out by a group of costumed performers

thrice—three times

rantings—wild, shouted words

assailed—attacked

pauper—a poor person

pyre—a fire built for burning a corpse

braw—Scottish for "fine" or "brave"

kirkward—Scottish for "toward the church"

Chapter 2

After the last tableau had finished, Maisie turned to talk to her new friends, but they seemed to have slipped away. Just then, Mrs. West came up and apologized for leaving her on her own.

"Oh, I've been fine," Maisie said. "First that Oxford student sat beside me, then those two delightful girls with the flowing white dresses came and talked to me."

"Which girls?" asked Mrs. West.

Maisie glanced around the room and spotted them in an alcove, drinking red wine. She pointed them out to her hostess.

Mrs. West stared at her and with an embarrassed laugh, said, "Oh, those two! They must be actresses from London. Well, if you're all right, I must see to my other guests." Then she turned and walked away hurriedly.

The party finished at about midnight. When Maisie went to her bedroom, she saw her new friends talking at the end of the corridor.

"Oh, I thought you'd gone home," she said.

"No, we're staying here," replied Yolande.

Then, with a sudden rush of enthusiasm, Maisie invited them into her room, and the three girls sat by the fire, chatting pleasantly. After a while, Yolande's friend, Hedda, asked Maisie if she could open the windows because the room seemed stuffy. Maisie hesitated for a minute, but then politely agreed. When Hedda drew back the curtains, she was surprised to see a sprinkling of snow on the ground. The moon illuminated the church and tower. Hedda gazed up at the starry sky and said excitedly, "What a glorious night it is! Let's go out for a stroll."

Maisie was excited, too, and followed her friends on to the terrace. Linking arms, they walked toward the churchyard gate. But as Maisie glanced back at the well-lit house, she was astonished to see only one set of footprints in the snow—her own! How lightly her friends must walk, she thought.

The three girls talked as they strolled, and the next thing Maisie knew they were standing at the top of the steps leading down to the stone burial vault. Yolande started to walk down them, but Maisie drew back in fear.

"You're not going down there!" she whispered.

"Yes, I am," Yolande replied in a friendly voice. "It's all right, we live here."

"This is our home," added Hedda, as if she were talking about a typical house. "We visited your bedroom, so now it's your turn to visit our home."

The girls seemed so eager to show Maisie their home that she felt she couldn't refuse. So she followed them down the steps, even though her legs were trembling. When she reached the bottom step, Hedda turned and gently held her by the wrist. They stood in front of the heavy bronze doors and Yolande took hold of the gorgon's head on each of the two ringed door handles. She gave a gentle push, and instantly the doors swung inward.

As Yolande crossed the threshold, her body was lit up with a luminous glow, and Maisie could see, to her astonishment, the dark outline of her skeleton inside her body.

Maisie was paralyzed with fear. "I can't go with you," she cried.

Hedda held her wrist tightly, as if she might drag her in. But Yolande reproved her, telling her that Maisie must only enter of her own accord. Then, still luminous but no longer transparent, Yolande faced Maisie and asked her, in a voice sweet as honey, "Won't you come in with us, my dear?" Maisie looked into her kind eyes, and her fear left her.

As Hedda stepped into the gloom, her body, too, was lit up and her skeleton showed through. Then it was Maisie's turn, and as she looked down, she could see her own bones, though not as distinctly as Yolande's and Hedda's.

Once her eyes grew accustomed to the gloom, Maisie saw that they were standing in a huge hall with vast, carved pillars and a domed roof like a mosque. As they walked down the hall, Maisie noticed crowds of people in the aisles and corridors leading off it. Some of the people were dressed in long, flowing gowns like Yolande's and Hedda's, while others wore tunics. As she passed more of these figures, they spoke to her in a strange, flowing language. Gradually, Maisie realized that she could understand their words, and, as she returned people's good wishes, she was astonished, but not frightened, to discover that she too was speaking this Language of the Dead.

The girls led Maisie into a shadowy chamber at the end of the hall and there, sitting on a huge stone throne at the foot of a sphinx, was a high priest, holding a scepter. He was attended by a strange assortment of followers. Some were dressed in animal skins and wore strings of saber-shaped teeth around their necks. Others had collars threaded with lumps of amber or jade. A few had armlets and necklaces of gold.

The high priest stood up, held out his arms with the palms of his hands facing up, and said, "Have you brought a willing victim as Guardian of the Tower?"

"We have," chorused the girls.

Maisie had a strange sense that she was taking part in an ancient ceremony. So, when the priest asked her if she had come of her own accord, she replied that she had. He then asked the girls if she was of royal blood. Yolande replied that Maisie was, as she was descended from the Welsh prince Llewelyn ap Iorwerth.

"It is well," announced the high priest. And then, turning to Maisie, he said, "From the earliest times, Britain's builders have believed that every building must have the soul of three maidens to guard it. One is the soul of the maiden whose body lies beneath the foundations; she is the guardian spirit against earthquake and ruin. One is the soul of the maiden who is buried halfway up the building; she is the guardian spirit against storm and battle. One is the soul of the maiden who flings herself off the roof when the building is completed; she is the guardian spirit against thunder and lightning."

A man dressed in Roman armor continued, "In olden times, all men knew these rules of building. But now, when men build with brick and plaster, they do not bother to give their bridges or their towers a guardian spirit. And so their buildings crumble and collapse."

The man stopped and the high priest held out his scepter.

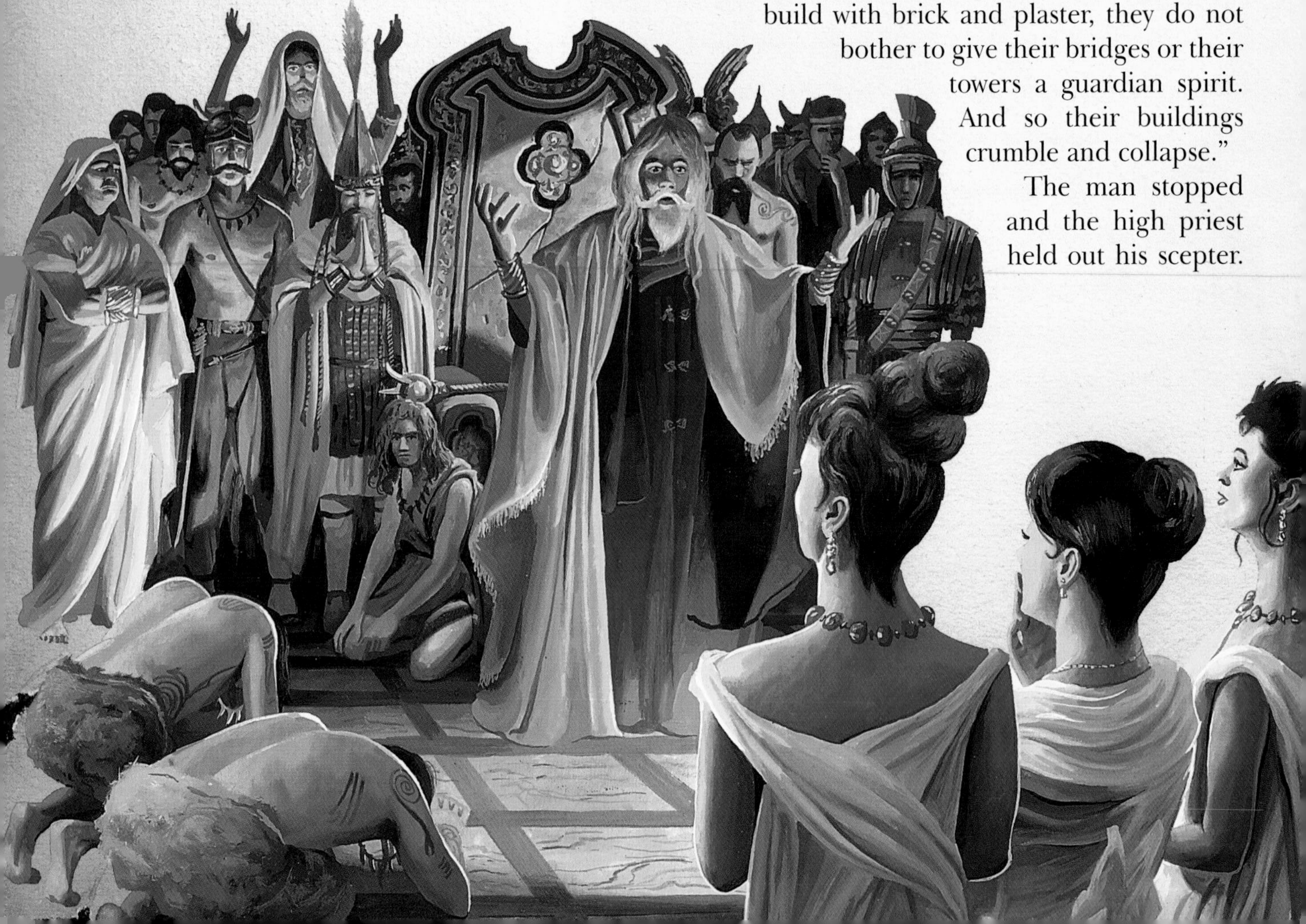

"We are the Assembly of Guardians and Dead Builders for Wolverden. Before this place was a Christian church, it was a temple of Woden, and before that a Stone Circle of the Host of Heaven. And before that again, it was the grave and burial mound of myself, Wolf, and afterward of my son Wulfhere. We all belong to this holy site, and you are the last to join us."

Maisie felt a cold thrill at being included in this ancient custom. She turned to Hedda and asked her who exactly she was.

"I am Hedda, daughter of Gorm, chief of the Northmen of East Anglia," explained her companion. "When I was taken prisoner by the Saxons, they baptized me. Wulfhere, who was building the first church and tower at Wolverden, asked me if I was willing to be buried under the foundation stone, and I agreed. I am the guardian against earthquake and ruin."

"And I am Yolande Fitz-Aylwin," added Yolande. "When the chancel was being re-built by Roland Fitz-Stephen, I chose to be buried in the walls. And now I am the guardian against storm and battle."

Holding her friends' hands tight, Maisie asked, "And what is my task?"

"Your task is to be the guardian against thunder and lightning for the new tower," Yolande explained. "The other guardians are buried alive, and so die a slow death of starvation and choking. But those who guard against thunder and lightning die in the air before they reach the ground, so their task is easier. Afterward, they live with us here forever, as our comrades. This glorious privilege is only offered to the purest and best among us."

Maisie, who had been gazing into Yolande's dark eyes, suddenly felt a surge of panic. "But I'm terribly afraid," she blurted out. "How shall I have the courage to climb the stairs and fling myself off the battlements?"

"You will not be alone," said Yolande reassuringly. "We will come with you and help you. Just think of dwelling here forever with us in peace."

She held out her arms to embrace Maisie, and the frightened girl fell into her arms, sobbing hysterically, "Yes, I will do as you ask me."

Yolande released her, kissed her twice on the forehead, and turned to the high priest. "We are ready," she said gravely. "The victim agrees and is willing to die. Lead on to the tower."

WORD POWER

alcove—a small area set back from a surrounding wall

gorgon—a female winged monster from Greek mythology

reproved—told off; rebuked

mosque—a place of worship for Muslims

sphinx—in Greek mythology, a monster with a woman's head and lion's body

scepter—a special stick, symbolizing power, held by monarchs at important ceremonies

chancel—the part of a church containing the altar and the choir stalls

Chapter 3

As the high priest got up from his throne, strange music swept through the underground palace. Maisie thought that she could hear flutelike instruments, drums, and reed pipes, but there was no sign of any musicians. Hedda and Yolande, with Maisie in between, stood behind the priest. His attendants formed two rows behind them as they moved into the huge hall to the sound of music.

When they reached the bronze doors, the priest pushed the handles. This time, the doors opened outward. As the priest then stepped out into the eerie moonlight, his body became luminous, and Maisie could see the clear outline of his skeleton inside. She gasped as she breathed in the night air. Its coolness made her feel wide awake. She realized that the atmosphere inside the vault had made her very drowsy.

The snow lay deeper on the ground now, and as the group made its way toward the tower, Maisie glanced back at the house. She could see that a light was still burning in her bedroom. When she turned back again, she was startled to see a bent figure emerging from the darkness of the church porch.

"I knew she would come," said a sing-song voice, "I knew Wolverden Tower would find another guardian."

As the figure approached, Maisie recognized the wrinkled face of Bessie. The old woman shuffled ahead of them until she reached the base of the tower. Then she pulled out a rusty key from her pocket and pushed it into the brand-new door lock.

"What turned the old will turn the new," she announced. Silently the key turned, and she opened the door. The high priest entered first and as he climbed the spiral staircase, he began to chant.

Maisie realized with a shock that she could no longer understand the Language of the Dead. Yolande and Hedda held her hands, and, using human language, encouraged her to climb.

Although the staircase was dark, the bodies of the climbers seemed to fill it with a bright light. Maisie walked up as though in a trance. She could hear the bells chiming, but as she passed the belfry, she noticed that they were not moving.

At the very top of the stairs, there was a ladder that led to a trapdoor. Suddenly Maisie felt that she could climb no more. As she glanced back down the staircase, she caught sight of old Bessie looking up at her with a horrible grin on her face.

"I won't be able to do it if that woman comes anywhere near me!" Maisie cried, squeezing Yolande's hand.

Yolande ordered Bessie to go back down. Then Maisie felt a rush of cold air as the high priest pushed up the trapdoor. He climbed onto the platform at the top of the tower, and, as if being pulled up by some unseen force, Maisie followed. Looking across the battlements, she could just make out the snow-clad hills in the moonlight.

The smell of a herb mixture that the high priest and some of his attendants were crushing up in a bowl, and of the aromatic sticks that other attendants were burning, suddenly made Maisie feel giddy. She heard Hedda saying, "She must face the east," and felt Yolande's light touch guiding her to the battlements.

Yolande then spoke in a solemn voice. "From this newly built tower you will fling yourself, so that you may serve mankind as its guardian spirit against thunder and lightning. Take care that no thunderbolt or flash of lightning ever strikes this tower, just as she that is below you preserves it from storm and battle, and she that is below her preserves it from earthquake and ruin." Then she held both of Maisie's hands and said, "Maisie Llewelyn, willing victim, step onto the battlements."

Obediently Maisie stepped up, the words "serve mankind" ringing in her ears. With her long white dress blowing gently in the wind, she held out her arms, as if she were a bird testing its wings before flying. Then she leaned forward to leap. But suddenly a pair of hands was grasping her shoulders and pulling her back. She struggled hard to get free—she was still

determined to become a victim—but the large, apparently human hands were too strong for her. She swayed and finally stumbled back onto the platform.

At that very moment, there was a batlike screech from one of the group. Instantly, the high priest and his followers raced to the battlements. Without hesitating, they flung themselves off and floated down to the ground, out of sight. Last to go were Yolande and Hedda, who held Maisie's hand one last time and gave her a look of regret that seemed to say, "Farewell! We have tried our best to save you from the burdens of living."

The sudden disappearance of her companions left Maisie in a state of shock. Half in a faint, she felt herself being gently lowered onto the hard stone floor. Someone was speaking to her, and even in her semiconscious state, she recognized the kind tones of the Oxford student.

The next morning, Maisie awoke in her bed in Wolverden Hall. Mrs. West was standing by the bed, talking to a man. Lying very still, Maisie tried to remember the events of the previous night. Had she really been in the vault? Did she really join the procession to the tower? She pictured herself standing on the battlements, and then recalled struggling against the firm grip of a pair of hands. She remembered seeing her friends leap off the tower, into the dark night, and the student holding her tight and covering her with his jacket. What happened next, she could not remember. How had she ended up in her bed? Then she became aware of the murmur of voices.

"Yesterday was unusually warm for the time of year, you see."

"But such a violent thunderstorm—it's not what we expected at all. I suppose the

WORD POWER

belfry—the part of a church tower in which bells hang

battlements—walls with notches in them, through which archers once fired arrows

aromatic—having a strong, usually fragrant smell

masonry—stonework

hallucinating—imagining things that are not really there

electrical disturbance must have affected the poor girl's head in some way."

Maisie realized that she was listening to a conversation between Mrs. West and a doctor. She sat bolt upright in bed and looked out of the window toward the church. Her heartbeat raced as she saw the jagged outline of Wolverden Tower, which had been half destroyed. With mounds of white stones shattered on the ground all around it, it looked as though it had been hit by cannon fire.

"What happened?" she cried out.

"Hush, hush!" said the doctor. "Don't trouble yourself about it."

"Did it... happen... after I came down?" she gulped.

The doctor nodded. "An hour after you were carried down from the top, a violent thunderstorm broke out. Lightning struck the tower and shattered it. It was such a terrible shame—Colonel West had planned to put up a lightning conductor the day after Christmas."

Maisie was at once filled with guilt. "It's all my fault!" she moaned sadly. "I have neglected my duty."

"Hush," the doctor said again. "You mustn't talk for a while. You have been in a deep trance."

But poor Maisie became agitated once again. "What about old Bessie?" she asked.

The doctor looked with surprise at Mrs. West and whispered something to her.

"You may as well learn the truth," he said to Maisie. "Bessie must have been standing below the tower. She was crushed under the falling masonry."

Maisie could feel her hands trembling, so she clutched the bedclothes tight. "One more question please, Mrs. West," she said in a quiet voice. "You remember the two girls that I pointed out to you in the alcove at the party and who sat beside me at the tableaux. Did anyone find them at the tower? Are they hurt?"

Mrs. West took Maisie's hand and stroked it gently. "My dear child," she said firmly, "there were no other girls. You have been hallucinating. I assure you, after the student left you, you sat completely alone for the rest of the evening's performances."

THE END

The Real & The Counterfeit

Retold from a story by Mrs. Alfred Baldwin

Will Musgrave had almost forgotten what Christmas in England was like, as he had spent it with his parents at their winter home in the South of France so often. This year, however, he resolved to pass much of the festive season at Stonecroft, the family home in Northumberland. He made his excuses to his parents and invited two of his college friends, Hugh Armitage and Horace Lawley, to join him.

Will spent Christmas and the day after with the Armitages at their Yorkshire home. The following day, he and Armitage drove north, picking up Lawley on the way. They arrived at Stonecroft that night, in high spirits and with keen appetites. The Musgrave home was a delightful refuge at the end of a long journey. The wide, hospitable front door opened into a brightly lit, oak-paneled hall, where a great fire burned cheerily. "Barker, I hope supper's ready and that it is something hot and plentiful. For we've traveled on empty stomachs through devilish cold and snow," said Will, before leading his guests up to their rooms.

"What a jolly gallery!" cried Lawley, as they entered a long, wide corridor, with many doors leading from it.

"It's the main thoroughfare," said Will, without slowing his pace. "It runs the length of the house, from the modern end to the back, which once formed the foundations of a Cistercian monastery."

The three men continued along the corridor, with Lawley and Armitage examining numerous portraits of long-departed Musgraves. Nearing the far end, Will spoke again. "I've had Barker prepare rooms for you opposite my own, so that we are close together."

The following morning, the friends arose to a white world. For as far as the eye could see, the ground was covered in a thick blanket of fine snow that was as dry as salt. The sky overhead was a leaden lid, showing all the signs of a deep fall yet to come.

"How very cheerful," said Lawley, as he stood, looking out of the window after breakfast. "But the snow will have spoiled the ice for skating."

"It's perfect for tobogganing, though," said Armitage. "If we can find the right slope."

"Well thought of, Armitage," said Musgrave, jumping at the idea.

"We'll also need something to slide on," added Lawley.

"That's easily found," said Armitage. "Empty wine cases are just what we need."

After breakfast, Will, Lawley, and Armitage rushed out into the open air to search for a suitable tobogganing slope.

"If the snow keeps firm, we'll walk over to see the Harradines at Garthside and ask the girls to come out sledding," said Will.

After a long and careful search, the three men found an ideal piece of land. For four hours, they worked with pickax and spade to make a toboggan slide.

"If we can get this bit of engineering done today," said Lawley, chucking a spadeful of dirt aside, "the slide will be in perfect order for tomorrow."

When their task was finished, the friends bathed and changed their clothes, then walked through thick falling snow to Garthside for tea with their neighbors, the Harradines. They returned to Stonecroft only after the Harradine girls and their brothers had agreed to join them for tobogganing the next day.

Late that night, the three friends sat chatting together in the library. They had played billiards until they were tired, and Lawley had sung sentimental songs, accompanying himself on the banjo. Then they lapsed into silence. Armitage, leaning his head back in his armchair, was the first to speak once more.

"Musgrave," he said suddenly, "an old house is not complete unless it's haunted. You ought to have a ghost here at Stonecroft."

Will suddenly piped up, "So we have, my dear fellow. Only it has not been seen by any of us since my grandfather's time. It is my life's ambition to meet our family ghost."

Armitage laughed. But Lawley said, "You would not say that if you really believed in ghosts."

"I believe in them most devoutly," Musgrave said, "but I want to have my faith confirmed by sight. You believe in them, too, I can see."

"I neither believe nor disbelieve in ghosts," countered Lawley. "I keep an open mind on the subject."

Will did not reply, but Armitage laughed out loud.

"I'm one against two, I'm afraid. Musgrave believes in ghosts. You're neutral, but open to conviction. I'm a complete unbeliever in the supernatural. People's nerves play tricks on them and that's that. If I were so fortunate as to see Musgrave's family ghost tonight, I still wouldn't believe in it. By the way, Musgrave," he added flippantly, "is it a lady or a gentleman ghost?"

"I don't think you deserve to be told," answered Will.

"Don't you know, a ghost is neither 'he' nor 'she'?" said Lawley. "Like a corpse, it is always 'it'."

"That's rather definite information from one who neither believes nor disbelieves in ghosts. How do you come by it?" asked Armitage.

"A man can be well informed on a subject though he reserves judgment about it," replied Lawley. "Musgrave believes in ghosts, but has never seen one. You don't believe and say that you would not be convinced even if you did see one. I think I have the only logical mind here. At any rate, time will tell. If ghosts do exist, we shall each be one in due course. And then, if we've nothing better to do, we may haunt our surviving friends, whether they believe in ghosts or not."

"Then I hope to die before you, Lawley, and become a ghost first," said Armitage. "To scare suits me better than to be scared. But Musgrave, do tell me about your family ghost. And I promise not to laugh."

"Well," said Will, turning to look into the fire, "Stonecroft, as I told you, is built on the site of an old Cistercian monastery. In fact, the back part of the house was built with stones that were once part of the monastery. The ghost is that of a Cistercian monk, dressed in the white habit of his order. Who he was or why

WORD POWER

Cistercian—belonging to a monastic order founded in Cîteaux, France, in 1098

devoutly—deeply; earnestly

habit—official monastic dress, in this case, a long white cloak with a hood

incredulous—unbelieving; skeptical

complacently—in a self-satisfied way; smugly

he haunts us, we do not know. He has been seen by members of the Musgrave family, once or twice in each generation, for the last three centuries. But he has not visited us since my grandfather's time. So, like a comet, he should be due again soon."

"How you must regret not having had the good fortune to see it yourself," said Armitage.

"My time will come," replied Will confidently. "I know where to look for the ghost. It has always made its appearance in the gallery. I have my bedroom close to where it was last seen. My hope is that if I open my door suddenly some moonlit night, I may find the monk standing there."

"In the gallery?" asked the incredulous Armitage.

"Midway between your two doors and mine," replied Will. "That is where my grandfather last saw it.

"He was awakened in the dead of night by the sound of a heavy door shutting and ran into the gallery where the noise came from. Standing opposite the door of the room I now occupy was the white figure of the monk.

"It glided the full length of the gallery, then simply melted like mist into the wall. The spot where it disappeared is on the old foundations of the monastery. It was probably returning to its own quarters."

"And your grandfather believed that he saw a ghost?" asked Armitage.

"How could he doubt it? He saw it as clearly as we see each other now."

Armitage sniggered in disbelief. "Forgive me, but I never can take a ghost story seriously," he said. "Ghosts are a trick of the light, nothing more than shadows cast by candle flames.

"This is the end of the nineteenth century. Electricity has turned night into day. And, by doing so, has destroyed the very conditions that produced ghosts or rather the belief in them. Darkness has always been bad for human nerves. Don't ask me why. That's quite simply the way it is. Ghosts, specters, apparitions, and phantoms are all superstitious rot as far as I'm concerned." And with that, Armitage looked around calmly and complacently.

"Perhaps I might have felt as you do if I had not begun life with the knowledge that our house was haunted," replied Will, with visible pride in the family ghost. "I only wish I were telling the story from personal experience."

At that Armitage made a vow to himself that, within a week, Will Musgrave would see his family ghost with his own eyes.

THE FACTS

Mrs. Alfred Baldwin (1845-1925) was born Louisa Macdonald, but took her husband's name when she married. All her ghost stories were first published in magazines, but some later appeared in a book called *The Shadow on the Blind* (1895).

Mrs. Baldwin's other claim to fame is that she was the mother of Stanley Baldwin, who was British prime minister three times in the 1920s and 1930s.

Chapter 2

Hugh Armitage thought of several ingenious schemes to make the Cistercian monk's ghost reappear at Stonecroft. It struck him that it would be a double triumph if both his friends saw the apparition. Musgrave believed in ghosts, and Lawley, though he claimed to be unsure, could be convinced of their existence.

Circumstances were favorable for Armitage's plot. The moon was rising late, and on consulting his almanac, he saw that in three nights' time it would come up at 2 A.M. An hour later, the end of the gallery would be flooded with light. But Armitage needed an accomplice who could sew, to run up a convincing imitation of a Cistercian monk's white robe and hood.

The next day, when the three friends took the Harradine girls out in their sleighs, Armitage spoke to the youngest, Kate. Pushing her sleigh over the hard snow, he bent forward and whispered, "I want you to help me play a practical joke on Musgrave and Lawley. Will you promise to keep it a secret?"

"Gladly. What sort of practical joke do you have in mind?"

"I want to make Musgrave believe he has seen the ghost his grandfather saw."

"What a good idea! He's always going on about it. But what if it startles him more than you intend?" asked Kate. "It's one thing to want to see a ghost and quite another to see it."

"Don't worry about Musgrave," Armitage replied. "We'll be doing him a favor, helping him see what he's wanted to see for so long. Lawley will catch sight of it as well. And two strong men are surely a match for one homemade ghost."

"Well, if you think it's a safe trick to play," said Kate. "How can I help?"

"Can you make something that will roughly resemble a white Cistercian habit? I'd do it myself, but I'm hopeless at sewing."

Kate laughed. "I can easily make something from a white bathrobe and fasten a hood to it."

Armitage told her the details of his scheme. On the chosen night, when the moon had risen and he was sure that the others were fast asleep, he would dress as the monk, put out the candles and go out into the gallery. "Then I'll slam the door loudly. That was the noise that roused the old grandfather, so it should bring them out of their rooms. Lawley's door is next to mine, Musgrave's opposite. So each will have a magnificent view of the monk at the same time."

"What if they find you out?" asked Kate.

"They won't. I'll be standing with the cowl over my face and my back to the moonlight. In spite of Musgrave's longing to see a ghost, I don't think he'll like it when he does. Nor will Lawley. They'll probably dart back into their rooms and lock themselves in. That'll give me time to get back to my room, strip off the habit, and hide it. Then, when they come to tell me what's happened, I can pretend that they have roused me with difficulty from a deep sleep. And one more ghost story will be added to the Musgrave family collection," laughed Armitage.

With that, he and Kate arranged to meet two days later so she could hand over the package containing the monk's habit. This was to take place on Thursday afternoon, when the other Harradines and their guests were coming to Stonecroft to try the toboggan slide.

Kate and Armitage managed to meet at the appointed time, having excused themselves from the tobogganing party.

"Please be careful," said Kate, handing the package to Armitage. "I've heard of people being frightened out of their wits by make-believe ghosts. I'd never forgive myself if Mr. Musgrave or Mr. Lawley were seriously alarmed."

"I'm more afraid of what they'll do to me if I'm discovered," said Armitage.

Kate smiled at this, and the two parted as twilight fell.

Once back at Stonecroft, Armitage took the back staircase to his room. After hiding the monk's habit, he ran downstairs to the drawing room, where his friends were enjoying tea and hot buttered muffins.

"Where have you been?" said Musgrave.

"I went for a walk along the turnpike road," replied Armitage.

Later, after dinner, the three young men sat in the library. Suddenly, as he took down a book from an upper shelf, Musgrave exclaimed, "Hello! It's my grandfather's diary with his own account of seeing the ghost in the gallery. Lawley, you may read it if you like, but I shan't waste it on an unbeliever like Armitage. What a coincidence! It's forty years tonight since my grandfather saw the monk's ghost." Musgrave handed the book to

Lawley, who read it with close attention.

"Does it persuade you?" asked Armitage.

"I'm still not convinced either way," said Lawley. Musgrave clearly did not wish to discuss the family ghost in Armitage's unsympathetic presence, so they dropped the subject.

The three men retired late, bidding each other good night and closing their bedroom doors behind them. Soon silence fell upon Stonecroft Hall, and the hour that Armitage had gleefully anticipated drew near.

Once his two friends were asleep, Armitage began to feel ashamed of his mischievous plot to awaken and scare them both. With a couple of hours still to pass, he sat down to write. As he bent over his desk, the big clock in the hall struck one so suddenly and sharply that he jumped. Lawley's snoring could be heard from the next room. "He must be sleeping deeply not to hear a noise like that!" Armitage thought.

When the clock struck again, Armitage was still at his desk. This time he expected it and it didn't startle him. Only the cold made him shiver. "If I hadn't made up my mind to go through with this mischief, I'd go to bed now," he thought. "But Kate's made the robe, so I've got to wear it."

Yawning, he threw down his pen and rose to look out of the window. It was a clear, frosty night, and the moon was rising.

Armitage turned from the window to begin his work. He slipped the white habit over his clothing, then marked dark circles around his eyes and powdered his face a ghastly white. Looking at his ghostly reflection in the mirror, he wished that Kate could see him.

Armitage opened the door and looked out into the gallery. The moonlight shimmered on the end window to the right of his door and Lawley's. It would soon be where he wanted it, making the scene neither too light nor too dark for his plan. Silently he stepped back again to wait. A feeling of nervousness came over him. His heart beat rapidly. He jumped when the silence was suddenly broken by the hooting of an owl. Having taken fright at the deathly pallor of his powdered face, he no longer cared to look at himself in the mirror. He peered into the gallery. The moon now shone where he intended to stand.

Putting out the light, Armitage stepped out into the gallery, opened the door wide, then slammed it shut with great force. Standing in the pale moonlight in the middle of the gallery, he waited for the door on either side to fly open and reveal the terrified faces of his friends. But there was no response from Musgrave and Lawley. Armitage cursed the ill luck that was making them sleep so heavily.

Slowly, the objects in the long gallery became clearer to Armitage, as his eyes grew used to the dim light. "I never noticed before that there was a mirror at that end!" he thought to himself. "And I didn't realize that the moonlight was bright enough for me to see my own reflection so far off. But is it my own reflection? It seems to be moving, even though I'm standing still! I know what it is! It's Musgrave dressed up to frighten me. And Lawley's helping him. That's why they didn't come out of their rooms when I slammed the door. We're both playing the same practical joke. Let's see which of us loses his nerve first!"

To Armitage's terror, the white figure glided slowly toward him, its feet not touching the floor. Armitage was determined to hold his ground. But a feeling crept over him that he had never known before. As the thing floated nearer, he opened his dry mouth and let out a hoarse cry.

Startled out of their sleep, Musgrave and Lawley ran to open their doors. In the gallery they saw two ghostly forms in the moonlight. As Armitage tried to push away the horror that approached him, the cowl slipped from his head. His friends recognized his white face, distorted by fear, and sprang toward him. Armitage staggered back into their arms just as the Cistercian monk passed them like a white mist and sank into the wall.

Once the real ghost had gone, Musgrave and Lawley were left alone with the counterfeit, their friend Armitage. They gazed in horror as they realized that he was dead, and that his white costume had become a shroud.

THE END

WORD POWER

almanac—a book containing information about the calendar and the movements of stars and planets
cowl—a large hood on a monk's habit
turnpike—a road barrier where travelers must pay a fee
pallor—paleness
shroud—a sheet in which a dead body is wrapped for burial

The Middle Toe of the Right Foot

Retold from a story by Ambrose Bierce

It is well known that the house where the Manton family once lived is haunted. In all the rural district near about, and even in the town of Marshall, a mile away, not one person of unbiased mind entertains a doubt of it. The evidence that the house is haunted is of two kinds: the testimony of witnesses who have seen it with their own eyes, and that of the house itself. There are many possible objections to the former, but facts that everyone can observe are convincing.

In the first place, the Manton house has been unoccupied by mortals for more than ten years, and with its sheds is slowly falling into decay—a circumstance which in itself the wise will not ignore. It stands a little way off the loneliest reach of the Marshall and Harriston road, in an opening that was once a farm. This is still disfigured with strips of rotting fence and half-covered with brambles. They run across stony soil that has not been plowed for many years.

The house itself is in tolerably good condition, though badly weatherstained. It is also in dire need of attention from a glazier, as the young boys of the region have smashed many of its windows. It is two stories high, nearly square, its front pierced by a single doorway with a window boarded up to the very top on each side. The corresponding unboarded windows above serve to admit light and rain to the rooms of the upper floor. Grass and weeds grow pretty rankly all about, and a few shade trees, somewhat the worse for wind and leaning all in one direction, seem to be making an effort to run away.

In short, as the Marshall town humorist explained in the columns of the *Advance* newspaper, "The proposition that the Manton house is badly haunted is the only logical conclusion." The public has another reason to believe that the dwelling is a place where supernatural phenomena occur. For one night about ten years ago, Mr. Manton rose and

cut the throats of his wife and two small children. Then he fled at once to another part of the country.

To this house, one summer evening, came four men in a wagon. Three of them promptly alighted, and the one who had been driving hitched the horses to the only remaining post of what had been a fence. The fourth remained seated in the wagon. "Come," said one of his companions, approaching him, while the others moved away in the direction of the dwelling, "this is the place."

The man addressed did not make a move. "By God!" he said harshly, "this is a trick, and it looks to me as if you were in it."

"Perhaps I am," the other said, looking him straight in the face and speaking in a tone that had something of contempt in it. "You will remember, however, that the choice of place was, with your own agreement, left to the other side. Of course, if you are afraid of spooks?"

"I am afraid of nothing," the man interrupted with another oath, and sprang to the ground. The two then joined the others at the door, which one of them had already opened, although with some difficulty as the lock and hinges were rusty. All entered. Inside it was dark, but the man who had unlocked the door produced a candle and matches so that they could have some light. He then unlocked a door on their right as they stood in the passage. This gave them entrance to a large, square room that the candle but dimly lit.

The floor had a thick carpeting of dust, which partly muffled their footsteps. Cobwebs were in the angles of the walls and hung from the ceiling like strips of rotting lace, waving in the air that the men's movements had disturbed. The room had two windows in adjoining sides, but from neither could anything be seen except the rough inner surfaces of boards a few inches from the glass. There was no fireplace, no furniture; there was nothing. Besides the cobwebs and the dust, the four men were the only objects there that were not a part of the structure.

The men looked strange in the yellow light of the candle. The one who had so reluctantly alighted was especially spectacular. He might have been called sensational. He was of middle age, heavily built, deep chested, and broad shouldered. Looking at his figure, one would have said that he had a giant's strength. His features gave the impression that he would use it like a giant, too. He was clean shaven, his hair rather closely cropped and gray. His low forehead was seamed with wrinkles above the eyes, and over the nose these became vertical. The heavy black brows were saved

WORD POWER

rankly—vigorously; in abundance

forbidding—hostile; threatening

pallor—paleness

bowie knives—hunting knives with short handles

scabbards—knife-holders; sheaths

principals—the main participants, here the duelers themselves

second—a person who acts as assistant to a competitor, for example in a fight

cordiality—friendliness; warmth

from meeting only by an upward turn at what would otherwise have been the point of contact. Deeply sunken beneath these, a pair of eyes of uncertain color, but obviously too small, glowed in the obscure light. There was something forbidding in their expression, which was not bettered by the cruel mouth and wide jaw. The nose was well enough, as noses go—one does not expect much of noses. All that was sinister in the man's face seemed emphasized by an unnatural pallor: he appeared altogether bloodless.

The appearance of the other men was commonplace. They were such persons as one meets and forgets that one has met. All were younger than the man described. Between him and the eldest of the others, who stood apart, there was apparently no kindly feeling. They avoided looking at each other.

"Gentlemen," said the man holding the candle and keys, "I believe everything is right. Are you ready, Mr. Rosser?"

The man standing apart from the group bowed and smiled.

"And you, Mr. Grossmith?"

The heavy man bowed and scowled.

"You will be pleased to remove your outer clothing."

Their hats, coats, vests, and neckwear were soon removed and thrown outside the door, in the passage. The man with the candle now nodded, and the fourth man—he who had urged Grossmith to leave the wagon—produced from the pocket of his overcoat two long, murderous-looking bowie knives, which he drew now from their leather scabbards.

"They are exactly alike," he said, presenting one to each of the two principals. By this time, the dullest observer would have understood the nature of this meeting: it was to be a duel to the death.

Each dueler took a knife, examined it critically near the candle, and tested the strength of blade and handle across his lifted knee. Their persons were then searched in turn, each by the other's second.

"If it is agreeable to you, Mr. Grossmith," said the man holding the light, "you will place yourself in that corner."

He indicated the angle of the room farthest from the door. Grossmith walked over there, his second parting from him with a grasp of the hand which had nothing of cordiality in it. In the angle nearest the door, Mr. Rosser stationed himself, and after a whispered consultation his second left him, joining the other near the door. At that moment the candle was suddenly extinguished, leaving all in profound darkness. This may have been done by a draft from the open door. Whatever the cause, the effect was startling.

"Gentlemen," said a voice, which sounded unfamiliar in the altered conditions, "gentlemen, you will not move until you hear the closing of the outer door."

THE FACTS

Ambrose Gwinnet Bierce (1842-19??) was born in Chester, Ohio. He served in the Civil War (1861-65), then began working as a reporter in San Francisco.

In 1871, Bierce published his first short story, called *The Haunted Valley.* Later the same year, he moved to England.

In 1875, Bierce returned to the U.S. and continued to work as a journalist, becoming known for his sharp, witty style. Many of his short stories, which were often written for newspapers, featured supernatural themes. A short story collection—including the story retold here—was later published under the title *Can Such Things Be?*

When he was 70 years old, Bierce announced that he was going to join Pancho Villa's rebels in Mexico. He was never seen or heard of again.

A sound of tramping ensued, then the closing of the inner door. Finally the outer one closed with a crash that shook the entire building.

A few minutes afterward, a farmer's boy met a light wagon that was being driven furiously toward the town of Marshall. He declared that behind the two figures on the front seat stood a third. It had its hands upon the bowed shoulders of the others, who appeared to struggle vainly to free themselves from its grasp. This figure, unlike the others, was clad in white and had undoubtedly boarded the wagon as it passed the haunted house.

Chapter 2

The events that had led up to this "duel in the dark" were simple enough. One evening, three young men of the town of Marshall were sitting in a quiet corner of the porch of the village hotel. They were smoking and discussing such matters as three educated young men of a Southern village would naturally find interesting. The men's names were King, Sancher, and Rosser.

At a little distance, within easy hearing but taking no part in the conversation, sat a fourth man. He was a stranger to the others. They merely knew that on his arrival by the stagecoach that afternoon he had written in the hotel register the name of Robert Grossmith. No one had seen him speak to anyone except the hotel clerk. He seemed to have no desire to do so, and to be singularly fond of his own company.

"I hate any kind of deformity in a woman," said King, "whether natural or acquired. I have a theory that any physical defect has a mental and moral defect of character to match."

"So," Rosser said gravely, "a lady lacking the moral advantage of a nose would find the struggle to become Mrs. King an arduous enterprise."

"Of course, you may put it that way," was the reply. But seriously, I once threw over a most charming young girl on learning quite by accident that she had suffered amputation of a toe. My conduct was brutal if you like, but if I had married that girl I should have been miserable for the rest of my life and should have made her miserable, too."

"Whereas," said Sancher, with a light laugh, "by marrying a gentleman of rather more tolerant views, she escaped with just a cut to the throat."

"Ah, you know to whom I refer. Yes, she married Manton, but I don't know about his tolerance. Perhaps he cut her throat because he discovered that she lacked that excellent thing in woman, the middle toe of the right foot."

"Look at that chap!" said Rosser in a low voice, his eyes fixed upon the stranger, who was obviously listening to the conversation.

"Curse his rudeness!" muttered King. "What ought we to do?"

"That's an easy one," Rosser replied. "Sir," he continued, addressing himself to the stranger, "I think it would be better if you removed your chair to the other end of the veranda. The presence of gentlemen is evidently an unfamiliar situation to you."

The man sprang to his feet and strode forward with clenched hands, his face white with rage. All were now standing. Sancher stepped between the two men, who seemed about to fight.

"You are hasty and unjust," he said to Rosser. "This gentleman has done nothing to deserve such language."

But Rosser refused to withdraw even a word. By the custom of both the country and the time, there could be only one outcome to such a quarrel—a duel.

"I demand the satisfaction due to a gentleman," said the stranger, who had become calmer. "I have no acquaintances in this region. Perhaps you, sir," bowing to Sancher, "will be kind enough to act as my second."

Sancher accepted the trust—somewhat reluctantly it must be confessed, for the man's appearance and manner were not at all to his liking. King, who during the conversation had hardly removed his eyes from the stranger's face and had not spoken a word, consented with a nod to be Rosser's second. A meeting was arranged for the following evening. The nature of these arrangements has already been explained. The duel with knives in a dark room was once a more common feature of Southern life than it is likely to be again.

In the blaze of a midsummer noonday, the old Manton house was hardly true to its grim reputation. The sunshine appeared to caress its walls warmly and affectionately. The grass greening the area in front of it seemed to grow with a natural and joyous exuberance, and the weeds blossomed quite like plants.

However, the bleak, lifeless trees on each side stood as a silent reminder of the misery and evil that the house had seen. The glassless upper windows also spoke of past neglect and sorrow. Even the heat shimmering over the stony fields around about could not completely dispel the gloomy atmosphere that hung over the scene.

This was how the house appeared to Sheriff Adams and two other men who had come out from Marshall to look at it. One of these men was Mr. King, the sheriff's deputy. The other man, whose name was Brewster, was a brother of the late Mrs. Manton. Under a state law relating to property abandoned for a certain period by an untraceable owner, the sheriff was legal custodian of the Manton farm. His visit was the result of a court order by which Mr. Brewster was to get possession of the property as heir to his dead sister.

By a coincidence, the visit was made on the day after the night that Deputy King had unlocked the house for another and very different purpose. His presence now was not of his own choosing. He had been ordered to accompany his superior and at the moment could think of nothing more prudent than to obey.

Carelessly opening the front door, which to his surprise was not locked, the sheriff was amazed to see, lying on the floor of the passage into which it opened, a confused heap of men's clothing. Examination showed it to consist of two hats, and the same number of coats, vests, and scarves. All were in a remarkably good state of preservation, although made somewhat dirty by the dust in which they lay. Mr. Brewster was equally astonished.

With a new and lively interest, the sheriff now unlatched and pushed open a door on the right, and the three entered. The room was apparently vacant. But as their eyes grew used to the dimmer light, something became visible in the farthest angle of the wall. It was a human figure—that of a man crouching in the corner.

Something strange in the figure's attitude made the three intruders halt when they had barely passed the threshold of the room. Gradually, its shape defined itself more and more clearly.

The man was upon one knee, his back in the angle of the wall, his shoulders raised to the level of his ears, his hands before his face, palms outward, the fingers spread and crooked like claws. The white face, turned upward, bore an expression of unutterable fright, the mouth half open, the eyes incredibly expanded. He was stone dead. Yet, with the exception of a bowie knife, which had evidently fallen from his own hand, there was not another object anywhere in the room.

In the thick dust that covered the floor there were some confused footprints near the door and along the wall through which it opened. Along one of the adjoining walls, too, past the boarded-up windows, was the trail made by the man himself in slowly reaching his corner. In approaching the corpse, the three men followed that trail.

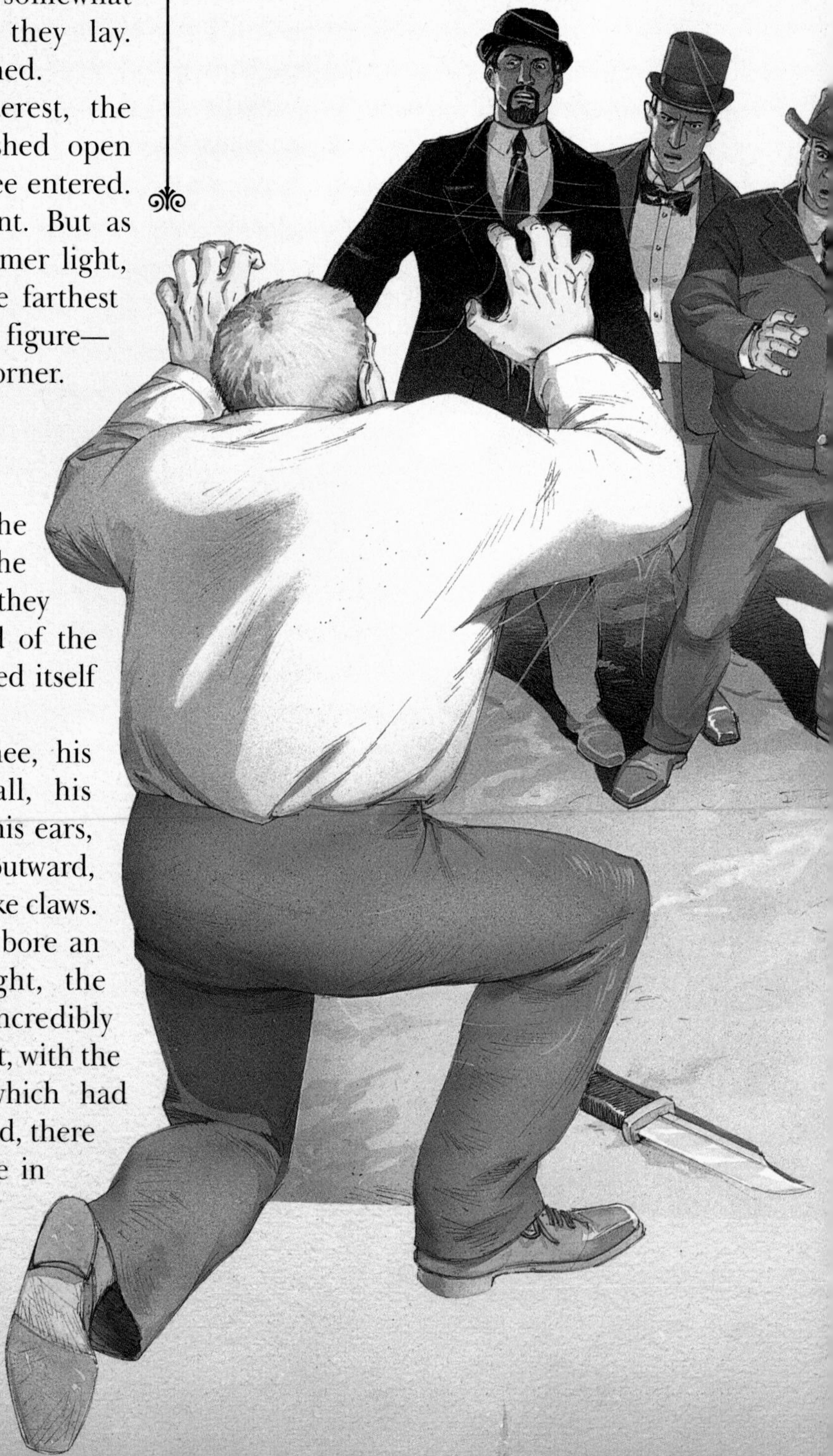

The sheriff grasped one of the outthrown arms. It was as rigid as iron, and the application of a gentle force rocked the entire body. Brewster gazed into the distorted face. "God of mercy!" he suddenly cried, "It is Manton!"

"You are quite right," said King, with an evident attempt at calmness. "I knew Manton. He then wore a full beard and his hair long, but this is definitely he."

He might have added, "I recognized him when he challenged Rosser. I told Rosser and Sancher who he was before we played this horrible trick on him. Then Rosser left this dark room at our heels, forgetting his outer clothing in the excitement, and driving away with us in his shirt sleeves. All through the proceedings we knew whom we were dealing with. We were paying him back for his evil crimes, murderer and coward that he was!"

But nothing of this awful story did Mr. King tell. Now he was trying to penetrate the mystery of Manton's death. It was obvious that he had not once moved from the corner where he had been stationed. His posture was that of neither attack nor defense. He had dropped his weapon and obviously perished from sheer horror as a result of something that he had seen. All these were extraordinary circumstances that Mr. King's disturbed intelligence could not rightly understand.

Groping for a clue in this maze of doubt, King's gaze moved slowly and mechanically downward. It fell upon something that, there, in the full light of day and in the presence of two living companions, affected him with terror. In the dust of years that lay thick upon the floor, leading from the door by which they had entered, straight across the room to within just a yard of Manton's stiff, crouching corpse, were three parallel lines of footprints.

The two outer sets of these light but definite impressions of bare feet were those of small children, the inner set a woman's. From the point at which they ended, they did not return—they pointed all one way. Brewster, who had observed them at exactly the same moment, was leaning forward in an attitude of rapt attention, horribly pale.

"Look at that!" he cried, pointing with both hands at the nearest print of the woman's right foot, where she appeared to have stopped and stood. "The middle toe is missing—it was Gertrude!"

Gertrude was the late Mrs. Manton, sister to Mr. Brewster.

THE END

WORD POWER

arduous – very difficult

exuberance – vigor; vitality

custodian – a person in charge of looking after something he or she does not own; keeper

prudent – sensible; wise

distorted – twisted out of its normal shape

rapt – totally absorbed; engrossed

The Portrait Painter

Retold from a story by Charles Dickens

I am a portrait painter and I live in London. One afternoon in May 1858, a gentleman and his wife were shown into my rooms. They told me that they had seen one of my portraits and said they would like to commission a picture of themselves and their children at their country house. I agreed and said that I would contact them in the fall, to arrange the date of my visit. They left me their card and departed. A little later, when I looked at the card, I realized that there was no address on it—the card simply stated their names, Mr. and Mrs. Kirkbeck. So I put it away and thought no more about the matter.

In September, I set off for the north of England and found myself, one evening, at a dinner party in a house on the Yorkshire-Lincolnshire border. Toward the end of the meal, I thought I heard the name "Kirkbeck" being mentioned farther down the table. I suddenly remembered the calling card and asked my neighbor if there was a family called Kirkbeck living nearby. He told me that there was and that they lived at the other end of Lincolnshire, at Alvingham. So next morning I wrote to Mr. Kirkbeck, saying that I believed he had visited me in May and commissioned portraits of his family. However, he had not left his address, so if he still wanted me to do them, he should write to me care of the post office at York.

Mr. Kirkbeck replied, and we arranged for me to visit the family the next weekend, and to return to paint the portraits a few weeks later. To get to Alvingham, I had to take the London-bound train and change at Retford Junction. It was a cold, foggy day when I boarded the train, and I had a carriage to myself until Doncaster, when a tall, veiled lady, who was dressed in black, got in. I offered her my seat next to the door, which is usually considered to be the ladies' seat, but she politely refused, saying that she preferred to feel the breeze on her face. Once she had settled her clothes and thrown back her veil, I could see that the lady was only about twenty-two or three, with auburn hair, dark eyebrows, and large eyes that stood out against her pale skin.

She seemed happy to talk, and I soon realized how lucky I was to have such a very charming companion with whom to while away the tedious journey. One thing puzzled me, though. She behaved as if she already knew me, or knew much about me, and several times referred to events in my life and places I had visited. The time flew by and when I got up to change trains at Retford, she offered her hand and said, "I expect we shall meet again."

I traveled on to Alvingham alone and found a carriage waiting for me. Mr. Kirkbeck was due to arrive by the next train, so I was taken to his house, where the servants showed me to my room. When I had unpacked and changed, I went down to the drawing room. From the doorway I could make out the seated figure of a lady, dressed in black, warming a foot in front of the blazing fire. As I came in, she rose and stood in front of the fire. The lamps had not yet been lit, so I could not see her features until, as I walked into the middle of the room, the lady swiveled around and smiled at me, as if she had been expecting me. In an instant I recognized my traveling companion from earlier in the day.

"I told you we would meet again," she said gently.

I was so taken aback to see her standing there that I couldn't reply. When I left her, she was on the train bound for London, and as far as I knew, there was no other railroad line, or other means of transport, that could have brought her to the house ahead of me.

When I finally found my tongue, I said that I wished I had used the same method of transportation as she had.

"That would have been rather difficult," she answered softly. But before I had a chance to ask her what she meant, a servant came in carrying lighted lamps and informed me that the master had just arrived and would be down shortly.

The lady then picked up a book with engravings in it and was just asking me if I thought that one particular portrait looked like her, when my hosts swept in, apologizing for being late. Mr. Kirkbeck asked me to take Mrs. Kirkbeck into dinner, and I held back for a minute, to allow Mr. Kirkbeck to lead the way with the lady in black. But Mrs. Kirkbeck stepped ahead as if she hadn't understood my gesture, so she and I walked into the dining room first.

Mr. and Mrs. Kirkbeck sat at either end of the table, with the lady in black and myself between them. During dinner I conversed with my hosts, who were very interested in the subject of portrait painting.

I had noticed that they did not seem to be talking to the other lady, and had not particularly greeted her when they came in; neither had they introduced me to her.

I therefore presumed that she must be the governess. It was only after dinner, when other members of the family, including a few of the Kirkbecks' children and their governess, Miss Hardwick, joined us in the drawing room, that I realized that the lady was not in fact what I thought she was.

At this stage of the evening, she came up to me and returned to the subject of painting. She asked me if I thought I could paint her portrait from memory. I told her it would be difficult and suggested that she could sit for me.

"No, that's quite impossible," she replied, firmly.

"Just once?" I asked. "Even once would be better than not at all."

"No, I'm afraid I cannot."

Then she said she was tired, shook my hand, wished me goodnight, and slipped out of the room.

When I myself went to bed, I lay awake wondering about my mysterious traveling companion. I recalled that I hadn't seen her talk to anyone apart from myself all evening, not even to say goodnight. I remembered the way she avoided looking at me as she firmly insisted that she could not sit for me.

When I came down to breakfast the next morning, she had already gone, and as no one mentioned her, I assumed that she was a relative of the Kirkbecks and that she must have left early to visit another member of the family nearby. The next morning, when a servant came into my room, I decided to question him about the visitor.

"Who was the lady who dined with us on Saturday night?" I asked.

"You mean Mrs. Kirkbeck, sir?" he replied.

"No, I'm talking about the lady dressed in black who sat opposite me at the table," I explained.

"Perhaps you mean Miss Hardwick, the governess, sir?" he replied again.

"No, it wasn't Miss Hardwick," I said patiently. "She joined us later."

"But there was no other lady, sir," the servant insisted.

I was now starting to feel less patient with the man's sluggish memory.

"Of course there was—she was the same lady who was sitting in front of the fire when I arrived. You must remember her!"

The servant stared at me, looking nonplussed. I could see that he thought I was ranting like a lunatic.

"I never saw any such lady, sir," he muttered, his eyes fixed firmly on the ground. The man then sped from the room before I could call him back.

Breakfast was rushed since I had to catch the early train to London, and I only had time to make the arrangements with my hosts for my return visit. But when I did return three weeks later, I questioned Mr. and Mrs. Kirkbeck about the lady in black. They were both quite positive that there had only been three people at the dinner table that night and that they knew nobody who fit the description I gave them.

WORD POWER

to commission—to place an order for something; to ask someone to do a task or duty

calling card—a card showing a person's name, similar to a business card

tedious—dull; boring

nonplussed—confused; at a loss

figment—invention; fantastic idea

I said no more on the subject, but now I was even more confused.

Who was this lady in black, and why had no one else seen her? Was she a figment of my imagination? Could I have dreamed up our train journey together, our talk before dinner, and her request for me to paint her portrait?

Chapter 2

It was nearly Christmas, and one afternoon, as daylight was fading, I was sitting at my desk writing letters when suddenly I sensed that someone was standing at my elbow, even though I had not heard anyone enter. I looked around, and there stood the lady in black. My surprise must have shown on my face, for she said, "I'm sorry if I've startled you. Perhaps you didn't hear me come in?"

She looked at me earnestly and immediately asked me if I had done any paintings of her. I confessed that I had not.

"This is sad news, as I urgently require one for my father," she replied. Then she produced an engraving of Lady M. A., similar to the one she had shown me at Alvingham.

"This might help you," she said. "They say this portrait has a strong likeness of me."

And, laying her hand imploringly on my arm, she whispered, "I beg you, paint my portrait. You cannot imagine how vital it is that you do so."

I could see that this was no light-hearted request, so I picked up my pencil there and then, and started to make a sketch of her. But my visitor would not pose for me and moved around the room, pretending to look at the pictures hanging on the walls. I managed to make two quick sketches before the room grew too dark to see my subject in any detail. I shut my sketchbook, and as I did so, she shook my hand firmly, said "goodbye," and walked to the front door. I watched as she stepped into the gloaming. She seemed to fade into the darkness, rather than disappear out of sight in the normal way. But perhaps it was just a trick of the light.

Would I ever see her again? What was I to do with the sketches I'd made? These matters troubled me. But I had work to do, and a few days later I had to leave for Leicestershire. I had sent ahead some large canvases, but when I arrived at my destination I discovered that they had gone to the wrong station and that it would take several days to get them back. I made use of the time by arranging to do some business in South Staffordshire. On my way there, I had to spend a night at Lichfield. Having settled down to an evening of solitude at the Swan Hotel, I remembered that an old acquaintance of mine once lived in the town. I rang for the waitress and asked, "Does Mr. Lute still live in Cathedral Close?"

"He does," she replied.

So I sent him a note, suggesting that he might join me for a couple of hours at the hotel. About twenty minutes later, a middle-aged stranger was shown into my room. He looked pale and gaunt. Holding up my note in his trembling hand, he explained that I seemed to have made a mistake. I apologized, and asked whether there might be another Mr. Lute living in Lichfield. He said there was not. Then I described my friend, and explained that he had married a lady named Fairbairn some two years ago.

"Ah, yes," he replied. "I believe you are referring to Mr. Clyne. He did live in Cathedral Close, as I now do, but he has since moved away."

As soon as he said the name "Clyne," I realized that this was, indeed, my friend's name. I apologized once more and admitted that I did not know why I had said "Lute" instead of "Clyne."

My visitor then took me by surprise.

"There's no need to apologize," he said. "As it happens, you are the very person I most wish to see. You are a portrait painter, are you not? I want you to paint a portrait of my daughter. Can you come with me now?"

I did not feel like painting anyone's portrait at that moment, let alone that of a stranger, so I explained that I could not as I was only to be in Staffordshire for the next two days. But the stranger was so insistent, and looked so weary, that I agreed and found myself accompanying him the short distance to his home. He was silent as we walked, and when we arrived, he introduced me to his daughter Maria and then promptly left the room.

Maria was a fair-haired girl of about fifteen, but her quiet, confident manner made her seem much older. She told me that her father had retired for the evening, as he was feeling unwell, and she invited me to sit by the fire. I explained that her father had asked me to paint a portrait of her or her sister, if she had one. When she heard this, she fell silent for a moment and gazed at the fire. Then she looked up, and in a quiet voice she related that her older sister Caroline, whom her father adored, had died nearly four months previously and that her death had thrown her father into a state of deep shock. He had often wished for a portrait of Caroline, and Maria thought that such a portrait might restore him to good health.

She paused, struggling to stifle her tears. Then she spoke.

THE FACTS

Charles Dickens (1812-70) is one of Britain's most famous authors. His writing was influenced by his childhood, when his father was always in debt, and by the harsh conditions of working people at that time. Another great influence was his love of ghost stories. When he was little, he had a 13-year-old nurse who was brilliant at telling a spine-chilling tale. Later Dickens used these stories. He certainly believed in the supernatural. When *The Portrait Painter's Story* was first published, Dickens was contacted by a man who said he was a real portrait painter and that the story Dickens told had actually happened to him!

"Oh, sir, it's no use hiding this from you any longer—Papa is no longer a sane person. Ever since Caroline's death, he says he is always seeing her. The doctor says we must keep all sharp objects out of his reach. Much of the time, like tonight, he cannot talk to us."

She begged me to return the next day and try to paint a portrait of her sister. I asked if they had any photographs or sketches of her, but Maria said no. I promised to try to do a portrait from Maria's description of her sister.

Next morning I started drawing. But though I did sketch after sketch, Maria confessed that none of them looked like Caroline. Toward the end of the day, Maria saw that I was growing tired and thanked me for my efforts.

"It is a great pity I cannot find the engraving of a lady who looks very much like Caroline. I am sure it would have helped you picture her," she continued.

"What has become of this engraving?" I asked.

"Oh, it has been missing from the book for about three weeks now."

"Can you remember whose portrait it is? I may be able to get a copy in London."

"It was a portrait of Lady M. A.," she replied.

Instantly I remembered the engraving the lady in black had pressed on me. I excused myself and fetched my sketchbook, with the engraving tucked inside it. When I showed my sketches and the engraving to Maria, she looked at them in disbelief.

"Where did you get these?" she whispered, with a hint of fear in her voice. But before I could answer, she took the sketchbook from me and rushed out of the room. When she returned, her father was with her.

Without even greeting me, he strode across the room and, scarcely able to contain his excitement, he blurted out, "I knew that I was right! It was you with my dear daughter, and it was she who sent me these sketches. Oh, thank you, kind sir," he said, stepping forward to shake my hand vigorously. "I will value these more than any other possession, except for my daughter Maria."

Mr. Lute no longer looked weary or gaunt, and as he held the sketches in his hands, Maria opened a book and showed me the blank page where the engraving of Lady M. A. had been, and I could see the glue marks where the print had been stuck down. Then she turned over the engraving that the lady in black had given me, and I saw that the glue marks on the back corresponded exactly with those on the blank page.

And so my story draws to a close. Mr. Lute did not want me to make any changes or additions to the pencil sketches of his daughter Caroline, but he begged me to start an oil portrait of her immediately. He sat by my side for hours, chatting cheerfully, occasionally suggesting corrections in my work.

The next day, he spoke about our chance meeting.

"I cannot explain how you came to write to me from the Swan Hotel," he continued. "But as soon as I saw you, I knew you were the man I had seen with my daughter at a dinner table in a country house, and later in a crowded room, and later still at a desk, writing or drawing. The doctors considered that I was suffering from delusions, but in fact I have seen Caroline many times since her death."

I finished the portrait in London and sent it to Mr. Lute, who has completely recovered his health. It now hangs in his bedroom, with the following words written underneath it: "C. L., 13th September 1858, aged 22." The thirteenth of September is not the date of Caroline Lute's death; it is the day this portrait painter first met her.

THE END

WORD POWER

gloaming—dusk

stifle—hold back, prevent

delusion—mistaken idea or belief

A Christmas Carol

Retold from a story by Charles Dickens

It was Christmas Eve when Jacob Marley died. Ebenezer Scrooge was the only mourner at his funeral. But over the next seven years, Scrooge barely gave his dead business partner a thought. He did not even remove his name from the sign over the door of their counting house. He was too tight-fisted to waste paint on it.

Hard and sharp as flint, Scrooge was a grasping, secretive, solitary old miser. His cold heart had made his thin lips blue and his walk stiff, yet real weather did not affect him. No amount of warmth from the sun on a summer's day could cheer him. Nor could any bitter wind chill him further. No one stopped him in the middle of the street to say, with a smile, "My dear Scrooge, how are you?" Beggars did not bother him, children ran away from him, even the dogs of blind men led their masters out of his path.

But what did Scrooge care! He had no time for people, only for money.

One Christmas Eve, Scrooge was sitting in his counting house, busily arranging money loans and debt repayments. It was cold and bleak outside—and not much better inside. Scrooge kept the smallest of fires in his office and always refused the requests of his poor clerk, Bob Cratchit, for more coal.

"A Merry Christmas, Uncle! God save you!" cried a cheerful voice suddenly. It was the voice of Scrooge's nephew, who was entering the office. His eyes twinkled and his cold cheeks were blushed with good cheer.

"Bah!" said Scrooge, "Humbug!"

"Christmas a humbug, my dear Uncle! You cannot mean that," said Scrooge's nephew.

"I most certainly do," replied Scrooge. "What right have you to be merry? You're poor enough."

"Then what right have you to be angry? You're wealthy enough!" returned Scrooge's nephew good-naturedly.

"What else can I be when I live in such a world of fools?" snapped Scrooge. "What is

Christmas time but a way of spending money you don't have. I wish every fool who is happy at Christmas could be boiled with his own plum pudding and buried with a stake of holly through his heart!"

"Come now, Uncle. Christmas is a time for good. It is a kind and forgiving and charitable time. I say, God bless it!"

Scrooge's poor clerk dared to applaud for a moment.

"One more sound from you, Bob Cratchit," yelled Scrooge, "and you'll start Christmas without a job."

"Calm down, Uncle, and please come to dinner with us tomorrow," said Scrooge's smiling nephew.

"No," replied the miser firmly.

"But we would love for you to be there."

"Pah. Love is the only thing in the world more ridiculous than a Merry Christmas. Good afternoon, sir."

"We have no quarrel, Uncle. Why cannot we be friends?"

"Good afternoon, sir," said Scrooge again, even more fiercely.

His nephew turned and left, still cheerful despite his uncle's bad temper.

Shortly afterward, two rich gentlemen walked into the office. They greeted the clerk, then turned to Scrooge.

"At this festive season, Mr. Scrooge, we try to help the poor. It is a time when want is most keenly felt. Thousands are in need of the most basic comforts."

"Are there no prisons?" asked Scrooge.

"Plenty of prisons, far too many in fact," sighed one of the gentlemen.

"Are the workhouses still in operation?" demanded Scrooge.

"I'm afraid to say they are," responded the other gentleman grimly.

"What a great relief!" cried Scrooge. "For a moment I feared that something had stopped their useful work."

The two wealthy gentlemen glanced at each other, and then one spoke.

"So as we were just saying, Mr. Scrooge, we are raising a fund in order to buy food and clothing for the poor. What would you like to contribute?"

"I would just like to be left alone," said Scrooge. "I don't make merry myself at Christmas, and I can't afford to make idle people merry. That's what workhouses and prisons are for."

"But sir, many would rather die than endure life in those awful places," protested one of the gentlemen.

"If they would rather die," said Scrooge, "they had better do it, and decrease the surplus population."

"But Mr. Scrooge..."

"It's really not my business," Scrooge interrupted. "It's quite enough for a man to understand his own business. There is no need at all to interfere in other people's. My business occupies me constantly. Good afternoon, gentlemen!"

Seeing clearly that further argument was useless, the gentlemen withdrew.

Scrooge resumed his labors as the fog and darkness thickened outside. Apart from warning away a group of carol singers, he stayed at his desk until the evening. Then he reluctantly shut the office.

"You'll want ALL day off tomorrow, I suppose?" growled Scrooge to his clerk.

"If that's quite convenient, sir," replied the poor clerk.

"It's not convenient," said Scrooge, "and it's certainly not fair paying a day's wages for no work."

The clerk observed that this happened only once a year.

"A poor excuse for picking a man's pocket every twenty-fifth of December!" said the miserly Scrooge. "I expect you to be back at your desk all the earlier the next morning!"

Scrooge sat all alone over a frugal meal in the same dreary tavern that he always visited. He spent the long evening reading newspapers and checking his bank books before going home to bed. He lived in gloomy chambers that had once belonged to his dead partner, Jacob Marley. They were in a grim building inhabited by no one except Scrooge himself.

As Scrooge reached out to open the front door, he gasped. The knocker, a lump of plain black iron, had changed its shape. Now it looked exactly like the face of Marley. As Scrooge stared in shock, the face disappeared and became the knocker again. Scrooge blinked in disbelief a number of times and shook his head violently.

"Bah! Humbug!" he shouted, entering the building and slamming the door hard. The crash resounded through the house like thunder. Scrooge was not a man to be frightened by echoes or fanciful visions. Still, he was a little uneasy as he entered his rooms and locked himself in for the night. Then he glanced at the old servants' bell that hung in the corner and was astonished to see it begin to swing all by itself.

At first, the bell swung gently. But then the swing became greater so that the bell rang out loudly. The sound was followed by a loud, clanking noise from the cellars. It gradually rose up through the house.

"It's humbug still!" said Scrooge. But as the clanking sound got closer and closer, the color drained from his thin cheeks.

Suddenly something flew into the room. Scrooge nearly fainted with fright. It was the ghost of his former colleague, Jacob Marley.

Scrooge had heard many people say of Marley that he had no heart. Now it seemed to be true. Marley was transparent—Scrooge could see right through him. But the ghost was wrapped in a large, heavy chain. It was made of cash boxes, keys, padlocks, accounts books, and heavy purses, all of solid steel. Scrooge felt the ghost's death-cold eyes staring right at him.

"What do you want with me?" he asked, his voice trembling.

"Much!" replied the ghost.

"You're not even real!" Scrooge said in a voice that sounded more bold than he felt.

At this, the spirit gave a frightful cry and shook its metal chain. This made such an appalling noise that Scrooge fell on his knees and clasped his hands in front of his face as though praying.

"Have mercy!" Scrooge cried. "I believe! I believe in you, oh, dreadful apparition."

"Listen, Ebenezer. I made this chain in life, of my own free will," said the ghost. "Perhaps you would care to know about your own chain? It was already the same length

WORD POWER

counting house—an office where people give out loans, collect debt repayments, count money, etc.

grasping—greedy

humbug—deceitful nonsense

want—lack of money, possessions etc; poverty

workhouses—grim, prisonlike institutions where the poor once lived and worked

reluctantly—unwillingly

frugal—containing little; meager

fanciful—imaginary; unreal

as mine seven Christmases ago. But I am sorry to say that it has grown a very great deal since then!"

"Tell me more. Speak comfort to me, Jacob," begged Scrooge.

"I have none to give," the ghost replied. "I cannot rest, I cannot stay, I cannot linger anywhere. When alive, I never roamed beyond the world of money and our counting house. But now, in death, I must travel forever. I have no rest, no peace, just the constant torture of guilt."

"But you were always a good man of business, Jacob," said Scrooge.

"Of business!" cried the ghost, wringing its hands. "Mankind was my business. The good of all people, rich and poor, that should have been my business, not money-making."

Hearing this sad cry, Scrooge started to shake rapidly.

"Hear me!" cried the ghost. "You will be haunted by three spirits. Expect the first when the bell tolls one o'clock. Without their visits, you cannot hope to escape the same dreadful fate as me."

The ghost flew out of the window. Scrooge looked out after him. The air was filled with phantoms, each wearing a chain like Marley's ghost. Some chains were short, some monstrously long. Scrooge recognized several of the ghosts. All were wailing in misery.

Eventually the creatures faded, leaving only mist. Scrooge tried to say "humbug!," but the word simply would not come out. Overcome by both terror and fatigue, he fell straight into his cold bed.

Chapter 2

Scrooge awoke to hear the church bells striking the hour. But something was wrong. The bells were chiming one o'clock, but he had fallen into bed after that time. Had an icicle frozen the clock's workings? Or had he slept through an entire day?

Before Scrooge could think further, a bright light filled the room, and the miser found himself face to face with a visitor. Scrooge jumped in fright. The unearthly figure before him was either a child or a very old man. Scrooge was so rattled and confused that he could not figure out out which. A strange light flickered around the figure, who wore a tunic of pure white.

"Are you the s-s-spirit, sir, whose c-c-coming was foretold to me?" stammered Scrooge.

"I am! I am the Ghost of Christmas Past—your past, Ebenezer Scrooge. I am here for your welfare."

The voice was soft and gentle, but deep and low at the same time.

"Surely my welfare would be better served by a good night's rest. I have work to do tomorrow," Scrooge protested.

The spirit said nothing, but took hold of Scrooge's arm. Suddenly, Scrooge found himself heading toward his bedroom wall, caught in the ghost's grip. He screamed, but miracle of miracles, he and the ghost passed right through the wall and out on to a country road, many miles from the city.

"Good Heavens!" gasped Scrooge. "I was born here."

Scrooge stared wide-eyed as many scenes from his past floated into view. Some were wonderful to behold, such as times spent playing with his younger sister. Others were much more tragic. Scrooge shuddered as he watched his father and teachers beat him. Then he cried for help as they locked him in his room night after night.

"These are but shadows of people that have been. They cannot see or hear us," said the ghost.

"Take me away, I cannot bear it," Scrooge begged. Scrooge's mood lightened when he saw a portly, gray-haired man at work in an office.

"Why, there's old Fezziwig. As a young lad, I was an apprentice of his, you know," Scrooge said with a smile.

The ghost and Scrooge watched Fezziwig shut his shop early on Christmas Eve, then hold a joyful party in his offices. Scrooge watched his younger self joining in the celebrations.

As the scene unfolded, Scrooge looked on and lost himself in the party. He remembered all the dances that the fiddler played, and watched as he, Scrooge, jigged and polkaed with the guests. He smiled, too, at the tremendous buffet of cold meats, mincemeat-pies, and ale that old Fezziwig had provided for the partygoers.

"Just three or four pounds worth of food and drink! Surely Fezziwig didn't deserve all the praise those silly people gave him," said the ghost as the party ended.

"Oh, but he did," replied Scrooge, "and not just for the party. He employed many people and could have made their lives hard and miserable, but he chose instead to make them happy..."

Scrooge's words tailed off as he fell into thought. The ghost watched him and smiled to itself before showing Scrooge a new, much later scene.

Scrooge was now a healthy young man with greedy, hawklike eyes. He sat under a tree with a beautiful woman, who was speaking.

"I have been replaced by another idol in your life, Ebenezer," she said. "There is no point in your denying it. I have seen it in your actions during the past few years. Money is all that interests you now. My decision to end our relationship may cause you pain. Part of me hopes it does, for you have caused me much. But, eventually, you will dismiss our romance as purely an unprofitable dream. May you be happy in the life you have chosen!"

Scrooge found hot, salty tears streaming down his face as he watched the scene. He tried to say "Bah! Humbug!" but the words stuck in his throat. So instead, in a broken voice, he said, "Spirit! Please remove me from this place."

Slowly, the ghost and the scene faded, and Scrooge found himself back in his bedroom. Utterly exhausted and upset, he fell into a deep sleep.

When Scrooge awoke, an unnatural light in his living room drew him toward it. What a transformation! The room was decked in Christmas decorations and warmed by an enormous fire in the grate. An enormous feast filled the floor.

"Come in and get to know me! I am the Ghost of Christmas Present," boomed a jolly giant clothed in a green robe with a white fur border.

Scrooge entered timidly, his eyes gazing at the floor. He was not the confident

WORD POWER

unearthly—supernatural; not of this world

rattled—uneasy; frightened

portly—fat; bulky

apprentice—a person who works for another while learning a trade from him or her

eked out—shared (a limited amount) in small portions

braces—metal splints or supports for legs

smarted—(here) felt mental pain

recital—a musical performance

Scrooge of before. The next instant, he and the ghost were standing unseen in the home of Bob Cratchit, his clerk. Scrooge looked on as the clerk's family celebrated Christmas as best they could.

Scrooge watched keenly as they eked out several small pans of boiled vegetables, arranging them thinly to fill each plate. He also observed Bob Cratchit carve every last sliver off the Christmas goose.

Scrooge counted the Cratchits' children. He had no idea that his clerk's family was so large. His eyes were drawn to the smallest of them all—a tiny, frail boy with his legs in braces. This was Tiny Tim. Scrooge found it hard to stop looking at him.

Every possible compliment that could be given to a meal was uttered by the family as they ate. No one suggested or even thought that it was sparse for Christmas Day, or small for such hungry people.

"A Merry Christmas to us all, my dears. God bless us!" cried Bob Cratchit, and all the family echoed his words.

"God bless us every one!" said Tiny Tim, his withered hand clasping his father's fingers tightly.

"Spirit," said Scrooge, with an interest that he had never felt before, "tell me if Tiny Tim will live."

The spirit shook his head.

"No, NO!" wailed Scrooge.

"If he is to die, he had better do it, and decrease the surplus population," said the ghost in reply.

Scrooge winced as his own words were repeated back to him. Then he hung his head and remained silent. But on hearing his own name, he looked up again. Bob Cratchit was proposing a toast to him.

"To Mr. Scrooge, the founder of this feast!"

"The founder indeed!" cried Mrs. Cratchit, angrily. "I wish I had him here. I'd give him a piece of my mind to feast upon."

"My dear," soothed Bob, "do not speak so harshly in front of the children on Christmas Day."

"I will drink a toast to you and our family, but not to that hard, unfeeling brute," she replied.

As Mrs. Cratchit said those words, the ghost whisked Scrooge away through the city. They journeyed through kitchens, parlors, and dining rooms. Then they left the city and visited farms, mines, and ships on the high seas. Everywhere they went, people were engaging in Christmas festivities.

Eventually, the ghost led Scrooge to his nephew's lodgings. There, a dozen guests were engaged in all sorts of party games and fun. The sound of laughter echoed through the house. Scrooge saw his niece, then heard her husband's voice.

"Honestly, Scrooge said that Christmas was a humbug!"

The guests all laughed, but Scrooge smarted.

"Shame on him," scolded Scrooge's niece. "But I think he's the one who misses out, not us."

"True. His wealth does him and others no service," said his nephew.

A little later, Scrooge's nephew and niece gave a recital on piano and harp. Scrooge normally hated music, but this seemed enchanting even to his ears. He became completely lost in its sweet sounds.

Scrooge applauded along with the guests when the recital finished. Without realizing it, he had become so light of heart that he joined in all the parlor games they played afterward. He was surprisingly good at charades, even though the guests could not hear any of his answers. At length, the ghost indicated that they had to leave.

"Can we stay just one more half hour?" Scrooge begged, just like a little boy. He was having so much fun. But the ghost shook its head, and they left the house.

"My time is nearly over," said the phantom, unveiling two wretched children, who had been hidden beneath his robe. They were miserable creatures, painfully thin, dirty, and frightened. Scrooge's heart went out to them.

"Are they yours, Spirit?" he found himself asking.

"No they are Man's," replied the ghost. "The boy is ignorance; the girl is want. Beware them both, especially ignorance. For if you don't pay attention to the lessons we have tried to teach you, doom will follow.

"Have the boy and girl no refuge?" cried Scrooge.

"Are there no prisons? Are the workhouses still in operation?" the ghost said, repeating Scrooge's earlier words. Then it disappeared.

Scrooge immediately found himself back in his bed and began to think about everything he had just seen. Suddenly, a chill ran down his spine, and he looked up. There before him stood another solemn phantom. Like a mist, it started drifting slowly along the ground toward him.

Chapter 3

Scrooge fell to his knees at the sight of the next ghost. The phantom in front of him was completely covered in a black cloak. Its power and mystery terrified him.

"You are the Ghost of Christmas To Come?" Scrooge eventually asked the spirit, but it remained silent. Filled with dread, Scrooge followed the phantom as it moved about the city. First, the two of them stopped to listen to some businessmen that Scrooge recognized. They were mocking a colleague who had recently died. Then the miser and the phantom arrived in the filthy city slums.

With the stench of decay all around, Scrooge and the phantom stood in a tiny hovel and watched a wizened old man buy items from three poor tradespeople. Scrooge realized that the three were selling clothing and possessions that they had taken from a dead man's house.

"If he wanted to keep 'em after he was dead, the wicked old crow," said one of them, "why wasn't he decent in his lifetime? Then he'd have had somebody to look after him when he died, instead of gasping his last alone."

The others agreed heartily, clutching the money that they had made.

"He frightened everyone away while he was alive, but has managed to profit us now he's dead! Ha, ha, ha!" laughed another of the tradespeople.

"Spirit!" said Scrooge, shuddering from head to foot, "I see the case of this unhappy man is not unlike mine. Merciful Heaven, what is this?"

Scrooge sprang back in terror at a new scene that appeared before him. There, a motionless figure wrapped

in a shroud lay on a bed, beneath a grimy, ragged sheet. Unwatched and uncared for, it was the dead man whose belongings were being sold.

The phantom pointed at the thin sheet. Scrooge could easily have removed it to see who the dead person was, but fear prevented him. He looked around. The house was not quite empty—rats were watching the corpse. Scrooge felt sick as he heard them gnawing nearby. What did they want in this room of death? He did not dare to think.

"Spirit, please let us leave this fearful place. If there is any man in this city who feels emotion as a result of this man's death, show me, I beg you."

The phantom spread its dark robe before Scrooge, then pulled it back to reveal a room where a woman and man were in conversation.

"He is dead," said the man.

"Oh, mercy!" exclaimed the woman and placed her head in her hands.

Scrooge felt a tinge of relief. Someone cared for this man at least. The woman kept her head bowed and her hands locked in prayer. But when she looked up again, she was wearing a broad smile and tears of happiness were streaming down her flushed cheeks.

"We are saved from him! Whoever arranges our debts in the future could never be as heartless as he was."

"Yes, my darling, we are saved! Hurrah!"

Aghast, Scrooge turned to the phantom.

"Please let me see some tenderness connected with a death, any death at all," he pleaded.

At this request, the ghost led Scrooge through several streets that were familiar to him. As they went along, the old miser looked here and there, hoping to catch a glimpse of himself. But he was nowhere to be seen. Then they entered Bob Cratchit's house and found Mrs. Cratchit and the children seated around the fire. Everyone was very quiet.

"Your father is late," Mrs. Cratchit said, her voice barely a whisper.

"He has walked slower these last few evenings, Mother," the eldest son replied softly.

The family remained silent until the door opened gently and in walked Bob Cratchit. How ill, how sad he looked. He tried to be sweet to his wife and children, but grief scarred his face. His children bustled around him attentively. His wife handed him some tea. He cradled it in his hands for a moment before breaking down.

"My little, little child!" cried Bob, over and over again.

Through his sobs, Bob Cratchit made every member of his family promise never to forget the dead Tiny Tim. Good, sweet Tiny Tim. Scrooge watched in dismay. He could not remember his heart ever feeling heavier than it did at this moment.

The ghost dragged Scrooge away from the grieving family and took him through the streets into a churchyard. It was an eerie place, overrun with grass and other plants. The ghost stood among the graves and pointed down to one of them. Scrooge advanced toward it, trembling. In his heart he knew that the grave belonged to the man they had seen lying dead and unloved.

"Phantom, will the events you have shown me happen no matter what, or can any be changed?" Scrooge asked. But the ghost remained silent. Then Scrooge bent down and read the gravestone. On it was his own name.

"No, Spirit, NO!" Scrooge screamed, gripping the phantom's robe.

The phantom started to shrink and change shape.

"Help me, Spirit. I am not the man I was before. I have changed. I WILL change. Don't leave me here! Speak to me," Scrooge pleaded.

Scrooge looked around him. The phantom had vanished and so had the graveyard. He was alive and back in his bedroom. He still had a chance to do something about all that he had seen.

"I will live in the Past, the Present, and the Future!" Scrooge cried. "Oh, Jacob Marley! Praise be for this!"

Scrooge started skipping around his bedroom and burst into laughter. His chuckle was impressive for a man who had not laughed for many years.

"I don't know what day of the month it is! I am as light as a feather and as happy as an angel."

WORD POWER

stench—a terrible smell

wizened—shriveled; heavily wrinkled

shroud—a sheet in which a corpse is wrapped for burial

aghast—horrified; appalled

Hearing the deafening peals of the church bells, Scrooge flung open the window and craned his head out. He spied a small boy below.

"What's today, my fine fellow?" cried Scrooge.

"Today?" replied the boy. "Why, Christmas Day, of course."

"Christmas Day!" said Scrooge to himself. "I haven't missed it. The spirits have done it all in one night."

Scrooge asked the boy to buy the enormous prize turkey in the butcher's window for him. He also promised to pay the boy a shilling when he returned with it.

"An intelligent boy, a delightful boy!" Scrooge exclaimed. "I'll send the turkey to Bob Cratchit!" he added, rubbing his hands with pleasure. "He won't know who's sent it. What a splendid surprise!"

Next, Scrooge shaved, dressed, and went out into the busy streets. He regarded everyone with a delighted smile and seemed so full of Christmas cheer that three or four strangers bid him "Merry Christmas." Scrooge had never heard such sweet words ringing in his ears before.

He had not walked far when he spotted one of the gentlemen who had visited the day before.

"My dear sirs," said Scrooge, greeting the gentlemen. "Please forgive me for my manners. May I now offer a donation of..." and he whispered a figure into one gentleman's ear. The gentleman sprang back in amazement at his words.

"Lord bless me! That's an awfully large sum of money, Mr. Scrooge. I don't know what to say to such generosity."

"Don't say a word. I think I owe a great many back payments. A Merry Christmas to you!"

"And to you, sir!"

Scrooge went to church, then walked about the streets watching people with great pleasure. It was as if he had never seen these people before, which in a way was true. In the afternoon he paced in front of his nephew's house a dozen times before he had the courage to enter.

"Bless my soul!" cried Scrooge's nephew. "Am I seeing a ghost?"

"No, it is I, your Uncle Ebenezer. Is there room at your table for a foolish old man, my dear nephew?"

Scrooge's nephew was delighted to welcome him. So were his niece and all the other guests. Scrooge had the most wonderful time, eating dinner, then playing parlor games late into the evening. What happiness!

The next morning, Scrooge rushed into his office to get there before Bob Cratchit. When Bob entered late, Scrooge put on his best angry face and told his clerk that this would not do.

"I'm so sorry Mr. Scrooge, sir," poor Bob said to his employer.

"I won't stand for this sort of thing any longer, you hear," Scrooge replied angrily.

Poor Bob trembled.

"So I'll be raising your salary. But before we discuss the matter further, rush out, and buy a sack of coal. We want the biggest fire in any office in this city. A Merry Christmas, Bob!"

Scrooge was better than his word. He doubled Bob's salary and became a second father to Tiny Tim, who lived long and well. He became as good a man as the city had ever known. He never saw another ghost and always kept Christmas well. May that be said of all of us. And as Tiny Tim said, "God Bless Us, Every One!"

THE END

The Signalman

Retold from a story by Charles Dickens

"Hello! Below there!" From above the steep railway cutting, I called to the signalman. He was at the door of his signal-box, holding a flag furled around its short pole. At first, I could hardly see him. An angry, red sunset forced me to shade my eyes with my hand. I seemed so high above the shadowy figure and he so far below me in the dark trench.

Strangely, instead of looking up, as I stood almost directly over him, the signalman turned and peered down the railway line. Why should he think my cry had come from that direction?

"Hello! Below there!" I repeated, my hand still across my eyes. At last, the signalman saw me.

"Is there a path I can take that leads down so that I may talk to you?" I asked.

The signalman watched me but did not reply. Just then there came a vague vibration. It quickly changed into a violent and pulsating rush of steam and air. I stepped back fearfully, suddenly aware that it might drag me down. Next moment, the train sped past. As it clattered away into the distance, the signalman refurled the flag he had waved.

I asked him again about the path. He stared oddly at me before finally, almost reluctantly, pointing to a spot above the cutting, some distance beyond.

"All right!" I called, starting toward it.

I came across a rough path that zigzagged down into the unusually steep cutting. I took care and time, for the stone walls of the deep embankment became ever more cold and damp. All the while, the signalman stood between the rails of the track that the train had just crossed. As I neared him, I stopped a moment and wondered why his sallow, bearded face gazed at me so intently. He appeared thoughtful and expectant.

Down and down I continued, until I reached the level of the track. What a lonely, dreary dungeon of a place it seemed. On each side, towering, wet walls of jagged stone blocked out all but a strip of sky. In one direction, the cutting curved away into the distance. The other way, it ended in a gloomy red light near the mouth of a forbidding black tunnel. So little sunlight found its way here that there was an earthy, deadly smell. A cold wind made me shiver, or was it the chilling thought that I had left the natural world far above me?

I was close enough to touch the signalman before he stirred, taking a step back and raising his hand.

"What a very lonely place," I began, awkwardly. "That's why I thought you might enjoy a visitor."

With a curiously puzzled expression, the signalman glanced at the red light by the tunnel, as if something were missing from it. Then he looked again at me with his fixed eyes and grim face. There was something alarming, almost unreal, about him. But then I stepped back and saw fear in his expression. Was he frightened of me?

"There's no need to stare! What's wrong?" I said, forcing a smile.

The signalman pointed to the red light and told me that he had thought, for a moment, he had seen me there before. When I assured him he was mistaken, the signalman relaxed and began to talk about his job. Duty meant he had little chance of escaping the shadowy cutting's damp air to climb up into the sunshine. There was little hard work for him to do. He just had to stay watchful and ready, sometimes by night as well as by day, as trains used the cutting.

Soon the man led me into his signal-box, where a fire gave out welcome warmth. There was a desk inside, too, and the telegraph machine, with its little bell, by which messages were sent up and down the railway line. For a while, the signalman spoke to me quietly about his past, particularly about misusing the many opportunities he had had when he was a young student. But he was interrupted several times by the little bell and had to read messages and send replies. Once he went to stand outside the signal-box door. Then he showed his flag to a passing train and called to the driver.

I was just thinking to myself how efficiently and safely the signalman went about his duties when he twice stopped talking to me and turned toward the little bell when it did not ring. At those times, the color drained from his face, and he stepped outside to study the red light by the tunnel's mouth. On both of these occasions, he returned to the signal-box with the same mysterious air.

"I am troubled, sir. I am troubled," he finally said in a low voice.

No sooner had the signalman spoken than it was clear to me that he wished he had remained silent.

"By what?" I asked.

"It is very difficult to say," came the reply. "If ever you make another visit, I will try to tell you."

I was more than a little curious and eagerly agreed to return the following night. As I left, the signalman shone a white light to help me find the path up out of the cutting again.

"When you are at the top, don't call out!" he warned in a way that made a chill run through me. "And don't call out when you come back down again tomorrow, either," he insisted. Then he continued even more mysteriously, saying, "What made you cry, 'Hello! Below there!' tonight? Those words. I know them well."

I explained it was simply that I had seen him below. But then the signalman asked another strange question that kept me wondering uneasily.

"You did not feel the words came to you in any supernatural way?"

"No," I replied, and left him.

The next night, the signalman was waiting for me at the bottom of the cutting, with his white light on. This time, I had been careful not to call out. Once again, we walked to his signal-box and sat down by the fire.

"As for yesterday evening, I took you for someone else who troubles me," the signalman said, in a voice that was little more than a whisper.

"Who is it?" I asked.

"I don't know. I never saw the face. The left arm is across it while the right arm waves urgently, like this," the signalman demonstrated. "At the same time, the figure cries out, 'For pity's sake, clear the way!'

"One moonlit night," the signalman went on, "I was sitting here in the signal-box when I heard a voice cry, 'Hello! Below there!' I jumped up and, from the door, saw a figure standing by the red light near the tunnel, waving as I showed you. The voice was hoarse from shouting, 'Hello! Below there! Look out!'"

I sat listening eagerly while the signalman explained how he had quickly snatched up his lamp and turned on its red light. Then he had hurried toward the strange figure, asking what was wrong. All the while, the figure masked its eyes with a sleeve.

"I was so close, I tried to pull the sleeve away," the signalman told me. "But the figure simply vanished! I ran on into the tunnel, my lamp held above my head. Yet the place was empty. All I could hear was the trickling water that dripped down the stained walls."

A sudden hatred of the place had then overcome the signalman, and he had hurried out of the tunnel again. He had examined the red tunnel light with his own red light, then sent messages along the line to check if anything was wrong. But the answer had come back, from both directions, that all was well.

While I listened, it was as if a frozen finger was moving right down my spine. I suggested that the figure's voice had been no more than a trick of the wind. But my companion had more to say.

"Six hours afterward" the signalman continued slowly, "there was a terrible accident on this very line. The unfortunate victims were carried out through the tunnel, over the exact spot where the figure had stood."

I tried hard to ignore the unpleasant shudder that his words sent through me and pointed out that amazing coincidences can occur. But, for the second time, the signalman had more to say.

"All this," he said, laying his hand lightly upon my arm and glancing over his shoulder with hollow eyes, "took place just a year ago. After six or seven months had passed, I had recovered from the terrible shock. Then, early one morning, I stood by the signal-box door and looked toward the red light again."

The signalman stopped and turned grimly toward me. Finally, he continued to speak with great seriousness.

"Then," he said, "I saw the mysterious specter once more."

WORD POWER

cutting—a deep trench cut in the ground to make an open tunnel for a rail track to run through

sallow—dull yellow

forbidding—sinister; menacing

telegraph—a communication system that sends and receives messages using coded electrical signals

Chapter 2

The signalman went on to tell me that the next time he had seen the mysterious figure by the tunnel, it did not cry out or wave its arm. Instead, it covered its face with its hands, as if in mourning.

"Did you go up to it?" I asked, as I sat by the fire in the signal-box, beneath the deep, gloomy railway cutting. This was my second visit. As it was late at night, the place seemed even less welcoming than before.

"No. I felt faint so I came in here to recover," he replied. "When I went back to the door and looked out, the ghost—for such, I believe, the figure was—was gone."

"And nothing more came of it?" I said.

The signalman looked grim. "On the contrary. That same day, as a train came out of the tunnel, I noticed anxious passengers waving desperately from a carriage window. I was just in time to signal to the driver to stop. He at once shut off steam and put on his brake. As the train pulled up, I ran after it and heard terrible cries. A passenger had died and was carried here, into the signal-box."

I listened, stunned and unable to speak for a moment. My mouth felt dry. Outside, the wind and telegraph wires wailed eerily.

"It's true, I tell you. That's exactly how it happened," insisted the signalman. "But that's not the worst of it. The specter returned a week ago. Since then it has appeared at the red light by the tunnel several times."

"What does it do?" I asked, breaking a thoughtful silence.

In answer, the signalman explained once

more how the mysterious figure screened its eyes with one arm and waved violently, crying: "For pity's sake, clear the way!"

At least now I could understand why the signalman was so disturbed.

"I have no peace or rest," he said, desperately. "The figure stands waving and ringing my telegraph bell. And it calls out to me: 'Hello! Below there! Look out!' in an agonized manner."

Suddenly, I remembered something odd.

"Did it ring the bell when I was here yesterday evening, causing you to go to the door?"

"Twice," nodded the signalman.

"Why, that proves your imagination is playing tricks," I cried, "because I swear the bell did not ring at either time."

The signalman, not so easily convinced, shook his head. He assured me that he had not been mistaken.

"The ghost's ring is a strange vibration in the telegraph bell," he said. "I'm not surprised you failed to hear it. But I certainly did."

"And was the specter there, by the tunnel, when you looked out yesterday?" I asked.

"Both times," came the firm reply.

I had an idea. "Will you come and look for it now?" I said.

The signalman bit his lip and unwillingly followed me to the door. Beyond was the red danger light and the black, gaping mouth of the tunnel. There, too, were the high, wet stone walls of the cutting, with the stars above them. But of the specter, there was no sign. Yet, when we went back into the box, the signalman was no less troubled.

"What is it trying to warn me about? Where is the danger?" he said, desperation in his anguished gaze. "I'm sure this third

time will lead to another terrible disaster, like the two before. But what can I do?" He wiped beads of fearful perspiration from his forehead with his handkerchief.

"If I telegraph a danger warning without any reason, I'll lose my job," he went on. "If only the figure would tell me where and when any accident was to happen. Then it might be avoided."

All I could do was to talk to the signalman, reassuring him and reasoning with him, until he finally calmed down. I even offered to stay until morning, but he would not hear of it. So I left him in that dismal cutting. While I climbed the pathway out, I looked back to the forbidding tunnel and the red light. There was something about it that I did not like, and I was thankful my lodgings lay well beyond its glow.

But now my own thoughts worried me. The signalman had sworn me to secrecy. I could not betray his trust. But was he in a fit state to continue working in such isolation? Would it be wiser, safer, if others knew the

WORD POWER

eerily—in a weird way; mysteriously

agonized—indicating suffering or sorrow; anguished

anguished—indicating suffering or sorrow; agonized

clammy—damp and sticky

truth? My mind raced. But, finally, I settled on what to do. I would offer to accompany him to seek, in strict confidence, the best medical opinion.

The signalman would be off-duty shortly after dawn. I had agreed to meet him again when he returned to his box, after dusk. I would speak to him then about my plan.

It was a pleasant evening as I set off for that meeting with the signalman. The sun was sinking when I reached the path near the top of the deep railway cutting. I was an hour early, so I decided to walk on a while, before making my way back. First, though, on an impulse, I stepped closer to the place above the cutting where I had originally seen the signalman.

A sudden, shocking dread gripped me. I could hardly believe my eyes. Below, by the railway tunnel, I spotted what looked like the figure of a man. His left sleeve was across his eyes, and his right arm waved urgently. But my horror passed when I realized that the man was real enough. He seemed to be demonstrating something to others nearby. The light by the tunnel had not been lit. But close to it was something I had not seen before. It was a tarpaulin-covered frame, no bigger than a bed.

I felt cold, and my hands were clammy. Something was wrong. A guilty fear welled up within me. I should never have left the signalman there, all alone. I should have alerted some other railway worker, who could have checked that he was fit to remain on duty. With growing panic, I hurried down the narrow path toward the men.

"What's wrong?" I called, breathlessly.

"Signalman killed this morning," came the crushing reply.

"Not the man from this signal-box?"

"Yes," nodded the group's spokesman.

He approached the frame and lifted the tarpaulin.

"You'll recognize him, then?" he asked. "Weird business. He was cut down by an

engine in broad daylight, with a lamp in his hand, too. His back was toward the engine."

The words sounded distant, unreal.

"Tom over there was driving," the spokesman said, as he pointed to the man who had been explaining how the accident had happened.

Tom took up the story as he stepped back to the tunnel mouth. "Coming around the curve in the tunnel, I was," he said, "when I suddenly saw the signalman at the end. There was no time to reduce my speed, and he didn't seem to hear the whistle. So I shut it off and shouted out to him."

"What did you say?" I asked.

"Hello! Below there! Look out! For pity's sake, clear the way!" Tom replied.

When I heard those words, which had so haunted the signalman, I shivered. I also began to consider more deeply why, by some strange coincidence, I had used the first of them when greeting him myself.

"It was dreadful," Tom said, and his voice echoed around that gloomy cutting. "I never stopped calling to him. I put an arm before my eyes so as not to see, and waved this arm. But it was no use."

THE END

THE GHOST CHAMBER

Retold from a story by Charles Dickens

Mr. Goodchild and Mr. Idle arrived at the house where they were to stay in broad, bright daylight. Then they stepped straight into the somber hall, which was full of old carvings and dark mahogany panels that gave it a mysterious character. Half a dozen noiseless old men, all dressed exactly alike in black, received them and glided up the stairs ahead of them. Then they filed off to the right and left of the staircase, as the guests entered their sitting room.

Mr. Goodchild and Mr. Idle passed a night in the house without seeing any more of the old men. Nor did it appear that any old men were missed or expected by any member of the establishment.

But soon, something strange began to happen. The door of their sitting room was repeatedly opened and shut. It was always opened at an unexpected moment, when they were reading, writing, eating, drinking, talking, or dozing. But when they looked toward it, it was clapped shut again, and nobody was to be seen.

On the second night of their stay, when the house was closed and quiet, the two men were reclining on sofas, smoking, drinking brandy, and talking. Mr. Goodchild took out his watch to wind it.

"What time is it?" asked Mr. Idle.

"One," said Goodchild.

As if he had ordered one old man, and the order had been promptly executed, the door opened, and one old man stood looking into the room.

"One of the six, Tom, at last!" said Mr. Goodchild, in a surprised whisper. "Sir, your pleasure?"

"Sir, *your* pleasure?" said the old man.

"Didn't I have the pleasure of seeing you yesterday?" said Goodchild.

"I cannot say for certain," was the grim reply. "I think you saw me, did you not?"

"Oh, yes," came the reply. "But I see many who never see me."

The old man looked chilled and cadaverous, and spoke very slowly. He seemed unable to blink, as if his eyelids had been nailed to his forehead. His eyes were two motionless spots of fire. He came into the room, shut the door, then sat down.

"Are you an old inhabitant of this place?" Goodchild asked.

"Yes."

"Perhaps you can decide a point my friend and I were discussing this morning. They hang condemned criminals at the castle, I believe?"

"They do," said the old man.

"Are the faces of the criminals turned toward the castle wall?"

The old man nodded. "When you are tied up, you see the stones of the wall expanding and contracting violently, and a similar expansion and contraction seems to take place in your own head and breast. Then suddenly there is a rush of fire and everything begins to shake, the castle springs into the air and you tumble downward."

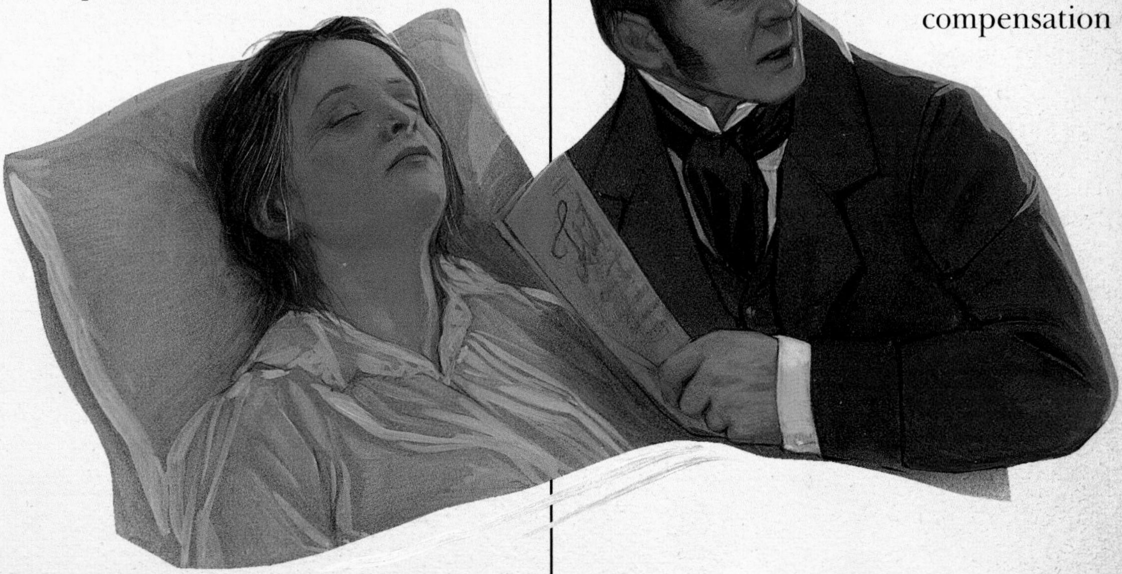

"A strong description," remarked Mr. Goodchild.

"A strong sensation," the old man replied.

Mr. Goodchild then saw what appeared to be threads of fire stretch from the old man's eyes to his own, forging a fiery link. He had the strongest sensation of being forced to look at the old man along those two fiery lines.

"I must tell you," said the old man, with a ghastly stare. And he began to tell the two men his terrible story.

Ellen had been a fair, flaxen-haired, large-eyed girl with no character and no purpose. A weak, credulous, incapable, helpless nothing. In this, she had perfectly reflected her father's character, not her mother's.

Ellen's mother had rejected the storyteller for money, putting him aside for Ellen's rich father. He had wanted compensation for being put aside, compensation in money. So when Ellen's father died, he had returned to Ellen's mother, even though he now hated her. He was bent on retaliation.

However, Ellen's mother had become fatally ill. As she lay dying, he could see that he would not get a penny from her. So he forged her signature on a document. It left all she had to her ten-year-old daughter Ellen, and appointed him the girl's guardian. Sliding it under the woman's pillow, he had bent down and whispered, "Dead or alive, you will make compensation to me in money."

Next he had been determined to make the foolish Ellen his bride. She had lived in his dark house for eleven years. With the collusion of an unscrupulous governess, the girl had been formed in the fear of him and in the conviction that there was no escape from him, that he was to be her husband.

Ellen had been twenty-one years and twenty-one days old when, upon a rainy night, he had brought her back to his gloomy house once more. By that time she had been his half-witted, frightened, and submissive bride for three long weeks.

On the threshold of the house, as the rain was dripping from the porch, she had turned to him and said, "Be merciful to me! I will do anything you wish, if you will only forgive me!" That had become her constant song, along with, "I beg your pardon," and "Forgive me!" He had felt nothing but contempt for her.

The two of them were alone in the house that night, as he had arranged that the people who attended them should come and go in the day. When he had entered the bride's chamber, he had found her withdrawn to the farthest corner, her hair wild about her face, her large eyes staring at him in vague terror.

He had said to her, "Ellen, here is a writing that you must copy out tomorrow, in your own hand. You should be seen by others engaged upon it. When you are done, call in any two people there may be about the house, and sign your name to it before them."

The next day, she had sat down at her desk and done as she had been told. That evening, when she gave the paper to him, he had asked her if she knew that it left her possessions to him in the event of her death. She had nodded.

He had then taken her by the arm, looked her in the face and uttered these fateful words, "Now, die! I have finished with you. I am not going to kill you. I will not endanger my life for yours. Die!"

From then on, he had sat before her in her gloomy chamber, day after day, night after night, looking the word "Die" at her when he did not utter it. As often as her eyes rose to meet his stern gaze, they read in it, "Die!" When, exhausted, she had dropped to sleep, she was awakened by the whisper, "Die!" When she had begged to be pardoned, she was answered, "Die!" When the rising sun flamed into the somber room, she had heard it hailed with, "Another day and not dead? Die!"

Shut up in the deserted mansion together, engaged in what seemed like an endless struggle, it had come to this—that either he must die, or she.

It was done, upon a windy

morning, before sunrise. She had broken away from him in the night, with loud and sudden cries—the first which she had uttered—and he had had to put his hands over her mouth. After that, she had been quiet in the corner of the paneling where she had sunk down. He had left her and gone back, with his folded arms and his knitted forehead, to his chair.

Then he had seen her coming, more colorless than ever in the leaden dawn, trailing herself along the floor toward him. She had been a white wreck of hair, and dress, and wild eyes.

"Forgive me! I will do anything," she had cried.

"Die!"

WORD POWER

cadaverous—like a corpse (cadaver)

flaxen—pale yellow, like the fibers of the flax plant

credulous—excessively trusting

collusion—cooperation, especially in order to deceive

bill-hook—a tool with a curved blade

loath to—unwilling to

Her large eyes had strained with fear, then reproach, then nothing. It was done. He had lifted her from the floor and laid her on the bed.

Ellen had soon been buried. Both she and her mother were gone, and he had compensated himself well.

He had decided to sell the house and travel. In order to get a better price for the house, he had hired laborers to trim the ivy that drooped over the windows and to clear the walks in which the knee-high weeds were growing. He had worked along with them, often later than they did.

One fall evening, when his bride had been five weeks dead, he was working alone at dusk, his bill-hook in hand.

"It's growing dark," he had said to himself, "I must stop for the night."

Then he had looked at the dark porch waiting for him like a tomb. He hated the house and was loath to enter it. Near the porch, and near where he stood, was a tree whose branches were waving before the window of the bride's chamber, where she had lived—and died. A branch of the tree had swung suddenly, and startled him. It had then swung again, although the night was still. Looking up, he had seen a figure almost hidden among the branches.

Chapter 2

The figure that the mysterious old man had seen in the tree was a youth. He had rapidly descended, then dropped from a bottom branch.

The man had seized the youth by the collar. "What thief are you?"

The young man shook himself free and stepped back, crying, "Don't touch me, you wicked murderer!"

"What!"

"I climbed this tree four years ago. To look at her. I climbed it, often, to watch and listen for her. I was a boy, when from that bay window she gave me this!"

Then he showed me a tress of flaxen hair, tied with mourning ribbon.

"She gave me this, as a token of her mourning and a sign that she was dead to everyone but you," he sobbed. "If I had been older, I might have saved her!"

The older man stood still, his bill-hook in his hand, looking at the younger man.

"The night you brought her back, I heard her beg your mercy and forgiveness. Three times from the tree, I saw you, slowly killing her. I saw her, lying dead on her bed. I have watched you, from the tree, for proof of your guilt. How, I do not yet know, but I will see you hanged. You shall never be rid of me. I loved her!"

The accused man moved toward the gate, but to get to it he had to pass his accuser. The back of the young man's head was turned toward him. It was as if the thing was done before he did it. The curved blade cleft the head and remained there. The young man lay face down on the ground.

He had buried the body that night, at the foot of the tree. But he had destroyed his triumph. Having rid himself of the bride and acquired her fortune without endangering his life, he now, for a death that had gained him nothing, would live evermore with a rope around his neck. Afraid to sell or leave the house, lest discovery of the body should be made, he was chained to it. So he had hired two old people, a man and his wife, as servants to help him in the house.

He had done the gardening himself and made an arbor against the tree, where he could sit and see the grave was safe. As the seasons had changed, the tree changed. In summer, the upper boughs had appeared to take the form of the young man. When the leaves fell in fall, he had thought that they were heaping themselves into a mound above the grave.

There was a search for the young man, but it had been unsuccessful and the youth was eventually forgotten. He, meanwhile, had grown richer. In ten years, his fortune had increased twelvefold.

But then, one night, a fierce and terrible thunderstorm had raged. In the morning, he had been informed by his serving-man that the tree had been struck by lightning, and that the trunk had split in half.

There was great curiosity to see the tree, but he had refused to admit visitors. There were certain men of science, though, who had wanted to dig it up by the roots to examine it. He had refused as usual. But they had bribed the old serving-man and stolen into the garden by night with their lanterns, picks, and shovels. Sleeping in a turret-room on the other side of the house, he had been awakened and got up.

From an upper window he had been able to see their lanterns, and them, and the huge mound of loose dirt. When they had found the body and were all bending over it, one of them said, "The skull is fractured," while another had pointed out, "There's a rusty bill-hook!"

He had been arrested and held for the youth's murder and was further accused of having poisoned his pretty young bride. Soon afterward he was tried, found guilty, and sentenced to death. His money had not been able to save him.

This was how the old man ended his sorry tale. Then he announced to Mr. Goodchild and Mr. Idle: "I was that man, and I was hanged at Lancaster Castle with my face to the wall a hundred years ago."

At this, Mr. Goodchild tried to rise and cry out. But the two fiery lines extending from the old man's eyes to his own kept him down, and he could not speak. Then the clock struck twice, and he saw before him two old men. The eyes of each were connected with his own eyes by two lines of fire. Each man was exactly like the other, and they addressed him as one.

"I had been dissected in the medical school, but had not yet had my skeleton put together, when people began to whisper that the chamber of my bride—a room in this very house—was haunted. It was haunted, and I was there.

"We were there. I, in the chair upon the hearth, she, a white wreck again, crawling toward me on the floor. But I was the speaker no more, and the one word that she said to me from midnight until dawn was 'Live!' Every night from midnight until dawn she approaches, never coming nearer, always only ever saying, 'Live! Live!'

"Eleven months of the year I endure this torment. But in the month that I was hanged—this month—the bride's chamber is empty and quiet. However, the rooms where I spent ten years in fear after killing the youth—these rooms—are haunted then. And they are haunted by me. At one in the morning, I am one old man. At two in the morning, I am two. By twelve noon, I am twelve old men, one for every hundred percent of my financial gain. So my suffering is multiplied by twelve. From that hour until midnight, I wait for the executioner. At midnight, I, in the form of twelve old men, swing invisible outside Lancaster Castle, with my twelve faces to the stone wall!

"This punishment will never cease until I make my story known to two living men together. If two living men could be here, with their eyes open, at one in the morning, they would see me sitting in my chair.

"Rumors that the room was haunted did once bring two men here, to disprove the existence of the ghost. They locked themselves inside the room and had their supper, then sat in front of the fire smoking their pipes. The next few hours passed in idle conversation.

"By a few minutes before one, the younger man, Dick, was dropping off to sleep. His companion tried desperately to keep him awake, but in vain. I suddenly

WORD POWER

cleft—split in two

arbor—a sheltered area in a garden, often surrounded by trees

dissected—cut into pieces for examination

ruffled—irritated; agitated

looked at Dick in horror, for it was almost on the stroke of one, and I felt that he was yielding to me. It was as if a curse was forcing me to send him to sleep, so that I would not be freed from my torment. Then one o'clock sounded, and the older man stood transfixed before me.

"To him alone, I was obliged to tell my story. To him alone, I was an awful phantom making a useless confession. It will ever be thus. The two living men together will never come to release me. When I appear, the senses of one of them will always be locked in sleep, and he will neither see nor hear me."

At this, it shot into Mr. Goodchild's mind that he was virtually alone with the grim specter, and that Mr. Idle's stillness was explained by his having been charmed asleep at one o'clock. Terrified, Mr. Goodchild struggled so hard to release himself from the four fiery threads that he snapped them.

Then he lifted Mr. Idle from the sofa and rushed downstairs with him.

"What are you doing, Francis?" demanded Mr. Idle. "My bedroom is not down here. I don't want to be carried, anyway. Put me down."

Mr. Goodchild put him down in the old hall and looked around wildly.

"What are you doing?" asked Mr. Idle.

"The one old man," cried the frightened Mr. Goodchild, "and the two old men."

"What do you mean?" said Mr. Idle.

"Tom, since you fell asleep..." began poor Mr. Goodchild.

"Asleep?" said Thomas Idle. "I haven't closed an eye! It's you who has been asleep."

"I? Nonsense," said Mr. Goodchild.

Mr. Idle completely refused to believe Mr. Goodchild's story of the one old man and the two old men. Each accusing the other of having been asleep, the two friends parted company at their separate bedroom doors. Both were a little ruffled by their disagreement about the matter.

Mr. Goodchild's last words were that every one of the sensations and experiences about which he spoke had been real and that he would write down a full account of them all. Mr. Idle returned that he might if he liked—and he did like. In fact, his account formed the terrifying story that you have just finished reading.

THE END

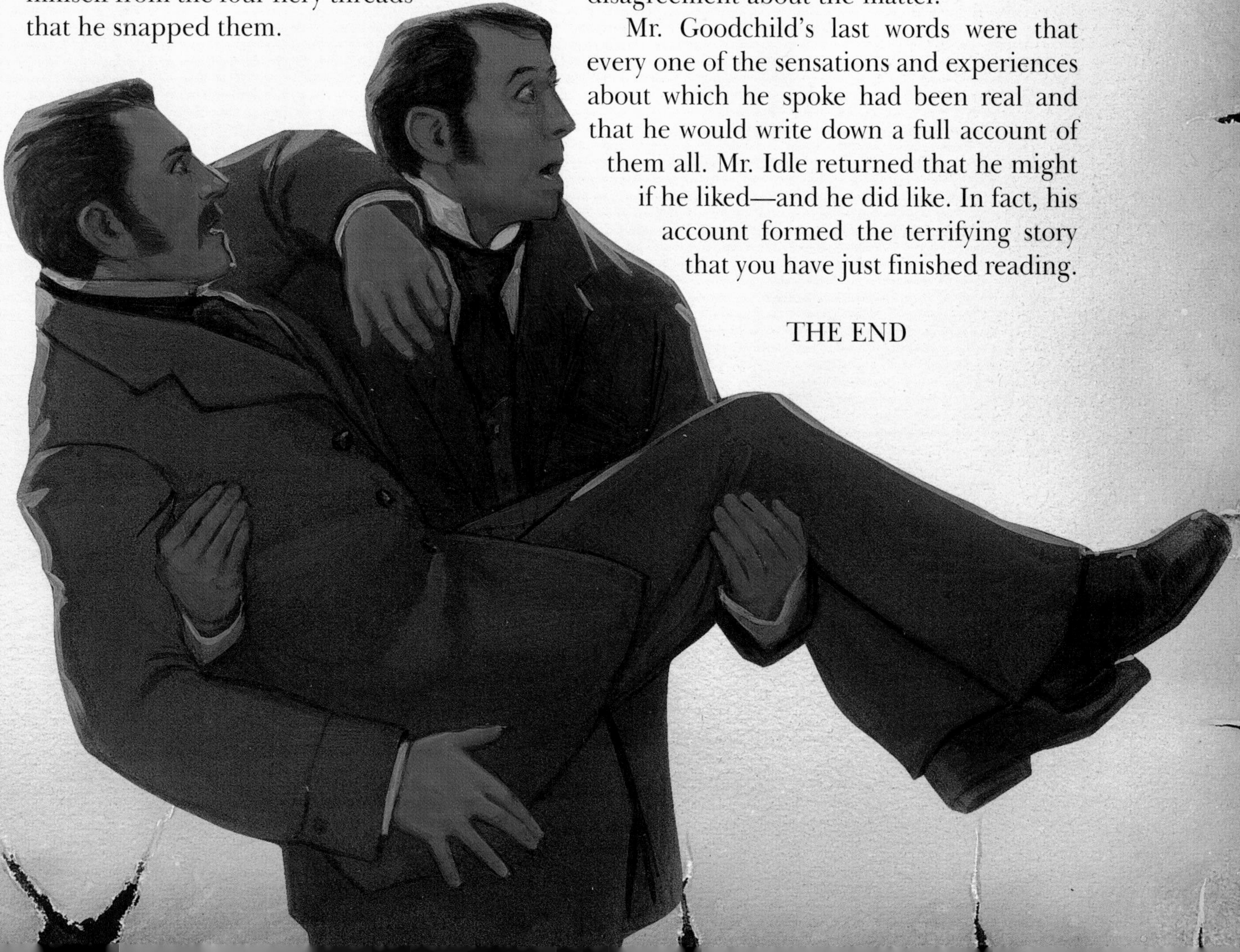

The Old Nurse's Story

Retold from a story by Elizabeth Gaskell

It was a cold winter's evening, and three children were playing in their nursery under the watchful eye of their old nurse, whom they called Hester. Suddenly a gust of wind rattled the windows, and the youngest child, a girl, left her toys and climbed into the nurse's lap. "Tell us a story, Hester," she pleaded. "A winter story."

The nurse looked thoughtfully at the children. "I think it's time I told you about your mother's first winter in Furnivall Manor." The children drew closer.

The nurse began: "When your poor grandfather died suddenly of a fever and your grandmother followed him just two weeks later, your mother, Mistress Rosamond, was only five years old. Poor lamb, she had only me to look after her, and I was not yet 18. Her guardian was Lord Furnivall, her cousin. He said that she and I should live with his spinster aunt in Northumberland. So one morning in September, we set off on the long journey to Furnivall Manor. Toward the end of the afternoon, we drove through iron gates and into a wild and rocky park, where wind and rain had bleached the oak trees white. The drive led up to a huge stately home, with a wing at each end. At the back of the Manor there was nothing but the bare fells.

"Little Rosamond clutched my hand tight as we were led into a vast, gloomy hall. We stared at the grand chandelier, the organ built into the wall on one side, and the enormous fireplace on the other. There were doors off the hall on each side, and we were taken through the west doors, beyond the organ, to a drawing room where a fire was blazing. There we met old Miss

Furnivall, a tall, thin lady with a wrinkled face and mournful eyes. She was very deaf and had to use an ear trumpet to hear us. Her companion, Mrs. Stark, seemed to live up to her name, for I had never seen such a stony-faced woman.

"I was delighted to be shown to our nursery rooms, where tea was laid out for us by James, the footman, and his wife, Dorothy. Miss Rosamond soon made herself at home, brightening up the house with her chatter and involving me in lengthy games of hide-and-seek all through the west wing. We discovered that the east wing was locked, and nobody ever seemed to enter it. Ivy grew across some of the windows, and huge branches swayed back and forth outside, making most rooms dark. We happily explored the east wing, opening boxes and dusty old books. There were many interesting paintings, too. One day I examined a portrait of a beautiful lady wearing a blue satin gown and white fur hat. She looked proud, almost scornful. And when I asked Dorothy who she was, she told me that I was looking at Miss Furnivall in her youth. 'That's Miss Grace, as she was called then,' explained Dorothy. 'Her older sister, Miss Maudie, was more beautiful still.' Then Dorothy pulled out a portrait of another proud-looking beauty, but told me not to tell anyone I'd seen it.

"One Sunday at the very end of November, I wanted to go to church with Bessy, the housemaid, so I asked Dorothy to mind Miss Rosamond. When Bessy and I stepped out of the church to walk home, we found the ground covered with snow. As soon as I returned to the Manor, I went to the kitchen to find Miss Rosamond. But Dorothy told me that my charge had stayed with the ladies in the drawing room. So I hurried there, but the two ladies were alone, working at their needlepoints in silence. Mrs. Stark then reported that Miss Rosamond had gone to find Dorothy an hour before. I began to panic, and, with Dorothy's help, searched the house high and low, in case the little girl was hiding. It was now pitch black outside, and from an upstairs window I suddenly saw, in a shaft of moonlight, a pair of small footprints in the snow by the front door.

"I tore downstairs, pushed open the door, pulled my cloak over my head, and followed the footsteps around the east wing to the base of a fell. I was sobbing with fear, and the air was so cold that my face felt numb. I could not imagine that anyone would be able to survive for long on such a night. As I looked up the hill, I caught sight of a shepherd trudging down, carrying something in his arms.

" 'Ha' you lost a bairn?' the shepherd shouted as he approached. As I ran up to him, I saw the white face and stiff limbs of Miss Rosamond in his arms, and my heart sank. I took her from him and held her close as the shepherd explained that he had found her curled up under two holly trees, farther up the hill. Back in the house, I took Miss Rosamond to the nursery fire, where, thank the Lord, I could feel the warmth returning to her body. At last she opened her eyes, and I resolved that I was never going to leave her on her own again.

WORD POWER

spinster—a woman who has never been married

fells—hills or high moors

footman—a servant in uniform

charge—a person in someone's care

bairn—a Scottish word for a child

resolved—decided firmly

fanciful—imaginary; unreal

"When Miss Rosamond woke the next morning, I feared she must have a fever, because she gave me a very fanciful account of what had happened the night before. She said that, on her way to find Dorothy, she had looked out from the window of the great hall and seen the snow. While she was staring at this beautiful white carpet, she suddenly saw a pretty little girl, beckoning her to come out to play. As she opened the door, the girl held out her hand, and together they went around the side of the house. Then the girl led her up the hill to some holly trees, where they found a lady crying in despair. When the stranger saw Miss Rosamond, she stopped, took her on her knees, and began to lull her to sleep.

"I tried to make Miss Rosamond see that she had imagined the whole scene, as there had been only one set of footprints in the snow. But she started to sob, 'I can't help it if there was only one set. I never looked at her feet, but she held my hand tight in her hand, and it was very, very cold.'

"Later that morning, Miss Furnivall asked for an account of the previous evening's events. The old lady started to tremble as soon as I mentioned Miss Rosamond's story of the little girl. Then, when I described the young lady under the holly trees, she threw her arms up and cried, 'Oh heaven, forgive me! Have mercy!' Mrs. Stark grabbed hold of her firmly, but Miss Furnivall kept shouting. 'Hester!' she roared at me, 'Keep her away from that child. It will lure her to her death.' As Mrs. Stark bustled me out of the room, I heard Miss Furnivall sob, 'Will you never forgive?'

"I did not know what to make of all this, but Miss Furnivall's outburst convinced me that I must never leave my charge alone. As the winter weather grew more stormy, I often heard the swell of organ music being played at night. One day I asked Dorothy who the organist was, but she said that nobody in the house played, and that it must have been the wind I heard. When I pressed Bessy about it, she told me that some people said it was the old lord playing, but why he played, especially on stormy nights, was a mystery to her.

"My unease turned to real fear, however, when one evening just before Christmas, Miss Rosamond and myself were playing in the great hall. Suddenly she cried aloud,

'Look Hester! There's the little girl outside in the snow.' I turned around, and there at the window was the figure of a small girl, with a dark wound on one shoulder that stained her pale dress. She was crying and seemed to be hammering at the window to be let in. But strangely, her banging hands made absolutely no sound.

"All at once, there was a deafening blast of notes from the organ. At that moment, Miss Rosamond started toward the front door, but I caught her just in time and then carried her, screaming, to the kitchen.

" 'What on earth's the matter?' asked Dorothy as we entered.

" 'She won't let me open the door for my little girl to come in,' cried Miss Rosamond, 'and she'll surely die if she's left out on the cold fells all night.'

"At these words, Dorothy's face turned as white as chalk, and I saw a look of terror in her eyes. But much worse was to come as the full horror of the events that had taken place at Furnivall Manor was revealed."

THE FACTS

Elizabeth Stevenson (1810-1865) was born in Chelsea, in London, England, but grew up in Knutsford, Cheshire. She married William Gaskell, a minister, and usually wrote under the name of Mrs. Gaskell. However, she published her first book, *Mary Barton* (1848), anonymously. Mrs. Gaskell is known mainly for her serious and yet humorous novels about small-town life and manners. Among the most famous is *Cranford* (1853), which she based on her own experiences in Knutsford. She also wrote a biography of her friend Charlotte Brontë, author of *Jane Eyre*, whom she first met in London in 1847.

Chapter 2

"Dorothy looked petrified as Miss Rosamond cried hysterically that she wanted to let the little girl in. So I made up my mind to take my charge away from that unhappy house the very next day. Once I had put her to bed, I told Dorothy of my decision.

"'You cannot take her from here, for she is a ward of court,' she explained. 'And I hope you would not desert her just because of some harmless sights and sounds.' But I insisted that I had to know the meaning of these apparitions; otherwise, I couldn't bear to sleep another night in the house. She sighed and then agreed to tell me.

"Slowly she began. 'Lord Furnivall was eaten up with pride in his two young daughters—Miss Grace (the present Miss Furnivall) and her older sister Miss Maude. When they were growing up, he declared that no man was good enough to marry them. His fierce temper only quietened when he played music. One summer, he invited a foreign musician to teach him the organ. The musician arrived from London and soon won over the lord with his fine playing. While his pupil practiced, the musician often took a stroll in the woods with one or other of the young ladies. He paid them great attention, and both fell in love with him. But one day, toward the end of the summer, he and Miss Maude slipped away and were secretly married.

" 'The musician returned to London, but promised to come back to the manor the following summer. He kept his promise, and this time he courted Miss Grace. He told Miss Maude that this was to prevent Grace from suspecting his true relationship to her. But Miss Maude had good reason to feel very possessive about the musician, for he was not only her husband, but also the father of her baby girl.

" 'The child had been born at a farmhouse on the moors some months before. When Miss Maude returned from her secret visits to the baby she adored, she grew fiery with rage to find her husband alone with her younger sister. The musician soon tired of her angry outbursts and so left Furnivall Manor a month earlier than planned.

" 'As winter approached, the old lord grew weak and had to walk with a stick. He also became even more crotchety than usual. The sisters were like a pair of wildcats together and only spoke civilly to each other in their father's company.

" 'The following summer, the musician returned, but the sisters fought over him so bitterly that one day he packed his bags and left. Afterward, not a word was heard of him. Blaming one another for his departure, the sisters moved their rooms to opposite ends of the house—Miss Maude to the east wing, Miss Grace and her maid, Mrs. Stark, to the west.

" 'Miss Grace, although still beautiful, soon began to look drawn and pale. But Miss Maude had color in her cheeks and appeared happier. This was because she had smuggled her baby daughter into her private rooms.

" 'I don't know how it happened, but it appears that one day the sisters met in the hall and soon began arguing loudly. Miss Maude taunted Miss Grace by telling her that the musician was her husband and that he had only pretended to love Grace. Miss Grace stormed back to her rooms and swore to Mrs. Stark that she would take her revenge on her older sister.

" 'One snowy night, just after the New Year, the servants heard the old lord's voice raised in anger. Then they heard a woman's reproaches and the cries of a young child. Finally, the crying stopped, and there was a deathly silence in the house. Later that night, the servants thought that they could hear a woman wailing out on the hillside. Early the next morning, old Lord Furnivall summoned them all. With Miss Grace standing by his side, he told them that his other daughter, Maude, had brought great disgrace on the Furnivall name and for that reason he had banished both her and her illegitimate child. He made everyone swear never to help either mother or daughter.

" 'Later that day, a shepherd found poor Miss Maude sitting under some holly trees on the fells with a crazy smile on her face. She was clutching her dead daughter. The child had a terrible wound on her shoulder, but people say that it was the bitter cold, not the wound, that killed her.'

"Dorothy stopped, and I sat in silence as the full horror of the tale hit me. It was no wonder that Miss Furnivall looked so sad and lifeless—I almost pitied her. But more urgently, I felt fear for the safety of Miss Rosamond. What if the ghost child should lure her out again?

"From that night on, I never let Miss Rosamond out of my sight. Every evening, Dorothy and I firmly bolted the doors and closed the window shutters an hour before dark. Even so, my charge still heard the crying from outside and always begged me to allow the ghost child in.

"One night, Miss Furnivall rang for me. Although Miss Rosamond was fast asleep, I dared not leave her alone, so I wrapped her in her warm robe and carried her downstairs. Miss Furnivall wanted me to unpick some stitching, so I laid Miss Rosamond on the sofa. As I worked, I could hear the wind rattling the windows. Miss Furnivall seemed unaware of the noise until she suddenly pushed herself up from her chair, held out a trembling arm and cried, 'I can hear voices... terrible screams... my father's voice!'

"Just then, Miss Rosamond sat bolt upright and shouted, 'My little girl is crying and crying!' She tried to climb down from the sofa, but luckily her feet got tangled in the robe and I caught hold of her. I held her tight, even though she struggled to get out of the room. Then I, too, heard voices—screams that seemed to be coming from the direction of the hall. Miss Furnivall was already walking out of the drawing room toward the hall, with Mrs. Stark behind her. So I followed, carrying Miss Rosamond in my arms.

"When we reached the hall, I noticed that the chandelier was alight and the fire was blazing, though it gave off no heat. The screams had grown louder and were coming from behind the closed door to the east wing. Suddenly the door swung back and out stumbled a beautiful woman, with a small girl clinging to the skirt of her dress. Behind them, a tall old man with gray hair and a face red with anger was shaking his cane in a frenzy.

"Miss Rosamond cried, 'Hester! It's the lady and my little girl. They want me to go with them. I must go!' And she tried to squirm out of my arms. But nothing could persuade me to let go of her, and I held her so tight that I thought I might crush her.

"The old man seemed to be herding the lady and child toward the front door when suddenly the lady turned around to face him defiantly. The next minute, she seemed to change her mind and spun around with her arms stretched out to gather the child close.

"Suddenly I heard Miss Furnivall cry out, 'No father! I beg you, don't! The child is innocent!' And then I saw that the old man had raised his stick high above his head. Standing beside him with a look of hatred on her face was a beautiful young lady in a blue satin gown and white fur hat. I suddenly remembered the portrait of Miss Grace—Miss Furnivall as a young woman—and knew that this was her.

"Miss Furnivall's words had no effect, and I watched in horror as the old man struck the child with the stick. At that very moment, the chandelier dimmed, the fire went out, and Miss Furnivall collapsed on the ground. But my first concern was for Miss Rosamond, who had fainted in my arms. I carried her upstairs and revived her by the fire. By the next morning, she had recovered her color, and she never talked about the lady or the little girl again.

"Miss Furnivall never recovered. That night she lay in bed, moaning, 'You can never undo what you did in your youth. Never!' A week later, she was dead.

"So, my dears, that is the story of your mother's first winter in Furnivall Manor. I suppose it must have been Miss Grace who told old Lord Furnivall about the child. And I suppose she must have regretted telling him every day, for the rest of her life."

THE END

WORD POWER

petrified—extremely scared

ward of court—a person placed in the care of a guardian by a court

crotchety—bad-tempered; cross

taunted—jeered at; mocked

reproaches—words or cries of blame

banished—sent away

illegitimate—child whose parents are not married

defiantly—in an openly challenging and aggressive manner

The Shadow

Retold from a story by E. Nesbit

It was a blustery winter's evening, and my friend Harriet and I had been having a wonderful time, dancing all night at a party in a big country house. Exhausted, we made for our bedroom. We were sharing it with a girl called Isabella, who was three years younger than us, and with another girl whose name we did not know. She was already in bed in the dressing room that was linked to the bedroom, as she had fainted earlier in the evening.

The fire warmed the room, which glowed in the light of the gas lamps and the candles on the mantelpiece. Even though the huge cedar branch outside our window scraped at the panes, we felt snug and safe. Soon we started to talk about ghosts, and each of us told a

ghost story. However, we always ended up laughing, as none of us believed in ghosts, and the stories were really rather silly. Harriet had just finished her tale when we heard a single tap at the door. We looked at each other in surprise. Then Isabella bravely called out, "Who's there?"

Silently, the door opened. To my amazement, there stood the reticent figure of Miss Eastwich, my aunt's housekeeper and companion. "Come in!" we said in unison. But Miss Eastwich remained in the doorway, staring at us as if she were made of stone. After a few awkward minutes, she started to speak.

"I saw that your light was still burning," she said, "and I wondered if ..." she paused and glanced at the dressing room door.

"It's all right," I answered quickly. "We haven't heard a peep from her. She must be fast asleep."

As Miss Eastwich was the most taciturn person I'd ever come across, I knew that there was no point in trying to make polite conversation with her. So I was just going to wish her goodnight when Isabella skipped across the room, flung a skinny arm around her neck, and dragged her toward the fire, saying, "You look frozen. Come in and get warm. Would you like a cup of cocoa?"

Miss Eastwich's pale eyes lit up, and for the first time in my life I saw a real smile on her face as she nodded her acceptance. Isabella seemed to have pierced the housekeeper's apparent coldness with her kind offer.

"This is really most pleasant," Miss Eastwich remarked as she took off her hat and coat and stretched out her hands toward the fire. Again I felt as if I were hearing her real voice—a softly spoken voice—for the first time. I explained to her that we'd been telling old ghost stories, but that most of them ended so neatly—usually with a murder or a hidden treasure—that we just could not believe them. Also, no one we knew had ever seen a ghost. Suddenly, Isabella clutched Miss Eastwich's arm and said, "Oh, do tell us a ghost story. I'm sure you know a perfectly horrid one."

Miss Eastwich hesitated, then replied, "Well, I do know one, but I imagine it would bore you."

I could see that she did not really want to tell her story, but Isabella insisted. Miss Eastwich looked at her imploring eyes, then said, more to herself than us, "It can't do any harm, I suppose. They don't believe in ghosts—not that it was really a ghost anyway—and they're all grown-up young ladies, not babies." Then she sank back into her chair, and we all fell silent.

Softly, Miss Eastwich began to tell her tale. "Twenty years ago, when I was just a little older than you all are, I had two very good friends, Mabel and Edward. I loved them more than anything else in the world. Then they married each other. After that, I did not see them for a year or two. One day, I got a letter from Edward. In it, he asked me to come and stay because his wife was ill, and he thought that I could cheer her up. He also said that their house, called The Firs, was gloomy, and that it was making him gloomy, too."

Miss Eastwich was staring into the flames of the fire. From her distracted expression, I could tell that she knew every

THE FACTS

E. (Edith) Nesbit (1858-1924) is best known for her classic children's books, including *The Treasure Seekers* (1899), *Five Children–And It* (1902), and *The Railway Children* (1904). However, she also wrote poetry, magazine articles, and short stories, frequently on supernatural themes. In 1910, some of her ghost stories, including *The Shadow*, were published in a collection called *Fear*.

line of that letter by heart. Slowly, she continued.

"I set off immediately to their house in the suburbs of London. I was expecting an old, gray-stone house, half hidden by shady trees. But the cab drew up in front of a cheerful, modern house, whose yard contained only a few low shrubs. Edward met me at the door, thanked me for coming, and asked me to forgive the past."

"What past?" interrupted Isabella.

I saw at once that Isabella had not understood how attached to Edward Miss Eastwich must have been, so I signaled to her to be quiet. Although Miss Eastwich was clearly flustered by the interruption, she managed to answer.

"Oh, I suppose he meant because they hadn't invited me to stay with them before. Anyway, I was very glad to be there. When I saw Mabel, who was pregnant, I could see that she was merely tired and perhaps a little excitable. It was Edward I was more worried about, as he seemed pale and distracted. As soon as Mabel went to bed that evening, I asked him what was wrong.

" 'Margaret,' he said earnestly, 'this is a peculiar house, and if it weren't new, I would think it was haunted.'

"I then asked him if he had seen or heard anything out of the ordinary, and he gave me a very strange answer.

" 'No, but something is definitely following me about. I can sense it. But whenever I turn around, all I see is my shadow. Mabel mustn't know that anything's wrong—she's such a delicate creature, you know.'

"Edward's nerves were clearly on edge, so I suggested that he take Mabel away from the house for a while so that they could both enjoy a break. But he explained that he couldn't persuade her to leave, as she had just got everything in order. 'I daresay I won't feel so agitated now that you're here, Margaret,' he added. 'I'm deeply grateful that you've come.'

"So I settled in, helped Mabel around the house, and tried to reassure Edward. The only problem was, I was beginning to feel ill at ease myself. I often had a powerful sense that something was behind me, particularly when I was on the stairs or in one of the corridors. But whenever I spun around, I could see nothing except my shadow. I was panicked by this sensation, which came upon me in daylight as well as at night.

"One evening I went down to the kitchen to heat up some milk for Mabel. While I was waiting for it to boil, I glanced around the darkened kitchen. A tall cupboard stood at the far end, its door partly open. In the gloom, I could just see the outline of someone crouching behind it. Thinking it might be Mabel, I called out her name. But then the gray shape darkened to black and seemed to flatten itself so that it lay like a pool of ink on the floor. I stood, frozen in terror, as I watched the pool contract, then flow back in toward the cupboard and vanish.

"I let out a loud scream, but then had enough sense to knock over the pan of milk. When Edward rushed in to see what had happened, I could therefore say that I had screamed because I had scalded myself. But he must have suspected something, because the next night, after Mabel had gone to bed, he said, 'Why didn't you tell me? It was in that cupboard, wasn't it? I've seen it, too, and in other parts of the house as well. Now we both know that it is not just our imaginations.' "

WORD POWER

reticent—shy; not wanting to intrude

in unison—together

taciturn—unwilling to speak; silent

imploring—begging; pleading

distracted—bewildered; confused

contract—become smaller

Chapter 2

"It was of little comfort to know that Edward had also seen the apparition, and soon I had even more reason to worry. A few days later, I began to see the figure all around the house, both during the day and at night. When I first spotted it, it was always crouching. Then it would flatten out and lie like a black pool on the floor. Finally, it would draw itself slowly into the nearest shadow. To add to my terror, that shadow was often mine.

"Worse was to come. Early one morning, I sensed that the shadow was nearby, when suddenly I heard a long, deep sigh. That sound was even more disquieting than the shadowy shape, as it seemed to come from directly behind me. But when I turned around, I could see nothing.

"I would have packed my bag and left that day had it not been for one thing. If I had departed, Edward would have had no one to discuss the apparition with, and so would probably have blurted out the truth to Mabel. In her condition, that could have had disastrous consequences.

"So I tried to be cheerful when Mabel was around, and Edward did his best to follow my example. But whenever he and I were alone, we could talk of nothing else but the terrifying dark shadow that seemed to be stalking the house.

"The weeks went by, and at last Mabel's baby—a girl—was born. Edward and I were glad to hear the doctors report that both mother and baby were doing well. As we sat in the dining room late that night, we felt happier than we had for many weeks. We had not seen or heard the shadow for three days, so instead of talking about its terrifying appearances, we discussed the plans for Edward and Mabel to move to the coast as soon as she was well enough. I was to oversee the removal of their goods to the new house that Edward had already bought. Edward thanked me profusely for being such a comfort to them both.

"Afterward, I went upstairs with a light step, confident that, for once, nothing was following me. As I passed Mabel's door, I stopped and listened. All was quiet, so I continued to my own room. But just as I was about to open my door, I felt a surge of panic once more and knew that there was something behind me. I turned slowly, clenching my hands to stop them from trembling, and there it was, crouching a little farther down the corridor. Then it flattened itself, seemed to change into an inky-black liquid, and flowed under the door of Mabel's room.

"I ran after the apparition and cautiously opened Mabel's door. The new mother was asleep, with the tiny baby curled up in the crook of one of her arms. As I stood there, I prayed silently that Mabel might never know the terrors that Edward and I had encountered, and that the baby would see only pretty sights and hear only pretty sounds.

"I returned to my room and slept deeply. But at dawn a howl coming from Mabel's bedroom woke me with a start. When I reached her room, I saw poor Edward clutching the dead body of his wife. I realized with horror that one of my prayers had been answered—but not in the way that I had intended.

"I will spare you the unhappy details of the next few days, except to say that when Mabel was laid in her coffin, I lit candles and placed them like sentries all around it. Edward came in but after a few minutes' silence I took his hand and led him out again. Just as we reached the door, we both spun around for we had heard that ghastly sigh once more. Edward looked as if he were going to run back to his wife's body—perhaps in his confusion he thought the sigh had come from her—when suddenly he froze rigid. There, lurking on the other side of the coffin, was the crouching shadow. Changing from gray to black, it slowly flattened itself into an inky pool, then slid into the nearest shadow—the shadow of the coffin itself."

WORD POWER

disquieting—worrying; disturbing

profusely—very much; plentifully

surge—sudden increase

crook—curve; bend

mesmerized—fascinated; hypnotized

Miss Eastwich's voice, which seemed to have become softer and softer as she neared the end of her tale, now stopped. I scanned her face and could see that she had quite forgotten her young audience. Isabella brought her round with one of her typically direct questions. "Did you ever see him again?"

Miss Eastwich replied, "Yes, my dear.

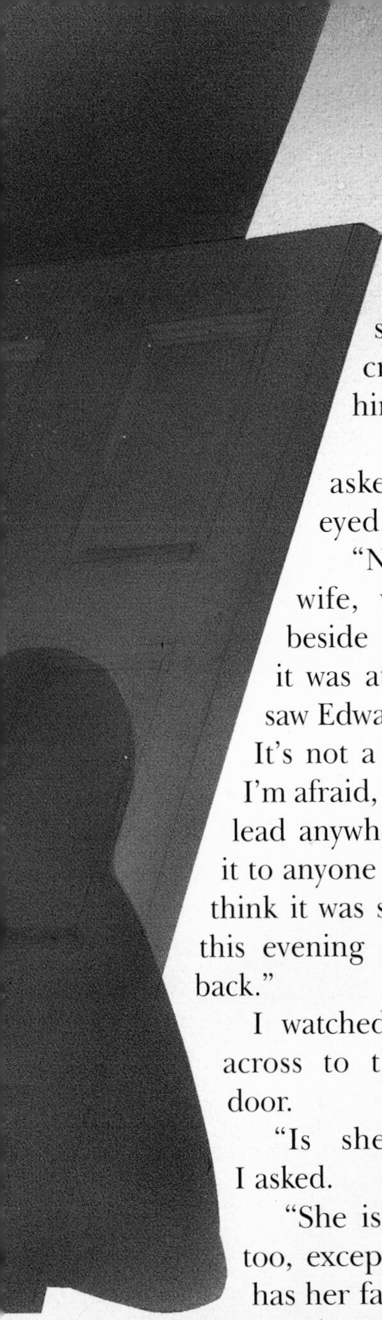

But just once. And that time there was something black crouching between him and me."

"The shadow?" asked Isabella, wide-eyed.

"No, it was his second wife, who was weeping beside his coffin. You see, it was at his funeral that I saw Edward for the last time. It's not a very cheerful story I'm afraid, and it doesn't really lead anywhere. I've never told it to anyone except you ladies. I think it was seeing his daughter this evening that brought it all back."

I watched her eyes wander across to the dressing room door.

"Is she Mabel's baby?" I asked.

"She is, and just like her, too, except for the eyes. She has her father's eyes...."

Miss Eastwich broke off suddenly, stood bolt upright, clenched her fists, and strained to see something beside the dressing room door that was not visible to the rest of us. At first, her stare was directed at a spot just below the handle, then seemed to drop down to the bottom of the door.

As she looked, her eyes grew wider and wider. Watching her, mesmerized, I suddenly heard a long sigh, which seemed to be coming from right behind me. Terrified, I glanced at Harriet and Isabella, and knew from their pale faces that they, too, had heard the sound.

Miss Eastwich was now making for the dressing room, so I grabbed a candlestick and shakily lit her way. She opened the door and crossed to the girl's bed. By the flickering light of the candle, we could both see that she was not sleeping. Her eyes were open, staring, and she was dead.

The doctor who examined the girl's body the next morning said that Mabel's daughter had died of heart disease, which she had inherited from her mother. But I saw the look of terror in those open eyes, and it seems to me much more likely that she inherited something from her father—the fear of the dark shadow. Miss Eastwich saw that look, too, and I thought her heart would break with sorrow at the sight of the young woman's corpse. But Isabella flung her arms around her new friend and smothered her with affection.

Afterward, my aunt let Miss Eastwich go so that she could be with her new charge, Isabella. The housekeeper remained in the service of the woman who had treated her so kindly for the rest of her life.

The Violet Car

Retold from a story by E. Nesbit

I am not used to writing, and I feel that I shall not say what I have to say unless I say it plainly. I have no skill to add to what happened, nor is any addition of mine needed to make the story clear.

I am a nurse, and I was sent for to go to a farm called Charlestown. There I was to look after a mentally ill woman. It was November, and the fog was thick in London, so my cab went at walking pace. As a result, I missed the train by which I should have traveled. I sent a telegram to Charlestown to tell them of the delay, then settled myself in the dismal waiting room at London Bridge station.

The time was passed for me by a little child. Its mother, a widow, seemed too crushed to respond to its questionings. I caught its eye and smiled. It would not smile, but it looked. I took out of my bag a silk purse, bright with beads and steel tassels, and turned it over and over. The child slid along the seat and said, "Let me." After that all was easy. The mother sat with eyes closed. When I rose to go, she opened them and thanked me. The child kissed me. We said our final farewells on the platform, then mother and child got into a first-class train carriage, and I into a third-class one.

I expected that there would be a conveyance to meet me at the station, but there was nothing. It was by this time nearly dark, windy, and rainy. I looked out, very perplexed.

"Haven't you engaged a carriage to fetch you?" It was the widow who spoke.

I explained.

"My car will be here soon," she said, "you'll let me drive you? Where are you going?"

"Charlestown," I said, and as I said it, I was aware of an odd change of expression in her face.

"Why do you look like that? There is nothing wrong with the house, is there, no reason why I should not go there?" I asked.

"No, oh no," she replied quickly. But I knew that there was a reason why she did not wish to go there.

"Don't trouble," I said, "it's very kind of you, but it's probably out of your way and ..."

"Oh, but I'll take you, of course, I'll take you," she said.

Then the car arrived. It had seats in the corners, and another little seat that pulled up when the door was shut. The child sat on it between us. The car moved smoothly, almost magically, along.

We drove quickly through the dark. We could see nothing except the black night and the light from the headlights. Finally we stopped and the chauffeur hauled down my trunk. It was so dark that I could not see the shape of the house, only the lights in the downstairs windows and the low-walled front yard. Yet I felt that it was a fair-sized house surrounded by big trees, and that there was a pond or river close by. In daylight the next day, I found that all this was so.

The chauffeur took my trunk up the path while I got out and said my goodbyes.

"Don't wait," I said. "I'm all right now. Thank you a thousand times!"

But the car stood, pulsating, till I had reached the doorstep, then turned and drove off into the distance.

I rapped loudly on the door knocker. The place was as quiet as death. The lights glowed from curtained windows, but there was no other sign of life. I wished I had not been in such a hurry to part from my fellow passengers and the great, solid presence of the car itself.

There was a pause. Then a bolt ground back, a key turned, and the door opened.

"Come in, oh, come in," said a woman's voice, and the voice of a man said: "We didn't know there was anyone there."

And I had shaken the very door with my knockings! I went in, blinking at the light. Then the man called a servant, and between them they carried my trunk upstairs.

The woman took my arm and led me into a comfortable room. In the lamplight I turned to look at her. She was small and thin. Her hair, her face, and her hands were all grayish yellow.

"Mrs. Eldridge?" I asked.

"Yes," said she. "I am so glad you have come. I hope you'll stay. I hope I shall be able to make you comfortable."

"I'm sure that I shall be extremely comfortable," I said, "but it is I that am to take care of you. Have you been ill long?"

"It's not me that's ill," she said, "it's him."

Now, it was this Mr. Robert Eldridge who had written to engage me. He had said that his wife was slightly deranged.

WORD POWER

conveyance—a vehicle that is designed to carry passengers

perplexed—confused; bewildered

pulsating—shaking rhythmically

deranged—mentally unstable; mad

dejected—miserable; depressed

"I see," said I. I thought it unwise to contradict her.

"The reason..." she was beginning, when his foot sounded on the stairs.

He came in and shut the door. He was a bearded, elderly man. "You'll take care of her," he said quietly. "I don't want her to get talking to people. She imagines things."

"And these illusions, what form do they take? What sort of things does your wife imagine?" I asked.

"She thinks I'm mad," he said.

"It's a very usual form. Is that all?"

"It's enough. And she can't hear things that I can hear, see things that I can see, and she can't smell things. You didn't see or hear anything of a car as you came up from the station, did you?"

"I came up in a car," I said. "You sent no one to meet me, so a lady gave me a lift."

The next day, I went out. I found that Charlestown was a large farm, but neglected. There was nothing for me to do but follow Mrs. Eldridge, helping her in her household duties.

I soon noticed that Mr. and Mrs. Eldridge were fond of each other. It was also clear that they had known sorrow and borne it together. She showed no sign of madness, except in the belief that he was mad.

In the mornings they were cheerful, after lunch they grew depressed, and as dusk was falling, they went for a walk. It always took the same direction, across the hills toward the sea, and they always returned pale and dejected. She sometimes cried afterward alone in their bedroom. He shut himself up in the farm office. After supper, they made an effort to be cheerful for my sake. But I knew that fear lived with these two. It looked at me out of their eyes. And I knew, too, that this was not her fear.

I quickly found that I was becoming fond of them both. They were so kind, so gentle. But the feeling grew that I must leave them—that there was, honestly, no work for me here.

"I ought not to stay," I said to Mrs. Eldridge one February afternoon. "You are both well. I oughtn't to be taking your money for doing nothing."

"You're doing everything," she said. "You don't know how much. We had a daughter of our own once. He has never been the same since."

"How not the same?" I asked.

"Not right in the head," she said.

"How?" I asked. "Dear Mrs. Eldridge, tell me. Perhaps I could help somehow."

"He sees things that no one else sees, and hears things no one else hears, and smells things you can't smell if you're standing there beside him," she said.

I remembered with a smile his similar words to me on the evening of my arrival. And I wondered which of the two Eldridges really needed my help.

"Have you any idea why?" I asked.

"It was just after our Bessie died," she said, "the very day that she was buried. The car that killed her—they said that it was an accident—was a violet color. They go into mourning for queens with violet, don't they? Our Bessie was like a queen to us. So it was right that the car should be violet, wasn't it?"

I realized now that the woman was not normal, and why. Grief had turned her brain. There must have been some change in my look, for she said suddenly, "I'll tell you no more."

One day soon after, I went for a walk. I followed the road toward the sea and walked along the cliff edge for some time. Then I turned back and reached a lane, where I came upon them. I heard the Eldridges before I saw them, and before they saw me. The voice of Mrs. Eldridge came first.

"No, no, no," it said.

"I tell you yes," he responded. "There—can't you hear it, that panting sound? It must be at the very edge of the cliff."

"There's nothing, dearie," she said.

"You're deaf—and blind—stand back I tell you, it's close upon us."

I came around the corner of the lane, and saw him catch her arm and throw her against the hedge, as though the danger he feared were close. Her eyes were on his face, and they held a world of pity, love, agony. His face was set in a mask of terror, and his eyes moved quickly as though following something down the lane, something that neither she nor I could see. Next he pressed his body into the hedge, his face hidden in his hands and his whole body trembling.

"And the smell of it!" he said, "Do you mean to tell me you can't smell it?" "Come home," she said. "It's all fancy. Come home with your old wife who loves you."

So together they made their sad way back to Charlestown farm, leaving me to wonder about the strange event that I had just witnessed.

Chapter 2

The next day I told Mrs. Eldridge what I had seen and heard in the lane. "And now I know," I said, "which of you it is that wants care."

To my amazement she said very eagerly, "Which of us, do you think?"

"Why, he, of course," I told her. "There was nothing there."

She sat down in the armchair by the window and broke into wild weeping. I stood by her and tried to soothe her as well as I could.

"It's a comfort to know," she said at last. "I haven't known what to believe. Many a time I've wondered whether it could be me that was mad, like he said. But there really was nothing there—and it's on him the judgment, not on me. Well, that at least is something to be thankful for."

So her tears, I told myself, had been of relief at her own escape. I looked at her with distaste. But her next words cut me like knives.

"It's bad enough for him as it is," she said, "but it's nothing to what it would be if I went off my head, and he thought it was his fault. Now I can look after him as I've always done."

I kissed her then and put my arms around her, and said, "What is it that frightens him?"

"I'll tell you. It was a violet-colored car that killed our daughter Bessie. And it's a violet-colored car that he thinks he sees—every day up in the lane. And he says he hears it, and smells the gasoline. And you can see he hears and sees it. It haunts him.

"You see, he picked her up after the violet car went over her. That was what turned him. I only saw her as he carried her in. But he saw her as they'd left her, lying in the dust. For days you could see the place on the road where it happened."

"Didn't they come back?"

"Oh, yes...they came back. But Bessie didn't come back. There was a judgment on them, though. The very night of the funeral, that violet car went over the cliff. It and every soul in it were dashed to pieces.

The man's widow drove you home from the train station on your first night here. Now there's my old man calling. He wants me to go for a walk with him."

She went, all in a hurry, and in her hurry slipped on the stairs and twisted her ankle. It was a bad sprain. I helped her to the sofa, and I bound it up. Then she looked at him as he stared out of the window. And then she looked at me.

"Mr. Eldridge mustn't miss his walk," she said. "You go with him, my dear."

So I went, understanding that he did not want me with him, but was afraid to go alone. And he had to go.

We went up the lane in silence. At that corner he stopped suddenly and dragged me back. His eyes followed something that I could not see. Then he said, "I thought I heard a car coming." There was sweat on his forehead and temples. Then we made our way back to the house.

Mrs. Eldridge had to rest her ankle, so again the next day I went with Mr. Eldridge to the corner of the lane.

This time he did not hide what he felt. "There—listen!" he said. "Surely you can hear it, too?"

I heard nothing.

"Stand back," he cried suddenly, and we stood back close against the hedge. Again his eyes followed something invisible to me.

"It will kill me one day," he said, "and I don't know that I care—if it wasn't for her."

"Tell me," I said.

"Did you ever hear tell of a violet car that went over the cliff?" he began.

"Yes," I said. "Yes."

"The day of my girl's funeral, you'd have thought the man who killed her would have stayed at home with the blinds drawn down. But not he. He was swirling and swiveling all about the country in his violet car, the very time we were burying her. At dusk—there was a mist coming up—he comes up behind me in this lane. He was new to the place and didn't recognize me, even though we'd been face to face at the inquest. I stood back, and he pulls up and calls out, with his lights full in my face: 'Can you tell me the way to Hexham, my man?'

"I'd have liked to show him the way to hell. But that was the way for me. I don't know how I came to do it. I didn't mean to. But before I knew anything, I'd said it. 'Straight ahead,' I said, 'keep straight ahead.' Then the car panted, and he was off. I ran after him to stop him, but I couldn't catch him. And he kept straight on—over the cliff. Every dear day since then, the car comes by, the violet car that nobody can see but me—and it keeps straight on."

"You ought to go away," I said. "You probably imagined the whole thing. I don't suppose you ever did tell the violet car to go straight ahead. I expect it was all imagination, and the shock of your poor daughter's death. You ought to go right away."

"I can't," he said earnestly. "If I did,

WORD POWER

inquest—an official inquiry into a sudden or violent death

earnestly—seriously; sincerely

delusion—a mistaken and unreasonable belief, often caused by mental illness

briskly—in a quick and businesslike way

someone else would see the car. You see, somebody has to see it every day as long as I live. And I'm the only person who deserves to see it. I wouldn't like anyone else to see it—it's too horrible."

I asked him what was so horrible about the violet car. I expected him to say that it was splashed with his daughter's blood. But he said, "It's too horrible to tell you."

I decided that I could cure him of his delusion. So I set myself to persuade him not to go to that corner in the lane, at that hour in the afternoon.

"But if I don't, someone else will see it."

"There'll be nobody there to see it," I said briskly.

"Someone will be there. Someone will be there—and then they'll know."

"Then I'll be the someone," I said. "You stay at home with your wife, and I'll go. If I see it, I promise to tell you. If I don't, I will be able to go away with a clear conscience."

I argued with him whenever I caught him alone. I put all my will and all my energy into my persuasions. Eventually, he gave way. Yes—I should go to the lane without him.

It was quite hard for me to go. This business of an imaginary car that only one poor old farmer could see probably appears to you quite ordinary. It was not so with me. You see, the idea had been the center of my life for months. This was the fear that I had known to walk with the Eldridges, those two good people, the fear that lay down and rose up with them.

I walked up and down the lane, wishing not to wonder what the hidden horror in the violet car might be. I was not going to be hypnotized into seeing things.

I had promised Mr. Eldridge to stand at the corner for five minutes, and I stood there in the dusk, looking up toward the hills and the sea. Everything was still. Five minutes is a long time. I held my watch and counted—four—four-and-a-quarter—four-and-a-half—five. I turned instantly. And then I saw that he had followed me.

He was standing a dozen yards away, and his face was turned from me. It was turned toward a car that shot up the lane. It came swiftly, and before it came to where he was, I knew that it was very horrible. I crushed myself back into the hedge, as I should have done to leave room for a real car.

As it neared him, he started back, then cried out: "No, no, no, no—no more, no more." With that he flung himself down on the road in front of the car, and its great tires passed over him. Then the violet car shot past me, and I saw exactly what the full horror of it was.

When I told Mrs. Eldridge what had happened, the very first thing that she said was: "It's better for him. Whatever he did, he's paid for now." So it looks as though she had known, or guessed, more than he thought.

I stayed with her till her death. She did not live very much longer.

You think perhaps that the old man was knocked down and killed by a real car, which happened to come that way of all ways, at that hour of all hours, and happened to be, of all colors, violet. Well, a real car leaves its mark on you where it kills you, doesn't it? But when I lifted up that old man's head, there was no mark on him, no blood, no broken bones. His hair was not disordered, nor his dress. And there were no tire marks in the mud.

The car that killed him came and went like a shadow. As he threw himself down, it swerved a little so that both its wheels should go over him.

Mr. Eldridge died, the doctor said, of heart failure. I am the only person to know that he was killed by a violet car, which then went noiselessly away toward the sea. And that car was completely empty. It was just a violet car that moved along the lanes swiftly and silently, and was empty.

THE END

The Dead Sexton

Retold from a story by Joseph Sheridan Le Fanu

Early one evening, a boy from the village of Golden Friars in Northumbria was returning home from a day out on the fells. He was walking along the lake shore, flinging stones at the water, when suddenly he noticed a darkly dressed figure. It was sitting on a low branch, hunched over something.

As the boy drew nearer, he recognized the thin, surly face of Toby Crooke, the village sexton. He seemed to be counting out silver coins with his long, bony fingers. The boy tried to creep by, but the sexton glanced up as he was passing and gave him an even more sinister look than usual. The boy broke into a run, and did not stop until he reached home.

None of the children in the village dared speak to the sexton. They never saw him smile or laugh or even hold a proper conversation. The bullet scar over his eye frightened them, even though the doctor said that Crooke must have received the wound as a soldier. But nobody in Golden Friars knew where he had been or what he had done during the 12 years that he had been absent from the village. The children had also heard many stories about his strange behavior and wild temper as a young man. So they kept well clear of his gray stone house beside the church.

Later that evening, the sexton's landlady, who had been sound asleep in her ground-floor bedroom, woke with a start. She could see the dark outline of a man with his back to her. He held a candle in one hand and seemed to be rummaging in the drawer where she kept her money.

Although she was frightened, she called out in a loud voice, "In God's name, what do you want there?" As the man turned to face her, the woman recognized the thin face of her lodger.

"Where's the peppermint you used to have in your bedroom, woman? I've got a pain in my innards," he said gruffly.

The woman explained that the

peppermint was finished, but that she would make him a hot drink if he liked. But he told her not to bother and strode out of the room.

In the morning, the local parson knocked at the landlady's door. He said that the sexton, who was normally very punctual, had not turned up to open the church. The two of them went to check his room, but he was not there.

Puzzled, the parson made inquiries in the village, but no one had seen the missing man. Then, in the middle of the afternoon, two boatmen rang the bell of the parsonage. When the parson appeared, they showed him a small, heavy church bell, which they had carried up from the lake shore.

"We think this is from the church steeple, Sir," said one. "We found it at the bottom of our boat, hidden under a piece of canvas along with the sexton's pick and spade. And the boat was not in her usual mooring place either, Sir."

The bell was indeed about the same size as those that hung in the church tower. There was still no sign of the sexton, so the parson hurried inside to get the key, then set off with the boatmen for the church. As he unlocked the door of the church porch, he spotted a sack, lying open on the floor. There was a length of rope beside it.

Without stopping to investigate, he pushed open the door that led to the tower. Feeling his way in the gloom, he started to climb the spiral stairs. Halfway up, there was a platform whose stone floor was illuminated by a shaft of light streaming in through an arrow-slit. The parson stepped on to the platform and asked the boatmen to continue to the top to count the bells. But before he could finish, one of the men let out a gasp.

"What on earth is that?" he cried, pointing to a dark mound on the far side of the platform.

The parson stepped across and bent down to feel it. To his horror, he found that he was touching the cold face of a dead man.

With the help of the boatmen, he dragged the body into the light. Instantly, he recognized the lifeless figure of his sexton, Toby Crooke. There was a deep gash across his pale forehead.

The parson sent the boatmen to fetch the doctor. When he arrived, he examined the body and announced that the sexton had been dead for many hours. His neck had been broken and his skull fractured by a terrible blow to his forehead. It did not take the men long to find the source of the blow. Lying on its side by the wall was a heavy church bell with blood and tufts of hair on the rim.

The boatmen carried the body down the stairs and out into the churchyard, while the parson and doctor followed behind. When they reached the porch, the parson saw the sack again and noticed that it was half full of bulky objects. He started to pull them out one by one. The first to emerge was a silver chalice belonging to the church, then a silver salver, a gold pencil case, silver spoons, and various other precious items. The doctor recognized the silver salver. It had been missing from his house for a month. The parson recognized the pencil case, which he had lost some time before.

They followed the boatmen to the George and Dragon Inn, where the body was to be laid in the coach house. As they walked, they began to piece together the events that had led up to the sexton's death. Over the past few months, Crooke had clearly stolen the objects that were now in the sack. It seemed that he had then planned to get away with his hoard, plus several of the church bells, by boat.

"He must have slipped on his way down the stairs and fallen back onto the platform, breaking his neck on the stone floor," explained the doctor. "The bell seems to have struck his forehead, then rolled away."

The word spread right through the village that the sexton had met a nasty end. Soon villagers crowded into the inn to see the body and to discuss the event. Over drinks, some said that they were sure Crooke was the highwayman who had killed a coachman on Hounslow Heath a couple of months before. Others claimed that he was the killer of a young girl over at Scarsdale.

When night fell, Tom Scales, the hostler, locked the door of the coach house and put the key in his pocket. Then he stood outside the front door of the inn, smoking his pipe. The evening was very still, and a bright moon hung in the frosty sky. Suddenly he could hear the distant sound of a horse's hooves approaching at a gallop.

He could tell that the horseman was traveling on the Dardale road, which entered the village beyond the bend at the parsonage. But although he was watching the road keenly, he did not see the rider coming around the bend. The next thing he knew, the horseman was thundering along the straight section of road between the parsonage and the inn.

WORD POWER

fells—hills or high moors

surly—bad-tempered; grumpy

sexton—a church caretaker

chalice—a cup used for communion wine

salver—a tray

hostler—a person who looks after horses at an inn

charger—a fast, powerful horse

cocked hat—a three-cornered hat

jackboots—high leather boots, often covering the knees

Tom Scales had never seen a horse gallop so fast, yet when the rider dismounted, the huge black charger had no trace of sweat on him. Indeed, it pawed the ground and snorted as if it was impatient to be off again.

"Take him, lad," commanded the stranger in a deep voice. "No need to walk him or rub him down—he never sweats or tires." Tom Scales noticed that the man was dressed in a cape, a cocked hat, and jackboots, just like someone from days gone by. But he said nothing and led the horse into the yard.

As they passed the door of the coach house, the animal stopped dead. Then it pawed the ground and lowered its head, as if it was listening for sounds from inside. Next it threw back its head and gave a piercing neigh, which sent a shiver down Tom Scales' back. The hostler tugged at the horse, anxious to get it into the stable quickly. He had never felt nervous with a horse before, but this one was different. It seemed to sense that there was a dead man behind the door. Worse, it seemed to be trying to communicate with the corpse.

Chapter 2

The doctor, attorney, innkeeper, and several others were smoking their pipes around the kitchen fire in the George and Dragon Inn. Suddenly, the strangely dressed horseman strode into the room. He had very piercing, dark eyes, sunburned skin, a crooked nose, and a deep scar running down his top lip. He raised his hat in greeting and asked the name of the village and the inn.

"George and Dragon?" he repeated, once he had been answered. "Come to think of it, I've been here before. What happy occasion brings so many faces together? Last time you all looked miserable, except for that most excellent man, Mr. Crooke. Where is he?" Glancing quickly over his shoulder, the stranger then boomed, "Isn't that him over there?"

There was a deathly silence in the kitchen as everyone stared at the far end of the room. The silence was broken by the innkeeper, who stood up and, thumping the table like an angry schoolteacher, announced, "He is not there, he can't be there, we can all see that he's not there." Then, in a calmer voice, he explained to the stranger that Crooke had "met with an accident" and was dead.

The others, all trying to speak at the same time, then provided the stranger with the details of the death. The stranger, however, was reluctant to criticize the sexton. "Why should he be damned for pulling down a church bell that he has been pulling at for ten years!" he said. "The man's in Heaven now, just as surely as you're not!"

The stranger then called to the innkeeper to bring several bowls of punch and invited everyone to drink as much as they wanted. While they drank, he requested a bed for the night. Then, as all the villagers started to drift homeward, he asked for a lantern so he could visit his horse in the stable.

Tom Scales, the hostler, was looking through the stable window to check on his horses when suddenly he felt a tug at his sleeve. He turned to find the dark-eyed stranger standing behind him. "They say there's something well worth looking at behind that door," the stranger whispered, pointing to the coach house. "I'll make it worth your while to show me."

Tom stared at the man's scarred lip, which seemed even more deformed in the moonlight, and nervously dug in his pocket for the key. Then, reluctantly, he walked over to the coach house, turned the key in the padlock, and stood back.

"What are you afraid of?" said the stranger, leading Tom over to the sexton's body, which was stretched out on a table. "He won't bite! Come, hold up the lantern while I take a good look."

Tom held up the light and stared at the sexton's waxy face. Then, as if in a nightmare, he clearly saw the sexton's eyes open and his lips move, as though he were trying to talk. The hostler was so terrified that for a full minute he could neither move nor speak. Then he gave a loud scream. The stranger swirled around, grabbed the lantern from him, and bundled him out of the door. Following behind Tom, he then kicked the door shut with his foot. As Tom fumbled with the key, the stranger hissed, "Give me the corpse, and I'll make you rich."

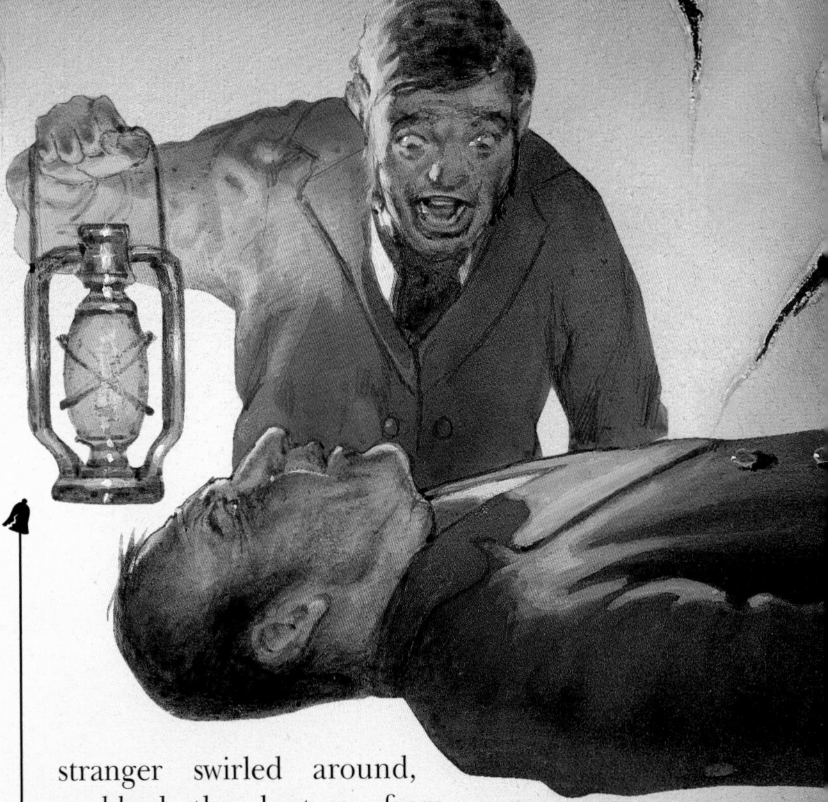

Tom did not even reply to this suggestion. He turned on his heels and ran back into the inn. By the time he had reached the kitchen, his face had drained of all color. The innkeeper offered him a drink of brandy to revive him.

"That man's evil, Mr. Turnbull," Tom spluttered. "There's something unnatural about that horse, too. It was making all the other horses in its stable sweat and fret, so I moved them next door. Please, Mr. Turnbull, let's fetch the parson in case you've got a devil or a demon under your roof!"

"Calm down," replied the innkeeper. "There's no need for that. We'll check the yard one last time before closing up."

Taking a lantern with them, they went out into the shadowy yard, glancing over their shoulders as they headed for the coach-house door. The padlock was still firmly in place.

"Seems fine," whispered Tom. "Let's go back in now, Mr. Turnbull."

"Not quite yet, lad," answered the innkeeper. "We'd better make sure the coroner will have a corpse to examine when he arrives tomorrow." He took the key from Tom, opened the lock, and slowly pushed the door until he could just fit his head around to peer in. Then he speedily shut it and locked up again.

"Safe as houses," he whispered to his companion. Just at that moment, they heard a jeering laugh from somewhere above them, and all the yard geese started to gabble furiously. Tom clutched the innkeeper's arm and shouted over the racket, "There he is! At the window, see?"

The innkeeper looked up at the open window of one of the guest bedrooms. There he saw the stranger leaning on his elbows, watching them.

"His eyes!" gasped Tom. "Look, they're like two burning coals!"

The innkeeper's eyesight was not as sharp as Tom's, and he wasn't sure if the stranger's eyes were red or black. But the man's laugh had frightened him enough.

"Time for honest folk to be asleep in their beds, sir," he shouted up.

"Do you mean as soundly as your sexton?" replied the stranger, and then gave another jeer that once more caused the geese to start up.

"Quick," said the innkeeper, pulling Tom behind him. "Hurry into the house."

When they were safely inside, the innkeeper said, "No man or beast shall steal a dead man out of my yard, as long as I can pull a trigger. Come with me to the gunroom, Tom. We'll keep watch all night if we have to."

The gunroom, which jutted out into the yard, faced the coach-house door on one side and the back door of the inn on the other. The innkeeper took down his blunderbuss, loaded it, opened the main window, covered himself with a heavy coat, and sat down. Tom locked the door of the room from the inside and took up watch at the smaller window overlooking the inn door.

An hour passed, and then another. Clouds blacked out the moon from time to time, throwing the yard into complete

WORD POWER

attorney—a lawyer

reluctant—unwilling

punch—a drink often containing a mixture of alcohol and fruit juices

coroner—a person who investigates suspicious deaths

blunderbuss—a short gun used between the 16th and 18th centuries darkness, but nothing stirred. The watchers had just heard one o'clock strike when suddenly Tom spotted the cloaked figure of the stranger. He was emerging from the back door and striding toward the stable.

Tom joined the innkeeper at the main window. Together they watched as the man led out his horse and opened the yard gate with one hard kick. Then he stood in front of the coach-house door, which seemed to swing open entirely of its own accord, and disappeared inside. In a few moments he came out, carrying the sexton's body. With one movement, he flung it over the horse's shoulders and sprang into the saddle.

"Quick! Fire the gun!" shouted Tom to the innkeeper. Then there was an ear-piercing crack, and Tom was hurled sideways against the window. The innkeeper lay flat on his back. There was total silence for a moment, until the watchers heard that jeering laugh once more, echoing around the yard. Tom crawled to the other window and saw the stranger galloping out of the gate, his black cloak flying out behind.

When Tom went to help the innkeeper up, he discovered that there was nothing left of the blunderbuss—it had shattered into tiny pieces. As for the dead sexton, nothing was heard or seen of him again.

THE END

Madam Crowl's Ghost

Retold from a story by Joseph Sheridan Le Fanu

I was only fourteen when I was sent to work with my aunt, Mrs. Shutters, who was the housekeeper at Applewale House in the village of Lexhoe. It was dark by the time I reached the village, where a horse and carriage was waiting for me. The driver put my box up on top and asked me where I was going. When I told him I was going to wait on Madam Crowl of Applewale House, he said:

"Oh, you'll not stay there long."

"Why?" I asked, nervously.

"Because they say she's possessed by an evil spirit, and she's a bit of a ghost, too. Have you got a Bible?"

I told him I had.

"Well, make sure you put it under your pillow every night. It will help to keep the old girl's claws off you."

I thought I saw the driver winking at his companion as he said these horrible words. But that didn't calm me—by now I was feeling both homesick and afraid. As the carriage rattled down a dark avenue, I leaned my head out of the window and saw the big black-and-white house that was soon to be my home. In the moonlight, I could make out the shadows of trees chasing each other up and down the front of the building, and dark shutters obscuring most of the windows.

I had never met my aunt before. As I stood in the hall watching her approach, the first thing I noticed was her pale face, black eyes, and very long, thin hands, which were covered in black fingerless gloves. She was kind to me and brought me up to her sitting room for supper. However, I knew immediately that she was a very silent woman, and that she probably thought children should be seen and not heard.

Mrs. Wyvern, a middle-aged woman who worked as the maid, was different. While I ate my supper, she chatted away, and said more in one hour than my aunt did during my whole stay at Applewale. When my aunt went up to the second floor to see her mistress, Mrs. Wyvern explained that a local woman sat with Madam Crowl when neither she nor my aunt were there.

"She's a troublesome old lady, Madam Crowl," she added. "You have to have your wits about you, as she's likely to walk into

the fire or climb out of an open window if you're not watching."

"How old is she?" I asked.

"She was ninety-three last birthday, and she can walk and talk and see and hear like the rest of us. But her mind's gone a bit. She's still dreadful fond of her dresses, though—you could fill seven stores with all the silks and satins and velvets she has. And I'm told she was a great beauty in her day. You'll have to sit with her, girl, and see that she gets up to no mischief, and bring her whatever she needs. You can ring the bell hard if she gets troublesome."

My bedroom was next to Madam Crowl's, but I didn't see or hear her for the first two days. Mrs. Wyvern told me that she was in one of her sulks and wouldn't let them undress her. Instead, she lay in her fancy clothes all night. The next evening I was sitting in my room, doing some embroidery, when I heard a sound like a bleating animal. It was coming through the open door that led into Madam Crowl's bedchamber. When it stopped, I could make out my aunt's voice saying, "Evil spirits can't hurt no one, ma'am, unless the Lord permits it."

The strange, bleating sound continued, and I deduced that it was Madam Crowl speaking, but I couldn't make head or tail of what she said. Then silence descended, and shortly afterward my aunt looked in on me. She told me that at last the mistress had fallen asleep. I wasn't to make a sound while my aunt went down to the kitchen to get a cup of tea.

I picked up a picture book and tried to read. But soon I found myself wondering whether the old lady really was asleep. My bedroom suddenly seemed too silent, so I got up and walked around so that I could at least hear the sounds of my own footsteps. As I got near the connecting door, I decided that there would be no harm in taking a quick peek at Madam Crowl's bedchamber.

The room was huge and lit by a blaze of candles—I counted twenty-two of them. It contained a four-poster bed with long, rich red curtains, which had been pulled shut, and the biggest mirror I had ever seen. I stared in amazement, thinking that it looked more like a scene from my picture book than a bedroom. By now I was feeling adventurous, so I checked that the old lady was not stirring behind the curtains, then gingerly tiptoed across the room to take a look at her. Slowly, I slipped my fingers between the thick curtains and pulled them back.

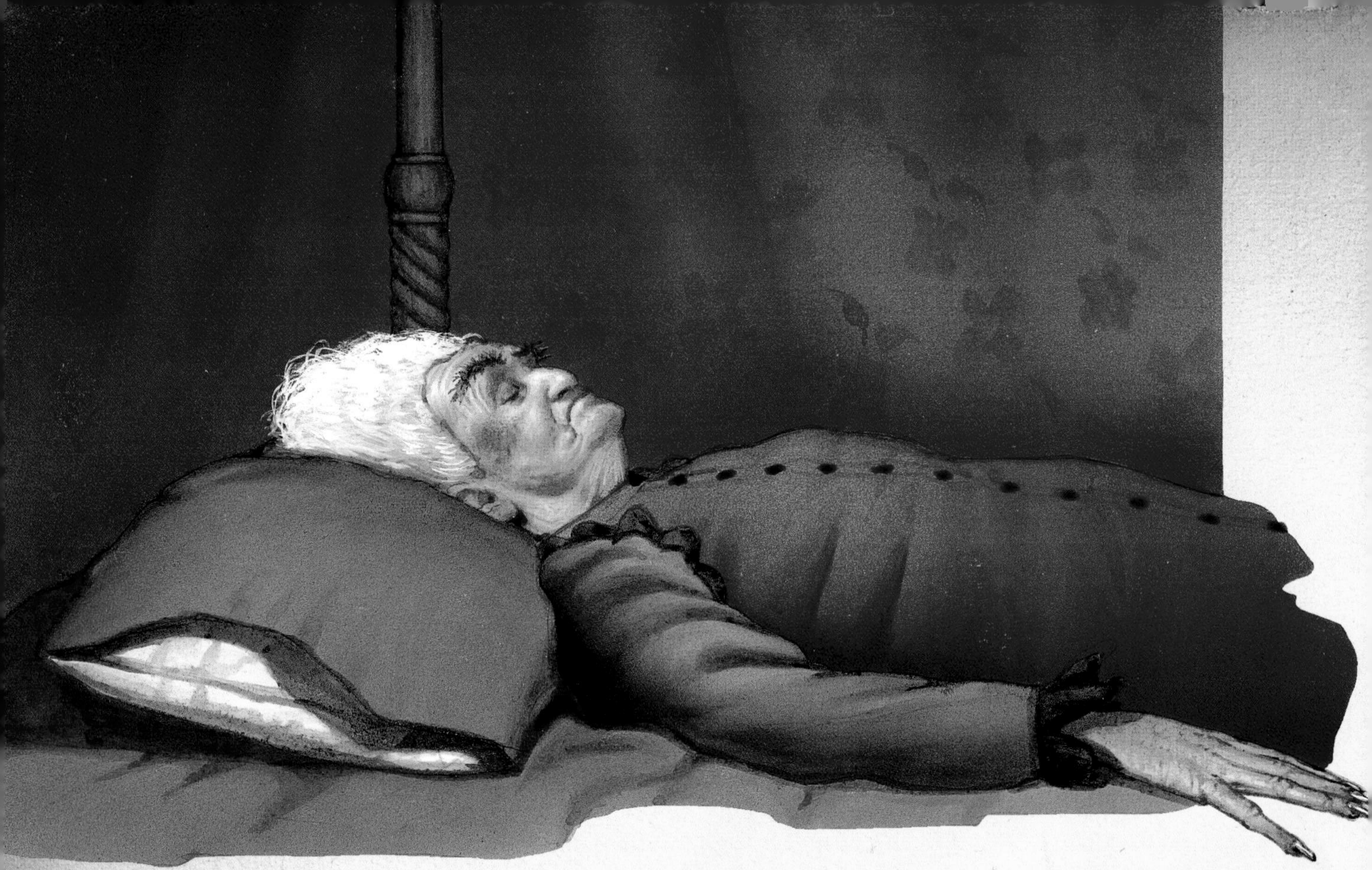

There, stretched out on the bed, was the strangest sight I'd ever seen. A lady with deeply wrinkled skin lay as still and lifeless as one of the stone effigies on the tombs at Lexhoe Church. She was dressed in a gorgeous gown made of scarlet and green satin and silk, with a powdered wig piled on top of her head and high-heeled shoes on her feet. As I stared more closely at her, I could see that her cheeks had been painted with circles of rouge, and her face and throat were coated in white powder. She was also wearing false eyebrows made of mouse fur. When I looked at her hands, which were stretched out by her sides, I saw that they were very long and pointed. I gave a shiver as I remembered the carriage driver's remark about Madam Crowl's "claws."

Before I had time to back away, the sleeping figure opened her eyes, sat up, swung her legs down onto the floor, and stood up in front of me with a loud clack of her heels. Then, piercing me with her glassy eyes, she stretched out an arm and pointed at me. In a high, hysterical voice she said, "You little rat. Why did you say I killed the boy? I'll catch you and tickle you until you're stiff as a corpse."

I don't know why I didn't turn and run right away. I wanted to, but I found that, just like a rabbit that's been dazzled by a strong light, I couldn't take my eyes off the old woman. I staggered back, but she came tottering after me, making a horrible zizzing sound with her tongue and pointing her bony fingers at my throat. I kept backing away, but she kept coming at me, her fingers only inches from my neck. Suddenly I felt the hard wall at my back—I was trapped! I let out a blood-curdling yell, and the next thing I knew, my aunt was standing at the door, shouting at Madam Crowl. The old lady turned around, and I ran as fast as my legs could carry me, straight through my room and along to the safety of my aunt's sitting room.

Mrs. Wyvern was in the room, and she chuckled as I related what had happened. But when I repeated Madam Crowl's words, the smile left her face.

"Tell me again what she said," she requested quietly.

"She said, 'You little rat. Why did you say I killed the boy? I'll catch you and ...' "

But before I could finish, Mrs. Wyvern interrupted me and asked, "And had you said she killed a boy?"

"No, Mrs. Wyvern. I hadn't said a word to her. I was too scared."

Then Mrs. Wyvern patted my hand and told me to forget all about it. But after that evening, I was never left alone with Madam Crowl again. Just a week later, I made an important discovery about the old lady's secret past.

WORD POWER

obscuring—hiding

deduced—figured out; concluded

gingerly—carefully; cautiously

effigies—models or statues of people

rouge—red powder used as a cosmetic

Chapter 2

One evening, Mrs. Wyvern told me the story of Madam Crowl's marriage to Squire Crowl many years before. The Squire was a widower and had a nine-year-old son from his first marriage. This boy was left to his own devices by his father and stepmother, and spent most of his time out and about on the estate. One morning his hat was found at the edge of a lake. The boy never returned, and it was presumed that he had drowned. But people later began to mutter that Madam Crowl knew more about his disappearance than she claimed.

In time, the people of Lexhoe forgot about the young boy, and Madam Crowl's own son inherited the estates when he came of age. It was his son, Squire Chevenix Crowl, who owned Applewale now, Mrs. Wyvern explained. The new squire didn't live at Applewale, but he still visited occasionally to keep an eye on his grandmother. As Mrs. Wyvern finished the story, I couldn't help thinking of Madam Crowl's hysterical words to me about killing the boy. Was it her stepson she had meant, or was she just talking nonsense? I didn't dare ask Mrs. Wyvern or my aunt, so I just kept my thoughts to myself.

Less than six months after I arrived at Applewale House, Madam Crowl started to grow weaker. Then suddenly her condition changed, and she began to toss and turn in the bed, ranting and raving and occasionally letting out a terrible shriek. Sometimes she thrashed about so wildly that she fell out of bed. When my aunt and Mrs. Wyvern went to pick her up, she held her wizened hands over her face and begged her helpers to have mercy on her. At the very end, she had convulsions, and when the parson came, she was not even capable of saying a prayer.

When Madam Crowl died, Squire Chevenix Crowl was away in France and could not get back in time for her funeral. His grandmother was buried in the vault under Lexhoe Church, and we all stayed on at the house to await the Squire's return. I expected that he would send me home to my family, since my aunt no longer needed my help. But in the meantime I was moved to another room, two doors away from Madam Crowl's former bedchamber. It was a large, square, oak-paneled room, simply furnished with a bed, a chair, and a table.

The night before the Squire was due to arrive, I went to bed as usual. However, I was so excited at the thought of going home to my mother and sister that I couldn't get to sleep. Shortly after the clock had struck twelve, I was lying awake with my face to the wall and my back to the door. Suddenly I noticed that the wall was glowing with an orange light, and that the shadows of my bed and chair were dancing up and down on it. Thinking that something must have caught fire, I turned around quickly. There, to my horror, stood the figure of Madam Crowl, dressed in satin and velvet. Her eyes were as wide as saucers, and there was a reddish light around the bottom of her gown, almost as if her feet were on fire.

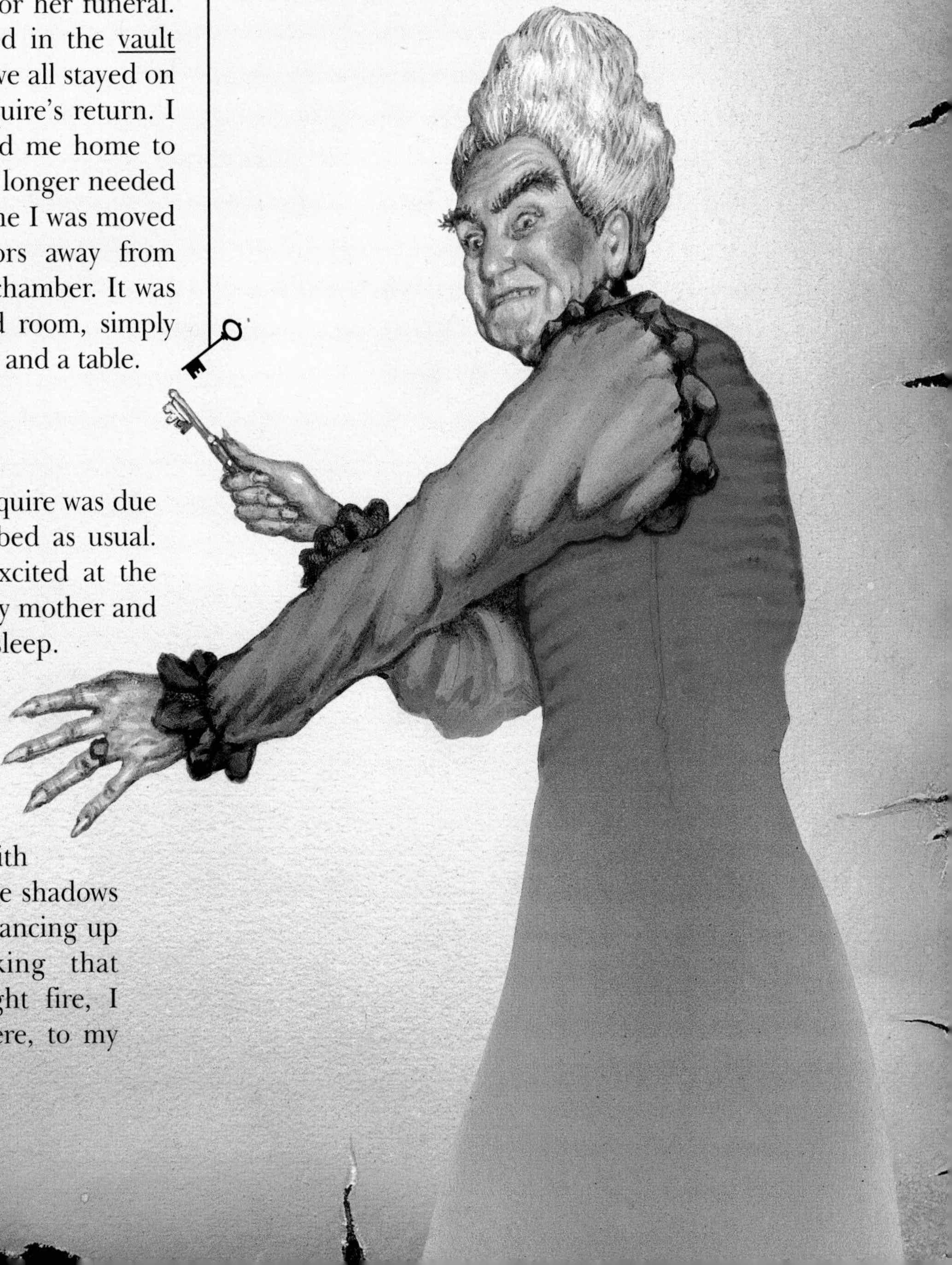

The old woman held out her shriveled hands in front of her, like claws, as she walked toward my bed. I was so terrified that I began to feel faint. But just at that moment a blast of cold air hit me, and I realized that the figure had passed by the bed and was now standing by a recess in the wall. Next, she held out a big key and opened a door that I had never seen before. She groped at something behind the door for a minute or two, then spun around, her face set in a hideous grin. Suddenly the room was plunged into darkness. I let out an ear-splitting yell and ran down the corridor, bumping into the walls until I reached Mrs. Wyvern's bedroom.

The next morning, I told the story of the night's events to my aunt. I was sure she would dismiss it as nothing more than a bad dream. But to my surprise, she held my hand and encouraged me to tell her every detail. When I explained that the apparition had opened a door in the wall, she asked me if the old woman had had a key in her hand. I told her that she had, a big key with a brass handle.

My aunt let go of my hand, went over to a cupboard, and took out a key identical to the one Madam Crowl's ghost had used. Then she asked me if it was the same. When I told her it was, she put it away again and let me finish my tale. When I had done so, she said that I would have to tell the Squire what I had seen.

At midday I was called into my aunt's sitting room to see the Squire. He was a handsome gentleman, who looked at me kindly and said, "Now what's all this I hear about you seeing strange sights in your bedroom? You know there's no such thing as ghosts or spirits. So why don't you sit down here and tell me all about it, from beginning to end." I told the Squire my story, and when I had finished he paused for a long time. Then he turned to my aunt and said, "The door this girl saw in her dream did exist, you know. One of my grandfather's servants told me that the family silver and jewelry used to be stored in a cavity behind the wall, and that the door to it was opened by a big key with a brass handle. It sounds as if it is the same key you found in my grandmother's chest, Mrs. Shutters. Let's go and see if there are any spoons or diamonds still hidden away behind the door."

I held my aunt's hand tightly as we followed the Squire into the bedroom. There was an empty cupboard against the wall in the recess. When the Squire moved it out of the way, we could see the

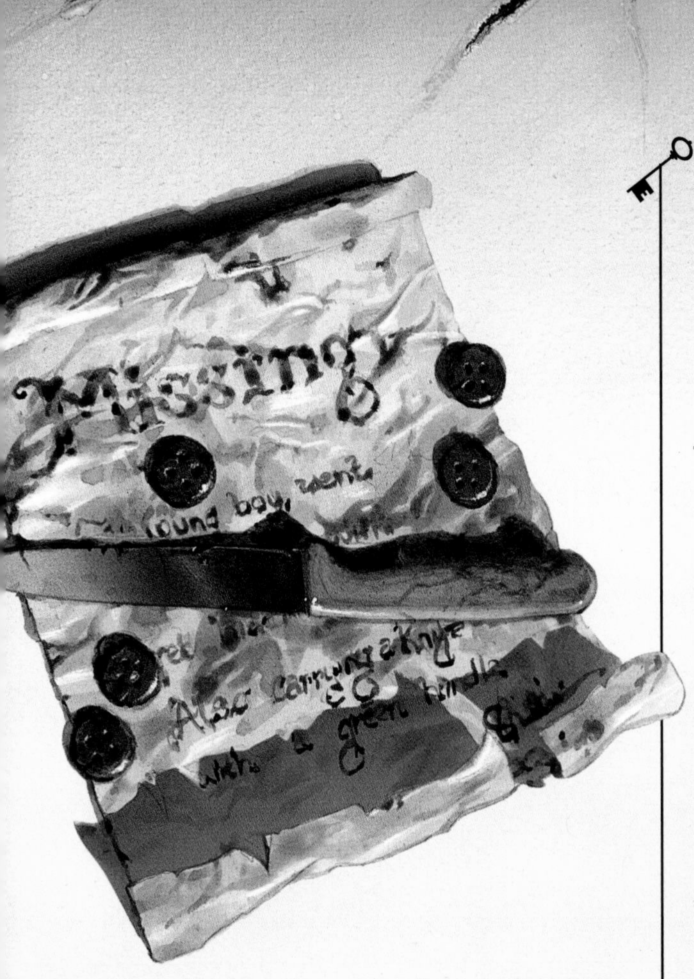

outline of a door frame in the middle of the oak paneling. The keyhole had been stopped up with wood. The Squire asked for a hammer and chisel. Then he quickly knocked out the wood, pushed the key into the lock, and turned it. The door opened with a loud creak.

Peering out from behind the Squire, all I could see beyond the door was total darkness. But as my employer held up a candle, I saw that inside was a tiny room. "There's something over there in the corner!" shouted the Squire. "Give me a poker, Mrs. Shutters."

As my eyes grew accustomed to the dark, I could make out a mound, shaped a bit like a crouching monkey, on top of a chest. The squire leaned forward and touched the mound with the poker. Instantly, it collapsed in a cloud of dust. Just before my aunt pulled me away, I could see that the crouched figure was in fact a pile of small bones and a skull. "A dead cat!" announced the Squire quickly, as he blew out the candle and closed the door firmly shut.

I left Applewale House that afternoon, with an extra dollar in my pocket from the Squire. God be thanked, I never saw Madam Crowl, in any form, again.

When I was a grown woman, my aunt came to stay with me. It was only then that I found out what had happened at Applewale after my departure. My aunt and the Squire had returned to the cavity and found a set of jet buttons and a knife with a green handle among the bones. Later, the Squire had sorted through his grandfather's papers. Among them was a copy of a poster his grandfather had distributed when he was searching for his son. The poster stated that the missing boy was carrying a green-handled knife and wearing a jacket with jet buttons. The bones in the hidden room most certainly belonged to Madam Crowl's stepson. She had shut him up to die in that dark hole, where his cries for help could not be heard.

THE END

WORD POWER

left to his own devices—left to look after himself

came of age—reached the legal age of adulthood

wizened—dried up and wrinkled

vault—an underground chamber with an arched roof

recess—an area that is set back from the surrounding surface

cavity—a hollow space; hole

jet—a type of hard black stone used for jewelry

The Pit And The Pendulum

Retold from a story by Edgar Allan Poe

I was sick and dying when, at long last, they untied me and let me sit. I felt my senses starting to leave me. The last words I heard were those of the dreaded death sentence as it was passed on me. After that, the voices of my judges—the Inquisitors—merged into one, and then I could no longer hear at all. Yet for a short while I could still see them in their black robes. I could still make out their thin, white lips as they shaped words of hatred for me. I saw their lips form the syllables of my name, and I shuddered. Looking around, I could just make out the fur-lined walls of the chamber. Then my gaze fell upon seven tall candles standing on the table ahead.

At first, the candles seemed friendly, like white, slender angels placed there to save me. Then a terrible wave of nausea flooded over me as the candles changed their identity. The angels had become specters with heads of flame. They would be of no help to me. Suddenly, a thought stole into my fevered mind. What sweet rest and peace there must be in the grave. The thought took time to sink in. As it did, I saw the Inquisitors, the judges of my fate, disappear. At the same time, the candles went out, and my bewildered mind seemed to be swallowed up in a mad and terrible rush toward hell. Then there was only silence, stillness, and blackness.

I lapsed into a strange and dreamlike state. At times, I think I was conscious, but I cannot quite describe how I felt. As for how long this strange state lasted, I cannot begin to tell. Now only several hazy shadows of memory remain in my mind. These tell of tall figures lifting me up, just as one lifts a coffin. They carried me down—down—still down, farther than I thought possible. Then I remember vague feelings of being unnaturally still and surrounded by flatness and dampness. But after that, all became madness.

Very suddenly, there came back to my soul some sound and movement—the movement of my own heart—and, in my ears, the sound of its beating. Then came a tingling sensation throughout my body, which lasted for a very long time. Then, again suddenly, I began to think and started to shudder with terror as I recalled the full horrors of my trial, the judges, my sentence, and the sickness that overcame me.

I still had my eyes closed, but I could tell that I was lying flat on my back. There seemed to be nothing holding me down. I reached out my hand. It fell heavily upon something damp and hard. I let it lie there for many minutes while I tried to imagine what it could possibly be. I still did not dare to open my eyes. It was not that I feared some ghastly sight. I was petrified that there was nothing at all to see. In the end, I became totally desperate. So I opened my eyes quickly. Then my worst fears were confirmed.

The blackness of night completely surrounded me. I struggled hard for breath. The depth of the darkness stifled me, but I tried to stay calm and think. It felt as though a long time had passed since I had received my sentence. The guilty usually perished in an *auto-da-fé*, and I remembered that one had been planned for the night that I was condemned to death. Yet I knew I was not dead, so what had happened? Had I been thrown back into my cell to await the next set of executions? No! The cells of the condemned were made of dry stone and had light. So what was this dark, damp place that I found myself in?

The most terrible of ideas then struck me and began to drive me toward madness again. When I regained my senses, I leapt to my feet. Every fiber of my body was trembling. I thrust my arms wildly above and around me in all directions. I felt nothing, yet was too petrified to move a step in case I found my way barred by the walls of a tomb—a tomb prepared for me.

Beads of sweat stood out on my forehead. Terrified, I waited and waited. Eventually, the suspense became too much, and I carefully shuffled forward with my arms stretched ahead of me. My eyes were straining from their sockets, in the hope of catching even a very faint ray of light. I walked many paces without finding anything other than total darkness. I breathed more freely. The space was quite big. It appeared that I had been saved from the very worst death of all—I had not been buried alive.

But other fears soon began to grow. I had heard stories about the terrible dungeons of the Inquisition. They were too ghastly to repeat, except in a low whisper. Would I be left to starve in this deep underground blackness? Or was there a fate even worse in store for me? I never doubted that the final result would be my death. I knew the Inquisition much too well to hope otherwise. I had only to learn when and how my dying would occur.

At last, my outstretched hands touched something solid. It seemed to be a stone wall, very smooth, slimy and cold. I traced a path along the wall, trying to follow it around, but I could not figure out the dungeon's size. I searched for my knife. It had been in my pocket when I had been led into the chamber of the Inquisition. I reasoned that if I could wedge the knife into a small crack between the stone blocks,

I could use it as a marker. But the knife had gone, along with all my clothes. They had been replaced by a simple robe of rough material. I tore a small part of the hem from the coarse fabric and placed it on the floor, so that it stuck out from the wall.

My plan was to walk right around my underground prison, and to use the fabric marker to tell me when I had completed the trip. Surely I could not fail to find it again? However, I had failed to consider the dungeon's size and my own awful weakness. The ground was extremely wet and slippery beneath my feet. I staggered onward for some time, before stumbling and falling over. I tried to get up but simply could not, and soon fell asleep where I lay.

THE FACTS

Edgar Allan Poe (1809-49) was a highly influential American short-story writer, poet and literary critic. He first became famous for a poem, *The Raven*, but today is better known for his powerful short stories. Poe wrote many horror tales, including *The Fall of the House of Usher* and *The Masque of the Red Death*. Many experts consider his dark tale *The Murders in the Rue Morgue* to be the world's first modern detective story.

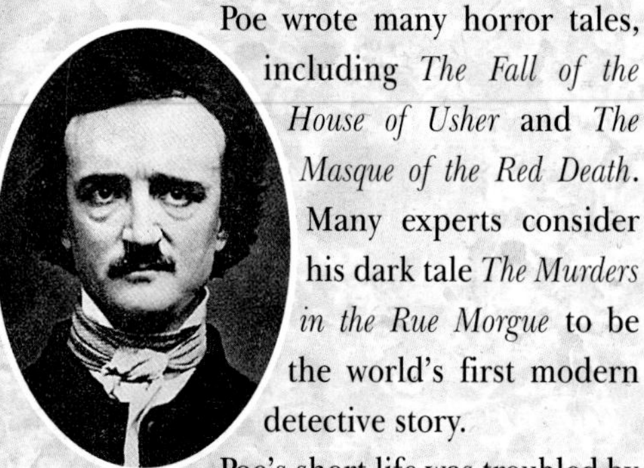

Poe's short life was troubled by poverty and alcohol problems. His death was as mysterious as anything he ever wrote. It may have been caused by drinking too much, by taking drugs, or by catching rabies. It has even been suggested that it occurred after someone had put an evil curse on him.

When I awoke, I found a small loaf of bread and a jug of water beside me. I was too exhausted to figure out how they might have gotten there. I just ate and drank greedily. With much effort, I began my tour around the dungeon once more, and eventually returned to the strip of material. I added up the number of paces I had taken—fifty-two before I had fallen and forty-eight afterward. The total of one hundred paces was equivalent to a distance of about fifty yards. I now had an idea of my prison's size, but not of its shape, as I had come across many angles in the wall on my trip.

There was little point in my research. I had no hope of escape or safety, but curiosity drove me on. I summoned up enough courage to leave the walls, aiming to cross the cell floor to the other side. I stepped slowly and cautiously. The floor felt solid but was covered in slime. I had walked ten or twelve steps when I slipped and fell on my face. The fall confused me, and it took some time for me to realize that there was something strange about how and where I lay. My chin was resting on the dungeon's floor, but my lips and the rest of my head were lower and touched nothing. My forehead was bathed in a vapor, and the smell of fungus and decay filled my nostrils. I stretched out my arm and felt around. It soon became clear that I was perched on the very edge of a circular pit.

As my hands groped wildly, I broke off a small stone fragment from the pit. Then I let it fall into the abyss and waited. It took many seconds for the stone to plunge into water. As the echoes rose out of the pit, I heard the sound of a door or a hatch above me opening and closing rapidly. For a moment, a faint gleam of light flashed through the gloom, but it faded away just as suddenly as it had arrived.

I congratulated myself on avoiding the doom prepared for me. If I had taken one more step before I had fallen, it would have been my end. But I knew all about the Inquisition and its tyranny. Its members killed some people simply by inflicting physical pain. But they subjected others to great mental torment first. For me they had chosen this, the very worst of all agonies. As a result of my long suffering, my nerves had been shattered. Now I trembled even at the sound of my own voice. I teetered on the brink of madness and was a fitting subject for the evil of the pit, or whatever terrifying new torture awaited me.

WORD POWER

Inquisitors—officers or members of the Inquisition, a medieval religious court that sentenced many people to death, especially in Spain

nausea—the state of feeling sick

auto-da-fé—a mass execution carried out by the Inquisition. The Portuguese words literally mean "act of faith."

vapor—a mist or gas

abyss—a very deep hole

tyranny—great but misused power

teetered—moved back and forth as though about to fall

Chapter 2

With my arms and legs shaking, I groped my way back to the wall. I decided that I would rather perish there than risk the terrors of the pit. My feverish brain now pictured many pits in various places around the dungeon. At any other time, I might have had the courage to throw myself into one and end it all. But now, I was reduced to being the greatest of cowards. I had read about these pits and knew that they were not intended to bring a quick, painless death to anyone who had the misfortune to fall in them.

It took many hours for me to calm down enough to sleep. When I awoke, I again found a loaf and a jug of water next to me. I had a terrible, burning thirst and gulped down the entire contents of the jug in one go. The liquid must have been drugged, because I then fell into a deep sleep. I don't know exactly how long it lasted, but when I came to, things had changed. My cell was no longer in complete darkness. Instead there was a glow that gave enough light for me to see the cell measurements. I had been quite wrong. It was no more than half the size that I had calculated.

I thought very hard about how I had made this mistake. I decided that I must have walked right past the strip of cloth that I had placed on the floor as a marker. It didn't matter. What could be less important in my situation? Yet I was not able to stop myself. I had gotten not only the size of my cell wrong, but also its shape and even what it was made of. It was square and only the floor was built from stone. The walls, by contrast, were constructed of huge plates of metal. The angles and depressions that I had felt on my trip around the room were simply where the plates joined.

Bathed in the strange, glowing light, I shuddered at what was painted on the sides of my prison. It was a collection of the most ghastly creatures. Hideous fiends, glowing white skeletons, and many other

monstrosities disfigured the cell walls. Their terrifying outlines were clear, but their colors seemed blurred.

I saw all this with extreme difficulty because I was now strapped to some sort of flat, wooden frame. The strap was wrapped around me many times, just like a bandage, only much stronger. Only my head and the bottom half of my left arm were free. I soon became aware that my mouth was dry, and I was hungry. With much effort, I was able to reach some food that lay in a dish by my side. I ate a portion of the spicy meat, which left me feeling even thirstier. Then I reached around hopefully for the jug of water that I expected would accompany my meal. To my absolute horror, the jug was not there. I realized that the evil Inquisitors now intended a raging thirst to overcome me.

In desperation, I looked across the prison floor. There was no water jug, but neither were there the dozens of holes that I had feared. Instead, there was one circular pit right in the middle. I had only just managed to escape its terrible jaws. But now another gruesome fate awaited me.

I looked up. The ceiling was about thirty or forty feet away and seemed to be made of metal, too. Then my eyes rested on a painting on the ceiling. It was a portrait of Old Father Time, but with one unusual alteration. In the place of the scythe that he normally carried, there was a massive pendulum, as on an old grandfather clock. Gazing up at the picture, I thought that I saw the pendulum move. Then I blinked and looked up once again. There was absolutely no doubting it. The pendulum was not part of the picture. It was real.

I watched the pendulum swing high above me for a long time. I was more amazed than fearful of its slow but deliberate movement. Then a strange scuttling sound on the floor startled me. Rats! Two, maybe three—all enormous in size—had managed to claw their way up from the depths of the pit. Quickly, they were followed by more. They seemed to be attracted by the smell of the meat—my food—beside me. I looked straight into their eyes, which were glinting with evil hunger, and used all my efforts to scare them away.

Some time later, when I next looked up, I was stunned. It took some time to get my poor, swooning mind to understand exactly what had happened. The pendulum had increased in length and was moving faster. I could now hear a definite hiss as it swung through the air. I estimated that it had grown about three feet since I had last observed it. This meant that, although it was still a long way from me, it had gotten closer. Now I could see the pendulum's evil design very clearly. Right at the end of its brass rod was a crescent of highly polished steel more than a foot long. I stared at it with despair and terror. Its lower edge was sharpened like a giant razor, and that edge was the closest part of the pendulum to me.

I could no longer doubt the doom that had been prepared for me by the torturers of the Inquisition. I knew that the hell-like pit they had tried to surprise me into was considered their most hideous punishment. I had avoided that by nothing more than a hair's breadth. But surprise was also known to be a vital part of their devilish plans. They had no intention of forcing me into the pit now that I knew about it. Instead they had devised, with fiendish cleverness, a different form of death for me. But it would be equally painful and terrifying.

For hour after awful hour, I watched and counted with dread the swings of the mighty, razor-tipped pendulum. Inch by inch, gradually, unceasingly, it crept down toward me. Its journey was painfully slow. Days of this unbearable torture passed until the blade swept so close that it fanned my body, and the smell of steel forced itself into my nostrils.

I prayed for the pendulum to descend more quickly so that it would finish me. I even strained upward, deliberately trying to throw my body into the path of the blade. There were moments, too, when madness completely overcame me, and I lay still, smiling at the glittering crescent above me,

WORD POWER

depressions—areas set back from a surrounding surface; hollows

disfigured—ruined or spoiled the appearance of

scythe—a farm tool with a large, curved blade used for cutting grass

cleave—split in two

ghoulish—overconcerned with unpleasant matters

lingering—very slow; drawn-out

just as a child smiles at a shiny bauble or new toy. But this was no child's toy. It was a deadly instrument of torture. And it was heading straight for me.

I eventually became unconscious and remained so for some time. When I came to, I found that the pendulum was no closer. Those demon monks—the Inquisitors—must have been watching me closely. They would only lower the instrument of my death when I was awake and could see it. I found myself sick and weak. I was desperately in need of food. I stretched out my hand and found a tiny portion of my meal remaining, the part spared by the rats. I ate and felt hope and joy—hope over a fragment of rotting meat and joy over its spicy flavor. My long period of suffering, the torment that my fiendish torturers had put me through, was slowly driving me mad.

The steel crescent at the end of the pendulum still passed back and forth. It was now so close to me that I could see where it would strike. It was designed to slice through the coarse robe I wore, cut my chest, and then cleave my heart in two. I took a ghoulish interest in exactly how the pendulum would strike me. As it was moving down so slowly, my death would be a lingering one. At first, the blade would only fray the robe I wore. It would return, again and again. Just cutting through the cloth would take many minutes.

I could not, no, dared not, think of what would happen after that. Instead I concentrated on the idea of the blade cutting through the cloth, as if by thinking hard I could stop its descent. Then I began to wonder what sort of sound the razor would make as it finally tore away my robe. I thought about this until my teeth were on edge. And still the swinging pendulum traveled grimly downward.

Chapter 3

Down, steadily down, the pendulum crept. I took a frenzied pleasure in seeing how fast it swung from side to side and yet how slowly it descended. It moved with the stealth of a tiger.

Down and relentlessly down! The sharp blade now vibrated within inches of my chest. I struggled violently, furiously, to free my left arm enough to grab the pendulum, hoping I could stop its daunting movement. But I could not free my arm any more. I remained tightly bound.

Down, still inevitably down! I gasped for breath with every sweep. My eyes followed the pendulum's journey with utter despair. I had one hope—hope even whispers to people lying in dungeons who are facing death from the evil Inquisition. It was that the pendulum would be lowered in one mighty, rapid movement and that I would be granted a quick end.

But the pendulum still descended at a snail's pace toward my trapped body. I could see that only ten, maybe a dozen, more sweeps would be required for the razor to make contact with my robe. My hope of a quick death passed, and a calm descended over me. There was absolutely nothing that I could do. It was inevitable. But then, for the first time in days, perhaps even weeks, I began to think clearly about the possibility of escape.

It occurred to me that the bandagelike strap around me was all that tied me to the frame underneath. Perhaps the first strokes of the razor would slice through it enough for me to free my left hand. Perhaps, then, I would be able to unwind the remaining strands and escape. But no! Surely my torturers or their minions would have foreseen this. They would be watching for such a move. I tilted my head up to look along my body. The straps completely bound me, going right across my chest where the pendulum would cut first.

I had just dropped my head back in anguish when an idea flashed through my mind. It was half-formed and scarcely sane. For many hours, as the pendulum swung, rats had scurried around my cell. I had become familiar with their menace and their wild, ravenous eyes. But they, too, had become familiar with me. They grew bolder and no longer feared my left hand waving back and forth. Over time, they had devoured almost all that remained of my meal, frequently fastening their fangs on my numb fingers. Their hunger and sharp teeth became the basis of my escape plan. Weak and barely sane though I was, I attempted to put it into action.

With the small amount of meat and spicy oil still on the dish, I rubbed as much of the bandage tying me as I was able to reach. I then lay still and waited. At first, the vermin seemed startled by my lack of movement. For a moment, they shrank back, and some returned to the pit. Then two of the boldest moved toward the frame and leaped onto my body, sniffing at my bonds. Finally, they signaled to the others to charge.

Legions of hungry rats hurried over, jumping onto the frame and crawling all over my body. By some sixth sense, they managed to avoid the pendulum's lethal swing as they pressed and swarmed upon me. They writhed upon my throat, stifling me. Their cold lips pressed against mine. Disgust beyond all reason filled me to the brim and chilled my heart. Yet, if I could only hold out for a minute, the struggle might be over. I could already feel the ties beginning to loosen. With superhuman effort, I continued to lie still.

My effort was not in vain. Eventually, the bands that had tied me hung in shreds. In one more moment, I would be free. But the end of the pendulum was now pressing upon my chest. Soon it had divided the robe that I wore. Twice again it swung, breaking my skin. Sharp pain shot through every nerve of my body. But the moment of escape had arrived. I slid sideways off the wooden frame to safety.

WORD POWER

daunting—very discouraging

minions—slaves; helpers

anguish—extreme misery; agony

ravenous—very hungry

vermin—animal pests

intensity—strong force or great brightness

I had scarcely stepped onto the floor of the prison when the pendulum, that hellish machine, stopped moving. I watched with fear as it was drawn up by some invisible force through the ceiling. I was free, but in the grasp of the Inquisition! My every move was being watched. I had escaped death in one grim form to be delivered up to it in another, equally grim. Nervously, my eyes ran along the barriers of solid iron that held me prisoner. A change had occurred, but at first I was unable to work out exactly what it was.

I now became aware of where the strange light was coming from. There was a gap, narrower than a finger's width, between the walls and the floor. I bent down to try to look through the gap, but could not manage it. Mystified, I stood up and noted how the light in the room had become brighter. The evil figures painted on the walls had come to life. Their colors, once so dull and hard to make out, now shone very brightly.

The light made the ghastly images even more terrifying than they had been before. Their demon eyes glared at me from a thousand different directions. They shone with a fiery intensity. However, even they were outshone by the wall itself, which now glowed a bright crimson red.

My nostrils were soon filled with the smell of red-hot metal. There could be no doubt of what my tormentors—those most wicked of men—planned! They were going to kill me by heating the walls of my cell. I began to shrink back from the glowing metal toward the pit in the center. Compared to the fiery destruction that had been designed for me, its coolness seemed almost welcoming. I stared into the pit, whose innermost nooks and crannies were now clearly lit. Oh, horror of horrors! I shrieked and buried my face in my hands, weeping and wailing bitterly.

Again, I looked up in fear. The heat had greatly increased. With it came a second change to my prison—a change in its shape. Once square, it was slowly turning into a diamond as its iron walls changed angle. There was a rumbling sound, a deep moaning of the red-hot walls as they moved. I neither wanted them to stop nor even hoped that they would. I could embrace them in the knowledge that they would soon bring me everlasting peace. "Death," I wailed desperately. "Any death but that of the pit."

What an utter fool I was! The glowing walls were intended to force me into the pit. It was scarcely possible that I could withstand their burning heat or, for that matter, the force of their movement. The diamond shape gradually grew flatter and flatter. Its widest part was in the center, where the pit lay waiting. I shrank back, but the moving, burning walls pressed me onward, closer and closer. My poor, hot body writhed in pain. Eventually, I was left with no foothold on the floor of the prison. I stopped my struggling, but the agony of my soul forced out one long, final scream of despair as I teetered on the brink.

Suddenly, there was a deafening sound of trumpets and the hum of human voices. Then came a harsh, booming noise, like a thousand thunderstorms. I couldn't believe it! The fiery walls had begun to retreat. An outstretched arm caught my own as I fell fainting into the abyss. It was the arm of a general from the French army. They had conquered the Inquisitors' stronghold and its dungeons. The Inquisition was in the hands of its enemies. I was saved.

THE END

The Open Door

Retold from a story by Charlotte Riddell

I am one of the few people left who love the country and hate cities. And the country was looking its best just then, as I walked through the leafy lanes of Meadowshire in late spring, wishing I could live there forever.

I had walked a long way before chancing upon a gentleman on a horse. I asked him if he might tell me the way to Ladlow Hall.

"That is Ladlow Hall," he answered, pointing over the fence to my left. I thanked him and was going on, when he said:

"No one lives there now."

"I know," I answered.

He bade me good-day and rode off.

But I am getting ahead of myself. I should explain how it was that I came to be in that place. Though only twenty-two, I was eager to leave my job as a clerk with realtors Frimpton and Frampton, in the City of London. Office work did not suit me, and I saw, in the wealthy tea trader Mr. Carrison's misfortune, an opportunity to advance my own prospects. Mr. Carrison had taken a long lease on Ladlow Hall, a country house, through my former employers. But he had found it to be uninhabitable due to a door that would not stay shut. Word had spread that the house was haunted.

"I can't live there," he said, when I put my proposal to him. "What's more, I can't get anyone else to live there. I can't get rid of it. Matters are at a deadlock. Others have failed to solve the mystery. But if you want to try, I will make this bargain with you. If, after staying in the house for a week, you can keep the door shut, I will pay you the sum of ten pounds."

"Leave ghost-hunting and spirit-laying alone, Phil," my uncle advised me.

But for ten pounds, six months' salary in my job as a clerk, I would have faced all the inhabitants of spirit land.

So, having armed myself with pistol and rifle, I set out to solve the mystery of the haunting of Ladlow Hall and to shut the open door.

From the main gate, a long avenue bordered by linden trees led straight up to the Hall.

Soon I stood looking at a square, solid house, three stories high. A flight of steps led up to the main entrance, which had four windows on each side. All the blinds were down. A dead silence brooded over the place. I fit the key in the lock, turned the handle, and entered.

Out of the bright sunlight, my eyes grew slowly accustomed to the darkness, and I found myself in an immense hall. Pictures hung all around the walls. In odd niches and corners stood statues and suits of armor. A magnificent oak staircase led to the upper rooms.

Mr. Carrison had given no instructions to identify the ghostly chamber. Indeed, I knew nothing of the story connected with it. But I did know that I had never before seen so many doors. Two of them stood open.

"I'll just shut them as a beginning," I thought, "before I go upstairs."

The doors were of oak, heavy and well-fitting. I closed them very securely, then ascended the staircase and entered the many bedchambers. Some were quite bare of furniture, others contained antique chairs, dressing tables, and armoires. Most doors were closed. I shut those that were open, then made my way into the attic.

I closed the doors throughout the house. Where there were keys, I locked the doors. Where there were no keys, I left them as securely fastened as possible.

When I reached the ground floor, it was nearly evening. To explore the whole house before dusk, I would have to hurry.

Next, I visited the kitchens and the offices of the staff at the rear of the great hall. However, there was no sense in lingering over the details of larders, pantries, and laundries. The mystery was scarcely likely to be there, hidden among the cinders and empty bottles.

Hurrying back into the hall through the gathering darkness, I felt very much alone among the statues and ghostly figures of men in armor. I would quickly look through the lower apartments, then decide which rooms I should occupy myself. With a hot cup of tea beside a blazing fire, I hoped I would not continue to feel quite so oppressed by the solitude of the place.

Though the sun had gone down, it was still light enough in the hall to see that one of the doors I had shut was standing open!

THE FACTS

Charlotte Riddell (1832-1906) was born into a wealthy family in Carrickfergus, Northern Ireland. Her father became ill when she was young, so he was no longer able to work. As a result, the family quickly sank into poverty. In 1855, a few years after her father died, Charlotte moved to London with her mother. To earn a living, she began to write. She published her first novel, *Zuriel's Grandchild*, a year later. During her lifetime, Charlotte produced about 46 novels, as well as many magazine articles and short stories. The stories included numerous tales of the supernatural, some of which were collected in *Weird Tales* (1882). Charlotte died in Hounslow, London, in 1906.

I turned to the door on the other side of the hall. It was as I had left it—closed. I had definitely discovered the room with the open door.

I shut the door once more, then walked to the grand staircase and back again. The door stood wide open. I went into the room and pulled up the blinds to take a better look. It was a dreary, gloomy room with dark, paneled walls, a black, shining floor, and windows high up.

Opposite the door through which I had entered, I was astonished to find a bed. It seemed out of place in a room so near the hall with all its noisy comings and goings. Beside it, there was another door that was locked. It was the only locked door that I had encountered in the house.

"Any crime might have been committed in such a room," I thought.

When I left through the open door, I shut and bolted it.

"I will go out and get some wood, then look at it again," I said to myself. When I returned, it stood wide open once more.

"Stay open, then!" I cried. "I will not trouble myself again with you tonight!"

As I spoke, there was a ring at the front door that echoed through the desolate house and startled me beyond expression.

It was the man who had brought my luggage from the station. I requested him to put it down in the hall. While finding some change to pay him, I asked where the nearest post office was. "Not far," he said. "If you want a letter sent, I can drop it in the box for you. The mail-cart picks up the bag at ten o'clock."

I had nothing ready to mail then and told him so. On his way out of the door, he paused with his hand on the lock and asked:

"Are you staying here all alone, master?"

"All alone," I answered, with as much cheerfulness as I could muster.

"That's the very room, you know," he whispered, nodding in the direction of the open door.

"Yes, I know," I replied.

"Been trying to shut it already, have

WORD POWER

lease—a contract for renting a house

spirit-laying—driving out spirits; exorcising

cinders—ashes from a fire

oppressed—burdened; overwhelmed

desolate—dreary; miserable

muster—find; summon up

game—daring; courageous

you? You are a game one!" And with that worrying comment he left.

I cast one glance at the door—it was open. Through the windows, moonlight streamed cold and silvery. I sat at a great table in the hall and wrote a brief letter to Mr. Carrison. Then I walked hurriedly out the door and down the long avenue, with its mysterious lights and shades. The scent of summer and the smell of the earth were delicious. If it had not been for the door, I should have felt very happy indeed.

The post office, in the village of Ladlow Hollow, was near an ancient bridge that spanned a stream.

As I stood by the door of the store, talking to the postmistress, the same gentleman that I had met that afternoon on his horse passed by on foot. He wished me goodnight as he went by, and then nodded familiarly to my companion, who curtseyed.

"His lordship ages fast," she remarked.

"His lordship?" I said, feeling puzzled.

"That's Lord Ladlow," she explained, and then nodded toward the retreating figure.

Walking back to the Hall, I had much to think about. Lord Ladlow indeed! My word. I had thought he was far distant. And here I find him, walking away from his own home.

Just then, I heard a noise in the bushes nearby. In an instant I was in the thick of the undergrowth. Something shot out and then darted deeper into the cover provided by the plants. I followed at once, but could catch no glimpse of it. I did not know the lie of the ground and, baffled and annoyed, had to give up the hunt.

In the house, the moon's beams were streaming down upon the hall. I could see every statue and every suit of armor. The scene seemed like something in a dream. I was tired and decided that I would not trouble about fire or food, or the open door, until the next morning.

With the intention of going to bed, I picked up some of my bags and carried them to a room on the first floor, then returned for the rest. Laying my hand on my rifle, I felt that it was wet. I touched the floor. It was also wet. Someone else had been in the house!

Chapter 2

The next morning, the postman came with letters from both Mr. Carrison and my uncle. I thanked him very much for his trouble.

"It's no trouble at all, sir," he replied. "I pass by here every morning, on my way to her ladyship's."

"Who is her ladyship?"

"She's the Dowager Lady Ladlow," he answered, "the old lord's widow."

"And where is her place?" I enquired.

"Through the shrubbery, round about a quarter of a mile up the stream."

The postman departed. I spent the rest of the morning considering the open door, examining it from within and without. So long as I was nearby, it remained closed. If I walked even to the opposite side of the hall, it burst from latch and bolt and swung wide. I could not lock it because there was no key. I was baffled.

At two o'clock, Lord Ladlow paid me a visit.

"You should be made aware of the rumors that there are about me," he said, as we walked in the park. "My uncle, the former Lord Ladlow, was murdered in that room. Many think I killed him. But I loved the old man. Even when he disinherited me for the sake of his young wife, I was sorry, but not angry. Then, when he wrote the will in my favor once more, I tried to persuade him to leave the lady a handsome sum, too.

"That night, my uncle was stabbed from behind in the neck, as he sat at his desk. After his death, his lawyer confirmed that he had made a new will, only three days previously, leaving everything to me. But that new will was never found. So my uncle's wife submitted the former will, which left her everything.

"Ill as I could afford to, I had to dispute the matter. The lawyers are at it still. I was soon linked with the murder, so, having lost my good name, I went abroad. While I was away, Mr. Carrison took the Hall. Till I returned, I had no knowledge of the open door. This mystery must be cleared up."

As Lord Ladlow spoke, I remembered that "something" in the shrubbery. So I told him that I thought there had been someone prowling mysteriously about the place just the previous evening.

"Poachers," he suggested.

I shook my head. "I think it was either a girl or a woman."

After Lord Ladlow had left, I returned to the house, and that door. If I shut it once, I shut it a hundred times. Do what I would, it opened wide the instant that I turned away.

At about four o'clock, Lord Ladlow's daughter, Beatrice, arrived on horseback.

"Papa sent me with this," she said, as she put a letter in my hand.

The letter said: "Buy your food yourself. Keep it locked away. Get your water from the pump in the stable yard. I am going to London. Should you want anything, Beatrice will help you."

I at once borrowed Beatrice's pony and led him under the window of the locked room, to which the room with the open door led. Once the pony was in place, I stood on its saddle and looked in. The room was bare—there were no chairs or table, and no pictures on the walls.

"That is where the murdered man's valet slept," said Beatrice. "It was the valet who discovered him on the night that he was killed. Poor man. He died from the shock."

I returned Beatrice's pony to her and watched her ride off across the park. Then I turned back into the lonely house.

Although certain that nothing human was keeping the door open, I sensed I was not alone in the house. This was apparent from details—a chair and papers moved, clothes touched. I surmised that, while I was asleep or at the post office, someone had wandered around the house. I was about to

write to Mr. Carrison for permission to break open the locked door when, early one morning, I spied a hairpin beside it.

Then it occurred to me. In order to solve the mystery of the open door, I must keep watch in the room to which it led.

It was a lovely morning. I opened the hall door to let in the fresh air. There, on the top step, I saw a basket full of fruit and flowers, with a card addressed to me. I selected a peach and ate it, but had barely swallowed the last piece when I remembered Lord Ladlow's message of caution. A strange taste lingered in my mouth. I smelled the fruit in the basket. It all had the same faint odor. I put some in my pocket and hurried away to visit the doctor in the village.

The doctor examined me and at once gave me some medicine. "It is fortunate you stopped at the first peach," the doctor said, "Someone has tried to poison you."

When I arrived back at Ladlow, the postman had left a letter from Mr. Carrison. It enclosed ten pounds and the news that Lord Ladlow had released him from the terms of the lease. As a result, Mr. Carrison no longer needed to let Ladlow Hall to me, so I could leave at once. Before leaving, however, I was determined to catch whoever had sent me the poisoned fruit.

The deep night shadows were closing over Ladlow Hall as I returned from my daily trip to the post office an hour earlier than usual. The moon had not yet risen. The house, silent and deserted, was as still as death.

I took a candle and went slowly up to my room, as though preparing to go to bed. Then I blew out the flame. Next, feeling a great thrill of terror, I slipped softly downstairs in the dark, went straight across the hall, and in through the open door. Noiselessly, I made my way to the other side of the room, sat in an easy chair near the bed, and hid behind a curtain.

Hours passed. The moon rose and crossed the sky. Then, at last, the sky grew lighter. Dawn was breaking. Soon the awful vigil would be over. Hush! What was that? The locked door opened suddenly, and a slight woman dressed in black came into the room. She went straight across to the open door, which she closed and bolted. Then, glancing around, she produced a key, crossed

WORD POWER

Dowager—a "dowager lady" is the widow of a lord. The title is used to distinguish her from the wife of the new lord, known simply as "lady."

valet—a personal manservant

surmised—guessed

vigil—a watch, usually overnight

entreated—begged; pleaded

to the cabinet, and opened it. I did not stir. She took out the drawers one by one and peered into the openings. What on Earth did she want? Then it struck me – SHE WAS SEARCHING FOR THE MISSING WILL!

I sprang from my hiding place and soon had her in my grasp. But, fighting like a wildcat, she tore free and ran toward the valet's room. I knew that if she reached it, she would escape. So I rushed after her, just caught her dress, and dragged her back. Before I knew it, she had taken the revolver out of my pocket and fired.

She missed. I fell upon her and seized the weapon. She would not let it go. But I held her so tight that she could not use it. She bit my face. She tore at my hair. She turned and twisted about like a snake. I did not feel pain, only a deadly horror that my strength was giving out.

The woman made one last, desperate plunge. I felt my grasp slackening. She felt it, too, and tore free, at the same instant firing again blindly. Again, she missed.

Suddenly, there came a look of total horror in her eyes.

"See!" she cried, and fled.

I saw in a flash that the door she had bolted was open. There, beside the table, stood an awful figure with uplifted hand. Then I saw no more, but felt something like red-hot iron enter my shoulder. At once, I fell senseless to the ground.

When the postman arrived later that morning and found that no one was stirring, he looked through the window. Inside, he saw me lying on the floor in a pool of blood. He was about to run to the farmyard to call for help when Lord Ladlow came riding up the avenue.

Together, they broke down the door, then laid me on the bed in that terrible room. I hovered between life and death for some time, but at length recovered enough to tell Lord Ladlow all I knew.

It seemed that the Dowager Lady Ladlow had regularly been sending her maidservant to the Hall to look for the missing will. Only by finding and destroying it could the Dowager be sure to keep the fortune that she had inherited. It was the maid I had seen as she searched for the document. But the ghost of the former Lord Ladlow, whom she had murdered, never left her to search in peace. Instead it always entered through the open door to haunt her. Now I begged the new Lord Ladlow to search for the will himself.

"Break up the cabinet if necessary," I entreated. "I am sure the papers are there."

And they were. His lordship finally got the money and property that were rightfully his. But the scandal was hushed up and the crime went unpunished. As one condition of Lord Ladlow's silence, the Lady Dowager and her maid went abroad immediately and never returned.

I am happy now. But there are times when a great horror of darkness falls upon me and I cannot endure to be left alone.

THE END

Frankenstein

Retold from a story by Mary Shelley

We found him adrift on an ice floe many leagues inside the Arctic Circle. The sled dogs that lay around him were already dead. In a few days he would join them. But before he died, he rested on my boat and relayed to me, Captain Robert Walton, his terrible tale.

This, in his own words, is the story of Victor Frankenstein.

I had the happiest of childhoods at my family's estate just outside Geneva. Along with me, my parents, and two younger brothers, Ernest and William, lived a girl called Elizabeth. My mother and father had taken her into our family when she was a young child. Elizabeth had golden hair, bright blue eyes, and a very gentle manner. I grew to care for her very much. As my two brothers grew older, my family hired a nanny, Justine, to help care for them. She was kind and understanding, and soon became like an older sister to us all.

The first deep sadness I encountered was when my mother died from scarlet fever when I was seventeen. It was shortly before I was to enroll at the university in Ingolstadt, many days' ride away in Bavaria. It was my mother's dying wish that Elizabeth and I should one day marry. But I needed to learn all that I could about science before I wed that beautiful, saintly girl.

I don't know when my interest in science started. I remember reading ancient texts from a young age. I also remember the excitement I felt when I was fifteen on seeing a violent thunderstorm erupt over the mountains near our home. After witnessing the incredible power of a lightning bolt reducing a tall tree to a stump, I was filled with wonder and read avidly about electricity. I was anxious to learn all that I could about the hidden secrets of nature—not for profit, but for the good of mankind. What glory!

I recall the long, tearful goodbye that occurred the day the carriage took me and Henry Clerval, my best friend, to Ingolstadt to study. I promised to visit as often as I could and felt great sadness as the carriage pulled away from my family and my beloved Elizabeth.

Henry did not care for science, but for the classics and tales of heroism and daring. He hoped that one day his name would be alongside those of the brave adventurers that he read about. His cheerful manner raised my spirits, and as we reached Ingolstadt, I wasted no time before enrolling at the university.

Over the next two years, I devoted myself completely to science. It became my whole life. I read widely, attended lectures, and sought out the company of great scientific minds, all the while learning everything I could. I met Henry often at first, but as my studies took over, I saw him less and less. In all that time I never visited my family.

Only a person who has experienced the lure of science can understand how and why I was so focused. In other subjects of study, you can go only as far as others have gone before you. But in science, there are always new challenges to meet and amazing discoveries to be made.

Over time, I was drawn to the study of human and animal life, and to ask myself where life came from. It was the boldest of questions, and I quickly became obsessed by it. Looking back now, I see that my enthusiasm was unnatural, for I underwent the most horrific experiences in my quest for an answer. Yet I not only endured them, but did so with great enjoyment and willingness.

To examine the causes of life, one must study death. I learned all there was concerning anatomy, but this was not enough. I knew I must also observe the natural decay of the human body. Like some supernatural fiend, I spent days and nights in hospitals, beside mortuary slabs, and in vaults and tombs, observing the processes of death and decay.

My attention was firmly fixed on the most gruesome of spectacles. I saw how the fine form of man wasted away. I saw how the wonders of the eye, the brain, and the heart became food for the worm. I examined every possible detail very closely. I catalogued everything that occurred in the change from life to death, and in doing so, hoped to learn how to reverse the process.

One day, that dream came true. I alone had discovered the most astonishing of secrets, the secret of transforming death into life. I am afraid, Captain Walton, that this secret must stay with me while I live and be buried with me when I die. For knowledge of it would lead you to misery and destruction. As it has me.

The discovery overwhelmed me for some time. I had still to prepare a container, a body, for my marvelous gift. I feared that I would be unable to build such a complex thing. Yet I dared not fail.

Returning to graveyards and slaughter-houses, I collected my ghoulish raw materials—body parts of the dead.

THE FACTS

Mary Shelley (1797-1851) was the daughter of British political philosopher William Godwin and the early feminist Mary Wollstonecraft. In 1813, she met the poet Percy Bysshe Shelley, and they married three years later. The idea for the story of Frankenstein came when the Shelleys spent the summer at Lake Geneva with the poet Lord Byron. He suggested that they each write a ghost story. Mary Shelley's was by far the most successful and was published in 1818. She wrote five more novels, including *Valperga* (1823) and *Falkner* (1837), but none recaptured the power of Frankenstein.

Mary Shelley's life was deeply sad. Her husband drowned in 1822, and only one of her four children survived infancy.

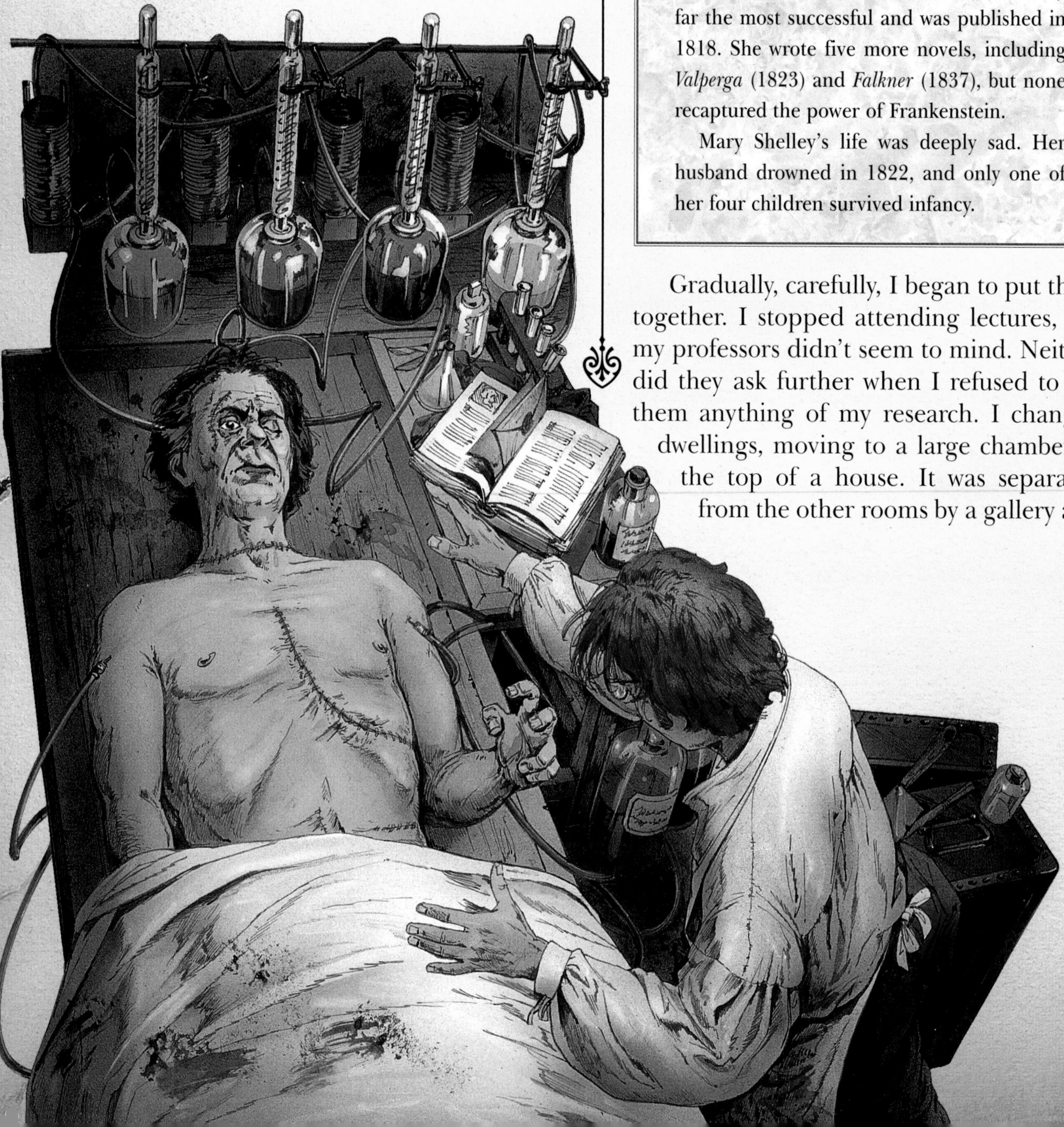

Gradually, carefully, I began to put them together. I stopped attending lectures, but my professors didn't seem to mind. Neither did they ask further when I refused to tell them anything of my research. I changed dwellings, moving to a large chamber at the top of a house. It was separated from the other rooms by a gallery and a long staircase. In this chamber I had my workshop, which would have disgusted any normal person.

It was a beautiful summer, but I only saw it from the smeared windows of my workshop. Although I missed Elizabeth and my family greatly, I never replied to their letters because I was so obsessed by my experiments.

Now my limbs tremble and my eyes swim at the memory. But at the time, nothing could take me away from my task. I worked all hours. The possibility of creating life from death drove me on through the toil. I grew dangerously thin, and my face was a ghostly white mask from which my eyes stared out of sunken, hollow sockets. When occasional thoughts of Elizabeth and my family stopped me from working, I slept on a filthy mat on the floor.

Nearing the completion of my work, I fell into a fever, making sleep almost impossible. When awake, I became so nervous that I would jump out of my skin at the smallest unexpected sound. I shied away from any human contact and didn't see Henry for many months.

Driven like a demon through that fall, I continued to work until one stormy night in November. After the claps of thunder and flashes of lightning had ceased, I stood back proudly. My work was finished. A living being was about to rise from where before there had been only death.

The night was pitch black. The only sound I could hear was the gentle churning of my tanks of chemicals. That, and the rain rattling against the filthy windows of my cursed apartment.

My creation was a giant figure of a man, fully eight feet tall, and designed to be a magnificent, handsome fellow. But when I looked at him properly for the first time, I saw something quite different. How can I describe my emotions at the catastrophe that lay before me? His limbs and head were in proportion, and I'd carefully selected his features to be beautiful. Beautiful? Great God!

His hair was shiny and black and his teeth pearly white, but these were the only good points. His yellow skin barely covered the muscles and blood vessels underneath. I looked aghast at his heavy brow and ghostly eye sockets, his shriveled, unnatural complexion, and his straight, black lips.

With my heart pounding, I watched in complete horror as one watery, pale eye opened and blinked. A breath rattled the creature's frame, and a convulsion shook its arms and legs. It was stirring...

WORD POWER

floe—a sheet of floating ice

league—a unit of distance equal to about three miles

scarlet fever—a disease whose symptoms include a rash and a red tongue

avidly—eagerly; enthusiastically

classics—literature of lasting importance, especially by ancient Greek and Roman writers

lure—an attraction or temptation

anatomy—the study of the human body's structure

mortuary—a building where dead bodies are stored before burial

aghast—overcome with horror

convulsion—a violent shake or jolt

Chapter 2

I stood in my laboratory staring at the figure that I had created as it started to come to life. Already, one hideous, dull eye had opened, and the enormous chest had started to heave.

I had worked so hard for so long solely to create life from death. For this, I had deprived myself of rest and health, of friendship and love. But now that I had finished, the beauty of the dream had vanished completely. As I watched the creature come to life, breathless horror and disgust filled my soul. Unable to watch as it rose to stand, I rushed out of the room.

I paced the courtyard outside my home for many hours before returning to my bed and falling asleep. But my sleep was disturbed by the wildest of dreams. I saw Elizabeth standing before me looking beautiful. I embraced and then kissed her, but as our lips touched, her features began to change. Finally, horror of horrors, I found myself kissing a corpse. I awoke full of dread to discover that cold sweat covered my forehead and my teeth were chattering.

In front of me stood the monster—my monster. His eyes were fixed on me. His jaws opened and he tried to make a sound, but nothing came out. His thin lips formed a hideous grin that wrinkled his leathery cheeks. I lay there silent, frozen with fear.

Next the creature dropped his ugly, square jaw open again and grunted. Then his arm stretched out toward me like a giant crane, and his massive, clumsy hand slowly, shakily unclenched. His first finger, bulging with unnaturally large muscles, was pointing straight at me. I could stand no more, so I fled down the stairs and out of the building. Why had I failed to notice how revolting the creature was as I worked to make it? Had I become weary of beauty and hardened to vile sights by my many visits to graves and slaughterhouses? Or was it that my work had driven me insane? For it was only now the monster was alive that I fully realized what I had created. It was ghastly—not merely ugly, but completely horrific. Disgust overcame me and I felt sick. What on earth had I done?

For some time, I don't know how long, I roamed the streets in a terrible daze. Then fortune smiled upon me and I heard a friendly voice.

"My dear Frankenstein!"

Henry Clerval stood before me.

"How very glad I am to see you after all this time!" he exclaimed.

Then Henry took me by the arm and started to lead me through the streets. As we walked, he chatted about my family. He told me that they were well, but missed hearing from me. I was so busy feeling guilty that it was only as we turned into my street that I realized we were heading toward my home—and my workshop. I started to tremble and tried to make excuses that would turn Henry back. But he just continued walking and said, "My dear Victor, I must find out what has been keeping you away from me and your loving family for so long."

It was all I could do to make Henry stay downstairs for some moments while I straightened up my lab. Laughingly he agreed, declaring, "You are a strange man, Victor Frankenstein. You're so serious about life."

I walked slowly up the stairs. Each step was harder than the last. For all I knew, the monster might still be roaming about inside

my rooms. My whole body shook with terror as I fumbled for the door knob. My heart was pounding so violently that I thought it would burst right out of my chest. Finally, I opened the door and ventured inside.

I could not believe my good fortune. The ghastly monster had gone. I checked and double-checked. Apart from a few pieces of upturned furniture, there was no sign that it had ever been there. It was almost as if I had completely imagined the creature. I quickly busied myself, hiding gory materials and my notes in cupboards and chests. Sweat poured from my brow until the salty beads temporarily blinded my eyes. Wiping them away, I glanced down at the spot where my floor rug should have been. It had gone, but I thought little of it.

Suddenly, Henry appeared in my room. In his opinion, I had kept him waiting long enough. The light there was much brighter than it had been in the streets outside, and my friend gasped when he saw my face.

"But Victor, how ill you look!"

"I have been working extremely hard," I replied and paused to wipe yet more of the sweat from my brow. Then I added, "But now I have finished."

My fever burned even more fiercely as I did my very best to entertain Henry and to act normally. I tried to make conversation, but could not remain calm. My voice and my laughter were harsh. I started to feel sick again and my head spun. When I attempted to offer Henry a glass of wine, my poor hands shook so much that I couldn't hold the bottle.

Suddenly, the awful realization of what had happened in my rooms only hours before struck me fully. I cast a nervous glance toward one of my dirty window panes. Then I thought I caught a glimpse of the monster outside the window and screamed. I fell into a fit as I thought I saw it enter the room. I writhed in agony as it seemed to grab hold of me and crush the life from my body. My vision blurred, and I couldn't breathe. The last thing I heard was Henry's cry.

My illness lasted for more than three months. Throughout that time, I remained in my bed in Henry's apartment. Sometimes I awoke and ranted until my lips frothed with foam. At other moments, I sat up then remained totally still, my eyes wild with madness. Most of the time I slept, but far from peacefully. This was all according to Henry, who nursed me. I remember nothing except for one long, continuous nightmare. In it, the monster that I had created was looming over me, its hellish features snarling and snapping.

As I slowly regained my health, Henry explained that he had not told Elizabeth and my father about my true condition in order to spare them grief. He had, instead, said that I was recovering at speed from an illness, but was still too unwell to write to them both. I thanked my dear friend from

WORD POWER

gory—horrific, involving lots of blood

writhed—twisted; squirmed

ranted—shouted violently

tonic—something, especially a medicine, that increases strength and wellbeing

devotion—strong and loyal attachment

rallied—recovered; felt better

fateful—important; significant

the bottom of my heart. How very kind and thoughtful he had been, yet again.

Henry suggested that I now write to my father, and then handed me a letter from Elizabeth. No doctor could have prescribed a better tonic. Elizabeth wrote of many lovely things. She told me that the estate was doing well and that my two young brothers were thriving under the care of the marvelous Justine. Most of all, the letter made clear Elizabeth's devotion to me. It truly warmed my heart.

I stayed at Henry's apartment for many more weeks while I rebuilt my strength. At times, as I looked over the letters from Elizabeth and my father, I felt wretched. How could I have ignored my loved ones for so long? How much time did it take to write a letter? The time it took to attach a muscle to a bone, that's all. As I thought this, I shuddered, and if I had been weaker might have lapsed back into illness. Yet I rallied when I considered the probable fate of my creation. How could it have survived with no education, no knowledge of the world? The monster was surely dead.

Eventually I composed a letter to my family. It was slow work and the result was brief, despite the many hours that I sat in front of Henry's writing desk. Why? Because I had so little to tell. I could and would not say a word about my scientific work, and work had been the only thing in my life for a very long time.

I felt much better when the letter was completed and started gradually to turn my thoughts to the future. Science now revolted me. I decided that I would have to inform my tutors that I could not go back to my studies. I was thinking over what I should do instead when a fateful letter arrived for me. It was from my father and the very worst thing that I had ever had to read. My young brother William, my kind, loving brother, so full of joy and happiness, was dead. According to the Geneva Police, he had been brutally strangled.

As if that were not enough, Captain Walton, I still have to tell you the worst of it. William's beloved nanny, Justine, had been accused of the evil deed. She was to be tried for his murder within the week.

Chapter 3

When I heard the terrible news about my brother William and his nanny Justine, I prepared to leave for Geneva. But Henry was inconsolable and would not join me. I urged the carriage driver on heartlessly, constantly pleading with him to drive the horses harder. For I was aware of the awful swiftness of justice in Geneva and feared for Justine. I knew that she could not possibly have murdered William. It was not in her nature.

I will not bother you with a description of the trial procedures, Captain Walton. They are similar the world over, and I may have missed certain details, for I was, like all my family, in a state of extreme shock.

The physical evidence against poor Justine was strong. She had been the last to see William, not far from where he died, and the locket my brother had always worn was found in her possession. Although she managed to stay calm throughout the trial, she broke down when the guilty verdict came and the sentence of death by hanging was passed. How unjust, how terribly wrong! My Father, Elizabeth, and I all protested, yet we were powerless—Justine's fate was sealed.

The following morning, Justine was executed. It was the darkest of days for me and the rest of my family. Afterward, I felt the need to visit the scene of my brother's death. So I left the others at home one night and went to the site. It was roped off and surrounded with flowers.

When I arrived, I fell to my knees and wept. Grief overwhelmed me, while above a storm erupted. The flashes of lightning reminded me of the destroyed tree that I had seen as a child, and of the time when I had created my monster. I had scarcely considered the terrible creature since I had received my father's letter. What if he were still alive and had come to Geneva? Could he have learned of my family? Would he have sought such dreadful revenge? I shook my head. No, it was impossible.

But making my slow way home, I had the most terrifying of encounters. I saw a massive, powerful figure standing some distance away. However, when the next lightning flash lit up the scene, the figure had gone. But I was dreadfully certain. It was, it must have been, my creation.

I now had a huge, guilty secret. Not one, but two people had died because of me and my infernal work. I won't trouble you with the full extent of my self-pity and grief. But I will say that I suffered dreadfully for my sins, or so I thought at the time. I even reached the point where I envied Justine her peace and rest. I am not afraid to admit that I thought of following her, of taking my own life. Only cowardice and fear of God's judgment kept me alive.

The glorious alpine landscape that surrounded my family's estate became my refuge. For many weeks, I took regular trips alone into the mountains. I could not face other people, however much they needed me. Nor could I tell them a word of what had happened. During this time, beautiful, unspoiled nature started to lighten my heart, and slowly my mood improved. One day, on a long trip past the glaciers, I vowed to return to my family and to take Elizabeth's hand in marriage.

As I thought this, I spied what looked like a man advancing toward me. As the figure loomed nearer, my heart trembled with rage and horror. It was the monster, the murderous wretch that I had created.

I stood firm as I waited for him to arrive. I was ready to fight him, to remove him from the planet or to die in the attempt. By the time that he reached me, I was more like a monster than he was. I screamed threats, gnashed my teeth, and snarled with anger, yet he was calm and had tears in his eyes. Finally, he spoke:

"Unhappy as I am, I will stand and fight you if I must. I am much stronger than you and will kill you, but I will not start the fight. I shall always be gentle with you because you made me. You should love me like a father. You think I'm a murderer, but you propose to murder me, your son."

Then the monster begged me to hear his tale. I was surprised by his voice. It was very loud and deep, but it also had a totally unexpected softness. However, I was even more surprised that he could speak at all. How had he learned to do so in such a short space of time? His thoughtful words intrigued me, too. So I decided to listen carefully to his story.

This is what the monster said: "I have only hazy memories of my beginning—I can recall your face before you abandoned me, and the sensation of great pain. I also felt what I later learned was coldness, and by instinct picked up a floor rug to cover myself. Then I left the place of my birth, your laboratory, and roamed the forests around Ingolstadt.

"For many weeks, by trial and error, I learned how to eat and drink, that fire warmed but was painful to touch, and much more. I also saw other creatures like you when I entered a village. I could not understand why they screamed and threw stones and sticks that hurt me until I saw my face in a pool of water. It was a terrible face, so I then understood why it aroused fear. Afterward, I stayed in the forest and avoided people, but I watched them and learned their ways of behaving and speaking. I also found books, taught myself to read, and gained much wisdom.

"I made my home secretly in a shed beside a run-down cottage. I watched every movement of the family that lived there, but did not make myself known to them. These people—an old man, a boy, and a girl—were gentle to each other. From them I learned what kindness and affection were and started leaving food for them.

"I so wanted to speak to them, but knew I must be careful. When I learned that the old man could not see, a plan started to form in my mind. He could not judge me from my appearance, so I would talk to him. One day, with great excitement, I waited for the boy and girl to leave, then approached the old man. He was understanding, and we spoke for some time. But when the boy and girl came back, they turned on me. The boy, whose kindness I had witnessed countless times, started to hit me over and over again with a heavy wooden club. I would not fight back and hurt him, so just took the blows. But they sickened my heart. If I was not able to convince even these fine people of my goodness, then what hope had I with the rest of mankind?

"Howling in despair, I left the cottage for good. Then my thoughts turned to you, my creator, who had caused me all this pain. I had seen the love that the old man gave his son and daughter. I hoped that if I found you, my father, you would see the error of abandoning me and love me, too. I remembered you muttering the word 'Geneva,' which I had learned was a town. So I decided that I would make my way there. I traveled only at night and always asked directions from a distance so that no one could see my hideous face. Eventually, after several months, I reached the outskirts of Geneva. There, tired and hungry after my long journey, I lay down to rest.

"But then a boy suddenly ran into the field where I was sleeping. Hoping to befriend him, I seized him as he passed by me. But he started to scream and to call me a monster. I tried to calm him, but his cries grew louder and louder. Then something in me snapped and in a reflex action, I wrung his neck as if he were a wild animal. One moment he was alive. The next he was dead. I found a locket on his body that contained two pictures. One was of a beautiful woman. The other was of you, my creator.

"At once I began to search for a hiding place and found a barn that I thought was deserted. But then I found a woman lying fast asleep in a corner. I bent over her and placed the locket securely in the folds of her dress. For some days afterward, I lurked in the area where the boy had died. I wasn't sure whether I still wanted to see you or whether it would be better if I simply left this world forever.

"But now I know what must happen. I cannot live among normal men. You have seen to that by making my appearance so terrible. So you must make another like me. One of my own kind, with the same awful defects, would not shun me. Create a bride for me and you will never see me again. Fail, and I will be with you on your wedding night to wreak terrible revenge."

As the monster finished his story, his eyes flashed with great anger, and he bounded away at incredible speed.

WORD POWER

inconsolable—very distressed; impossible to cheer up

infernal—relating to or suitable for hell; completely evil

alpine—typical of the Alps Mountains, for example, in having snow-covered peaks, grassy meadows, etc.

reflex—an immediate response that occurs without a person choosing to make it

defects—faults; flaws

shun—turn away from; avoid

wreak—cause (something bad, such as injury or damage)

Chapter 4

Two days after I had encountered the monster, and with the very heaviest of hearts, I headed for England. My family was dismayed and insisted that Henry accompany me. For several weeks we traveled through England and Scotland. It was a pleasant enough time, but the task I still had to do soured my heart, and I could not begin work on it until Henry left me. He was a dear friend, but I could not share with him, or with any man, the dreadful secret of my endeavors.

Finally, Henry and I parted company as I headed for a quiet island off the coast of Scotland, there to create a bride for my monster. I felt sick as I started, but quickly recovered my enthusiasm and interest. I was a scientist once more, fascinated by my work of creation. The same frenzy that overcame me before occurred again. However, many weeks later, my doubts and fears returned. By then, just one more night's work was needed to bring the female creature lying in front of me to life.

That morning, I had received a letter from Henry asking me to join him in the Scottish town of Perth. Thinking of Henry, my father, and Elizabeth jolted me out of my work fever. Only then, looking down at the face I had constructed, was I shocked by the creature's resemblance to Justine. How had that happened? For the first time during those weeks, I questioned what I was doing. To make a bride for the monster might rid me of him forever, but what if his bride turned out to be a murderer like him? And what if the hideous monster pair bred? My responsibilities as a scientist started to weigh heavily on me.

Suddenly I was disturbed by a scratching sound at the window. I looked up to see the creature anxiously awaiting his bride, a hideous leer on his face. He had somehow followed me to this lonely isle. One more look at his vile, distorted features was

enough for me. I reached for my surgeon's knife and plunged it deep into the female form that was lying on my work bench. The evil creature outside howled as I hacked and tore at the figure until my arms and body were covered in blood. Then he vanished.

The next day, I cleared up the awful mess that I had made and threw the remains of my second creation into the sea. Then I set sail from the island. A great storm kept my boat at sea for more than a week. When it finally ran aground, another ordeal awaited me. I was arrested and imprisoned for the murder of a man whose body had been found the day before.

I was left to rot in jail for an age before I learned who the dead man was—my best friend, Henry Clerval. Even before the police said that he had been strangled with unnatural force, I knew who his murderer was. I protested my innocence, but the terrible news had made me desperately weak, so I lacked the energy to argue sanely. Instead I ranted and raved, loudly claiming that the monster was responsible for the evil crime. But the authorities did not believe me. Luckily, the judge was merciful and summoned my father, who convinced him of my innocence. At last, I was set free.

The journey back to Geneva was grim. My exhausting work, my time in prison, and the dreadful news of Henry's murder had all combined to make me very ill. So it was many months before I was well enough to marry my dear Elizabeth.

Our wedding day was magnificent. Our family and many friends were present, and the entertainment was wonderful. Of course, the deaths of Justine, William, and Henry were in our minds, but

Elizabeth's happiness and my new calmness helped cheer up my father and the guests.

When all the celebrations were over, my bride and I said farewell to the gathering and took a boat across Lake Geneva. The sunset was beautiful, and I held Elizabeth close. I thought that, perhaps, after all the terrible trials of the past, the nightmare was over at last. But I could not forget that the monster had taken its revenge on my poor, innocent friend. As my thoughts turned to Henry, I tearfully whispered,

"It should have been me."

"Quiet, my darling. Not on our wedding day," Elizabeth had gently chided. She was so full of love and peace that I dared not tell her my awful secret—that three people close to her had died because of me.

By the time we had crossed the lake, the

sunset was over, and clouds were building up in the evening sky. As we reached the inn where we were to spend our wedding night, the weather turned and gentle rain dappled Elizabeth's lace dress.

"It has been the most perfect of days," Elizabeth remarked. I took her hand. She was right. But as the weather became stormier, I found that I could not rest. Instead, I began to think about the monster's threat to be with me on my wedding night. So I decided to take a walk around the inn, just to clear my head.

The rain lashed the outside of the inn hard, and I struggled through the deluge. At length, I completed my tour. Then, as I was heading back through the inn door, I heard Elizabeth screaming in terror.

Instantly, I raced up to our wedding suite and flung the door open.

It was too late. The monster had already struck again. My darling Elizabeth lay on the bed with one arm outstretched and purple bruises ringing her neck like jewels. I ran screaming and raging out of the inn, brandishing my pistol. Just for a moment, I glimpsed the creature and fired a shot. It howled, and I fired again, but it loped off into the shadows at great speed.

In a frenzy, with no time for grief, I raced home to my father. The servants told me that the terrible news had already reached him, and he had been taken ill. I sat by his bedside willing him to recover, but he never opened his eyes again. Heartbroken by the demise of so many members of his family in a few short years, the poor man had simply lost the desire to live. He passed away peacefully.

Yet there could never be peace for me. I had lost almost everyone that I held dear. Lying beside the tombstones in my family's plot at the local graveyard, I wept bitter tears of revenge. I vowed to pursue the evil beast that I had created for the rest of my life. I swore that I would rest only when it had been hunted down and destroyed. I have chased that infernal creature to the very ends of the Earth, Captain Walton, but still it torments me.

Victor Frankenstein finally grew so weak that I cannot with accuracy record his last words to me, Captain Robert Walton. What I can say is that they formed a plea for me to finish his work—to hunt down and kill the monster that he had created.

I let him drift off to sleep, hoping that he would regain his strength, and made my way up onto the deck. I needed the crisp, icy air to help me think clearly. I was deeply troubled by his story. It upset me greatly that this intelligent fellow had been taken to the brink of madness and death by the monster. I decided that he must already be insane, yet his story had seemed so real.

I stood there for some time until a crashing sound caused me to rush below decks. There in my room, leaning over Victor Frankenstein, was a huge brute of a man. I knew at once. The tale had indeed been true, and now Frankenstein's monster was standing before me.

"I did not kill him," the monster said, looking up at me. His yellow eyes were spouting tears, which were rolling down his hideous, leathery face. I was taken aback by the creature's ugly appearance, but also surprised by the softness of his voice as he continued:

"He was my father and my mother, and he treated me cruelly. He abandoned me when I was hardly born. He made me a female companion and then tore her apart in front of my eyes. I took revenge on the man I hated, but out there on the ice, I discovered that I still loved him as my creator. I came back to ask his forgiveness, but he was already dead when I reached your cabin."

Pitying this grief-stricken creature, I offered to take him back to civilization. But he refused.

"Civilization? With its sticks, its stones, its screams, and its guns? No. I have done wrong, but I cannot repent. Frankenstein made me with a mind and a body, but without a soul. I am no more for this world. I have resolved to die out here on the ice."

With those words, the monster leaped out of the cabin window and onto a floating chunk of ice, which was carried away by the sea currents. No one heard or saw him ever again.

THE END

WORD POWER

leer—an ugly, sneering look

distorted—twisted out of a normal or usual shape

chided—scolded

dappled—marked with spots of two or more different colors

deluge—heavy rainfall; downpour

brandishing—waving in a threatening way

demise—death

The Body-Snatcher

Retold from a story by Robert Louis Stevenson

Every night of the year, rain or shine, four of us sat in the small parlor of the George at Debenham—the undertaker, the publican, Fettes, and myself. Fettes was an old, drunken Scotsman, a man of education obviously, and a man of some wealth, since he did not appear to work for his living. He had come to Debenham years ago and was now an adopted townsman.

Fettes' place in the parlor at the George, his absence from church, and his disreputable vices were much talked of in Debenham. He drank rum—five glasses every evening—and for most of the night sat, glass in hand, in a melancholy alcoholic daze. We called him the Doctor, as he had some special knowledge of medicine, and had been known to set a fracture. But beyond these slight particulars, we had no knowledge of his past.

One winter night, there was a sick man in the George, a rich landowner who had had a stroke. The great man's still greater London doctor had rushed to his bedside.

"He's come," said the publican.

"The doctor?" said I.

"Himself," replied our host.

"What's his name?"

"Macfarlane," said the publican.

Fettes, almost through his third tumbler of rum, and stupidly befuddled, seemed to awaken suddenly, as if rising from the dead. "Macfarlane?" he said, quietly. Then his voice became clear, loud, and steady. "Not Dr. Wolfe Macfarlane?"

"Yes," said the publican.

"Do you know him, then, Doctor?" asked the undertaker.

"God forbid!" was the reply. "And yet, there can't be two of them. Is he old?"

"Well," said the publican, "his hair is white, but he looks younger than you."

"He's older, though. It's the rum you see in my face—rum and sin. He may have an easy conscience and a good digestion. Conscience! Hear me speak. You would think I was some good, decent Christian. But no, not I."

"You do not share the publican's high opinion of this doctor," I said.

Fettes ignored me and then declared, "I must see him face to face."

There was a brief pause. A door closed sharply on the second floor, and afterward a step was heard upon the stair.

"That will be the good doctor now," said the publican.

Fettes stood and walked up to the foot of the stairs, just in time to meet the man.

Dr. Macfarlane was alert and vigorous. A well-dressed figure, with a gold watch chain and gold glasses, he was obviously wealthy and successful. It was a surprising contrast to see our parlor drunk—dirty, pimpled, and dressed in his threadbare old cloak—confront him on the threshold.

"Macfarlane!" he said loudly, with no friendliness in his voice.

The great doctor pulled up short on the fourth step. He was evidently shocked at the familiar manner in which he had so unexpectedly been addressed.

"Toddy Macfarlane!" repeated Fettes.

Macfarlane stared at the man before him. "Fettes!" he said, in a startled whisper.

"Ay," said the other, "me! Did you think I was dead, too?"

"Ssshhh!" exclaimed the doctor. "This is a surprise. I hardly knew you, at first. But I'm overjoyed to see you—overjoyed. Must dash, however, the carriage is waiting and I mustn't miss my train. Give me your address and I'll be in touch. We must do something for you, Fettes. You appear to have fallen on hard times."

"Money?" cried Fettes. "From you? The money that I once had from you is lying exactly where I threw it in the rain."

This abrupt refusal cast Dr. Macfarlane back into embarrassed confusion.

A horrible, ugly look came and went across his face. "No offense meant, dear fellow," he said. "In that case, I'll leave you my address."

"I don't wish to know the roof that shelters you," Fettes interrupted. "I just

heard your name and feared it might be you. I wished to know if, after all, there were a God. But now I know that there is, in fact, none. Begone!"

At that, the great London physician hesitated. There was a dangerous glitter in his glasses. But the presence of so many witnesses made him decide to flee, and he darted, like a serpent, for the door. As he passed, Fettes clutched him by the arm and said, in a whisper that was painfully distinct, "Have you seen it again?" Macfarlane pulled his arm away and fled.

The next night, we were all standing breathless by the barroom window, and Fettes, at our side, was sober and deathly pale.

"God protect us, Mr. Fettes!" said the landlord. "These are strange things you have been saying."

Fettes looked us each in the face. "That man Macfarlane is not safe to cross."

And then, without finishing his glass, he went forth, into the black night.

We three turned to our places by the fire, and our surprise soon turned to curiosity. We sat late, discussing the possible causes of Fettes' agitation. Over the following days and weeks, I wormed out the true story. There is probably no other man alive who could narrate to you the following foul and unnatural events.

In his young days, Fettes had studied medicine in Edinburgh. He was well mannered, attentive, intelligent, and liked by his masters, one of whom was a certain teacher of anatomy, whom I shall here call Mr. K. In the second year of his attendance, Fettes acquired the position of second demonstrator in Mr. K's class.

The operating room and lecture room were his responsibility, and part of his duty was to supply, receive, and divide bodies for dissection. With a view to this responsibility, he lived in the same building as the dissecting rooms. Here, after a night of drinking, his hand still tottering, his sight still misty, he would be called out of bed before dawn by the shady individuals who supplied the corpses. He opened the door to these men, helped them with their tragic burdens, paid them their price. Then, when they had gone, he remained alone with the bodies. From such scenes he returned to snatch another hour or two of slumber, to recover from the night's drinking and to refresh himself for the labors of the day.

The slave of his own desires and low ambitions, he was almost insensible to the fate of the fellow humans whose corpses he took in. Although he was extremely cold and selfish, however, Fettes was careful enough to avoid any kind of inconvenient drunkenness or punishable theft. He also wanted the respect of his masters and fellow pupils. So he always made sure to do particularly well in his studies.

The supply of corpses was a continual trouble, both to Fettes and to his master. In that large, busy class, they were always running out of cadavers. Getting replacements was not only very unpleasant in itself, but threatened highly

WORD POWER

publican – owner of a pub or bar

melancholy—sorrowful; sad

threadbare—shabby; with the raised fibers worn away to reveal the threads beneath

anatomy—the study of the structure of human and animal bodies

demonstrator – an assistant who carries out practical work, experiments, etc., for example, during lectures

dissection—cutting something into pieces to examine its structure

insensible to—unaffected by

cadavers—corpses

dangerous consequences to all concerned. It was the policy of Mr. K to ask no questions in his dealings with the trade. "They bring the body and we pay the price," he often used to say. "Ask no questions," he would tell all his assistants firmly, "for the sake of your own consciences."

There was no understanding, however, that the corpses were those of murder victims. If that idea had been suggested to Mr. K, he would have recoiled in horror. On the other hand, the very lightness of Mr. K's speech upon so grave a matter was a temptation to the men with whom he dealt.

Fettes had certainly often remarked upon the freshness of the bodies he received. He was often struck, too, by the abominable looks of the ruffians who brought them to him before dawn. Putting these two facts together in his private thoughts led him to suspect the worst. But he understood his duty to have three branches: to take what was brought, to pay the price, and to avert his eyes from any evidence of crime.

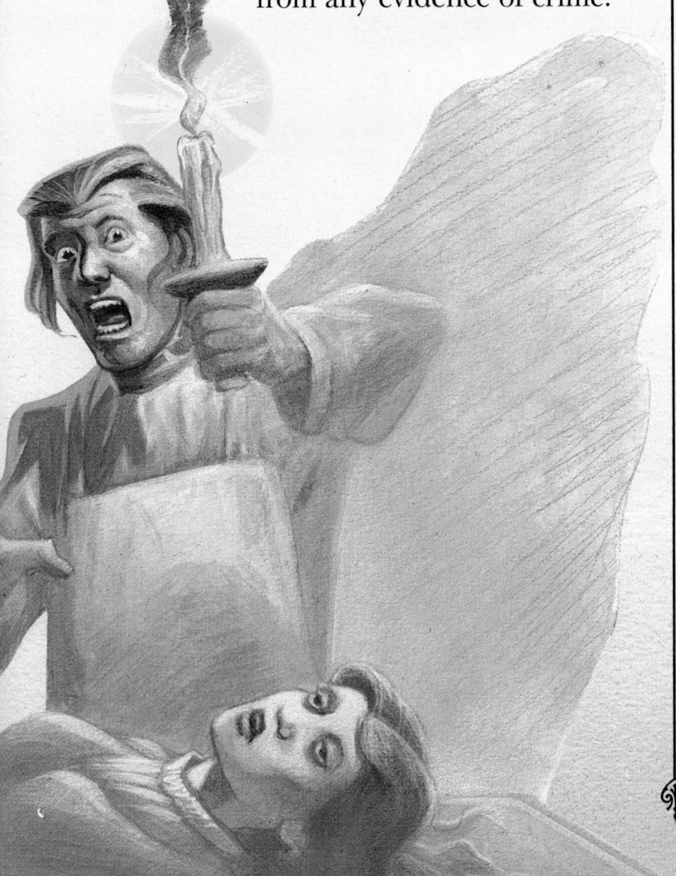

THE FACTS

Robert Louis Stevenson (1850-94) was born in Edinburgh, Scotland, and studied law at the city's university. While he was still a student, he began to write magazine articles. Then, after he became a barrister, he turned his hand to books. The first of these was *An Inland Voyage* (1878), about a canoe trip that he had made through France. Later he wrote short stories such as *The Body-Snatcher* (1884) and novels such as *Dr. Jekyll and Mr. Hyde* (1886), as well as poetry and plays. Stevenson married an American, Fanny Osbourne, and in 1890 they both went to live on the Pacific island of Samoa. He died there four years later at the age of 44.

One November morning, his silence was put sharply to the test. He had been awake all night with raging toothache, but had fallen into an uneasy slumber when he was awakened by an angry knock at the door. It was cold and windy outside. The men had come much later than usual, and seemed more than usually eager to be gone.

Fettes, sick with sleep, lit their way upstairs, then leaned his shoulder against the wall, dozing. But as the visitors stripped the sack from their sad merchandise, Fettes' weary eyes lighted on the dead face. He started. Taking two steps nearer the body, with the candle raised, he cried aloud, "God Almighty! That is Jane Galbraith!"

The men answered nothing, but just shuffled nearer the door.

"I know her, I tell you," he continued, horrified. "She was alive and hearty only yesterday. It's quite impossible that she can now be dead; it's quite impossible that you should have gotten this body fairly."

Chapter 2

The two men who had delivered the corpse looked threateningly at Fettes. Then they demanded their money and he paid them. When they had departed, Fettes examined the girl. She was, indeed, Jane Galbraith. Marks upon her body were evidence of a violent death. Panic seized him. But after reflecting upon the danger of interference in such a business, he decided to ask the advice of his immediate superior, the class assistant.

The assistant was a young doctor, Wolfe Macfarlane, a favorite among the students. He was clever but completely unscrupulous. Fettes and he were close, often working side by side. When bodies were scarce, they drove into the country in Macfarlane's trap, stole a corpse from a graveyard, and returned before dawn.

When Macfarlane arrived, Fettes told him the story of Jane Galbraith. Macfarlane examined the corpse.

"Yes," he said, "it looks fishy."

"What should I do?" asked Fettes.

"Do? Do nothing."

"Someone might recognize her," objected Fettes.

"Well, say you didn't. And there's an end. You could get Mr. K into the most unholy trouble, not to mention the rest of us. What defense would we have? Practically speaking, all our subjects have been murdered. As if you hadn't always suspected it yourself."

"Suspicion is one thing, proof another."

Macfarlane tapped the body with his cane. "Look—I'm as sorry as you are that this is here. The best thing is not to recognize it. Any man of the world would do the same. That's why Mr. K chose us."

Fettes agreed to imitate Macfarlane. The girl was duly dissected, and no one appeared to know who she was.

Some weeks later, after work, Fettes dropped into a tavern and found Macfarlane with a stranger. A small, pale man with coal-black eyes, his name was Gray.

Gray somehow seemed to exercise remarkable control over Macfarlane, ordering him about and commenting rudely on his servility. He liked Fettes, however, and confessed to him some of the evil deeds that he had committed. He appeared to be a very loathsome rogue.

"I'm bad, but Toddy here's the boy, aren't you, Toddy?"

"Don't call me that," snarled Macfarlane.

"Hear him! He'd like to practice knife-throwing on me," remarked Gray.

"We've a better way than that," said Fettes. "When we medical men dislike a dead friend, we dissect him."

Gray laughed, but Macfarlane looked up sharply at his friend. Next, Gray ordered a sumptuous feast for the three of them. Then he commanded Macfarlane to pay, which he did. It was late when they separated and Gray was incapably drunk. But Macfarlane's fury at the insults he had been obliged to swallow seemed to have kept him sober.

Fettes saw neither man the next day. However, at four the following morning, he was awakened by a knock at the door. It was Wolfe Macfarlane with his trap. In the trap was one of those ghastly packages that Fettes had come to know only too well.

"Have you been out alone?" he cried.

Macfarlane didn't answer. But, when the body was upstairs and laid out on the table, he said, "You'd better look at the face."

Fettes stared at him a moment, then did as he was asked. He had almost expected the sight that met his eyes, and yet, the shock was cruel. It was Gray, dead and naked, on a coarse layer of sackcloth. Fettes was speechless.

"Richardson may be given the head," said Macfarlane grimly.

Richardson was a student who had long wanted to dissect a head. "Now, you must pay me. Your accounts must add up correctly," said Macfarlane.

Fettes cried, "Pay you! For that?"

"I daren't give it to you for nothing and you daren't take it thus. It would compromise us both. The more things are wrong, the more we must act as if all were right. Where does Mr. K keep his money?"

There was an instant's hesitation, then Fettes made his decision.

"There," he answered hoarsely, pointing to a cupboard.

Macfarlane took a sum from the drawer.

"Now, enter it in your book," he said.

To avoid a quarrel with Macfarlane, Fettes did as he was told.

"And now," said Macfarlane, "it's only fair that you should pocket the lucre. I've had my share already."

"Macfarlane, I have risked hanging to oblige you."

"Oh, come now!" cried Wolfe. "You acted in self-defense. Suppose I got into trouble, where would you be? This second matter flows clearly from the first. Gray is the continuation of Jane Galbraith. You can't begin, then stop. There is no rest for the wicked."

"My God!" cried Fettes. "What have I done? When did I begin? There seemed to be no harm in taking on the post of demonstrator."

"There are lions and lambs in this life," said Macfarlane. "You're like Mr. K and me. You were born to hunt. Three days from now you'll laugh at this."

With that, Macfarlane left. Fettes could see, now, how weak he had been. Once, he realized, he had controlled Macfarlane's destiny. But now he was merely his paid, helpless accomplice.

Fettes outlived his terrors, just as Macfarlane had predicted. Soon he was congratulating himself on his courage. Before the week was out, he was whispering to Macfarlane that he had joined the lions and left the lambs behind.

At length, Mr. K was again short of bodies. But then news arrived of the funeral of a farmer's wife, at a place called Glencorse.

Macfarlane and Fettes, the two body-snatchers, set forth late one afternoon, well wrapped in cloaks. There was a cold, lashing rain. The young doctors stopped once, near the churchyard, to hide their tools. Then they stabled their horse at a nearby inn and sat down to the best dinner the place could provide.

Over brandy, Macfarlane handed over a pouch of gold to Fettes.

"A compliment for you," he said.

Fettes readily accepted the money and announced: "I was an ass till I knew you. You and Mr. K between you, you'll make a man of me."

Macfarlane laughed. "I tell you, it required a man to back me up the other morning, when I brought Gray's body in."

Fettes smiled proudly. "There was nothing to gain by my dissent. And I knew I could count on your gratitude." He pocketed the gold. "Hell, God, the Devil, right, wrong—men of the world like you and me despise them. Here's to Gray!"

After dinner, they paid their bill and left the inn, taking the road toward Glencorse. There was no sound but that of their trap and the unceasing rain. Though it was pitch dark, it was not until they reached the graveyard that they allowed themselves to light one of the trap's lanterns. Then, propping the lamp against a tree, they began their unholy labors.

Deep in the grave, the two men dug until they heard their shovels scrape on the coffin lid. But then Macfarlane hurt his hand on a stone. He angrily picked it up and flung it carelessly away. Immediately there was a crash of broken glass as it smashed the lantern. The lamp then bounced down the bank, leaving the men in almost total darkness.

The doctors were so near to finishing their task that they decided to continue in the dark. Removing the body from the coffin, they bundled it into a sack and carried it to the trap.

On the road back to Edinburgh, Macfarlane and Fettes sat side by side with their unnatural cargo propped between them. As the trap jumped among the deep ruts, the body fell upon one and then upon the other. This began to play on the nerves of the two companions. Macfarlane made some jest about the farmer's wife. Fettes did not laugh.

Fettes peered at the bundle and a chill crept into his soul. The sack seemed somehow larger than before. As they passed, farm dogs howled tragically. Fettes began to think that they were howling in fear of the hidden corpse.

"For God's sake," said he, "let's have a light!"

Macfarlane, terrified, stopped the horse immediately and got down. It was not easy to light the remaining lamp in the darkness and pouring rain. Eventually, the wick's flickering flame shed a wide circle of misty brightness around the trap. Only then did it become possible for the two young men to see each other and their ghastly burden.

Macfarlane stood quite motionless. Fettes was full of dread, as horror mounted in his brain.

"This is not a woman," said Macfarlane.

"It was a woman when we put her in," whispered Fettes.

"Hold that lamp up high, I must see her face."

Fettes took the lamp. Macfarlane untied the sack and drew it down from the head. Then each man yelled wildly and leaped down into the road. The lamp fell, broke, and went out. The horse, terrified by the commotion, bounded off toward Edinburgh at a gallop. With him went the sole remaining occupant of the trap—the dead and long since dissected Mr. Gray.

THE END

WORD POWER

unscrupulous—without principles; immoral

trap—a two-wheeled, horse-drawn carriage

servility—slave-like behavior; submissiveness

sumptuous—splendid; extravagant

compromise—expose to suspicion or risk

lucre—money

dissent—disagreement; refusal

commotion—upheaval; agitation

Dr. Jekyll and Mr. Hyde

Retold from a story by Robert Louis Stevenson

Mr. Utterson was a respected lawyer who lived in London. He was a serious man, who did not allow himself many pleasures. But he was surprisingly tolerant of other people's weaknesses and was a loyal friend.

One of the pleasures he did allow himself was to take a walk through the streets of London on a Sunday with a relative of his named Richard Enfield. Although Mr. Enfield was younger and very much a man about town, the two men greatly enjoyed their rambles together.

One Sunday morning, they wandered down a side street in a busy part of the city. The two companions admired the freshly painted shutters and gleaming brass knockers of the houses as they strolled along. But then Mr. Enfield stopped at a courtyard, on one side of which rose a drab two-story building. The gable end, which faced onto the street, had no windows, and the house's peeling door had neither bell nor knocker. Pointing with his cane, Mr. Enfield asked the lawyer, "Have you ever noticed that door before?" Mr. Utterson replied that he had.

Mr. Enfield then said, "Let me tell you a strange story to do with that door.

"A few months ago, I was walking home alone in the early hours of the morning when, all of a sudden, I could quite clearly see two figures ahead of me, illuminated by the streetlights. One was a man who was striding along one road, and the other was a young girl of not more than ten, running as fast she could down a street that crossed it. I could see that the pair were going to collide on the corner of the two streets, but before I could shout out to warn them, they had knocked into each other. The girl spun to the ground and, to my horror, the man trampled right over her and walked away, ignoring the girl's piercing screams.

"Fired with anger, I tore after the man, grabbed him by the collar and started to lead him back to where I could see a crowd gathering around the girl. To my surprise he didn't put up a struggle, but gave me such an evil look that I felt myself breaking out in a sweat. The girl's family was there, and soon a doctor arrived. Luckily, the child was not seriously injured, but she was suffering from shock. The family turned on the unrepentant man and threatened to ruin his reputation. But the man merely snapped, 'Naturally I wish to avoid such publicity. Name your price.'

"The girl's family demanded a hundred pounds in damages. He agreed and told us to follow him.

"Where do you think he led us? To this very door, which he opened, at that late hour, with a key and returned, holding ten pounds in gold coins and a check for the rest. The check was in the name of a respected gentleman who had a reputation for good works. Naturally, we suspected that it was a forgery, but the man offered to cash it personally next morning.

"So the girl's father, the doctor, and myself held him at my chambers until the morning, when we accompanied him to the bank. To our surprise, the check was honored and the money handed over to the girl's father. And when I thought about it afterward, I could only presume that this despicable man had some sort of hold over the gentleman who had signed the check—quite possibly the man was blackmailing him."

Mr. Utterson stared thoughtfully at the doorway. Then he asked his companion for the name of the evil-looking man.

"His name was Hyde," replied Mr. Enfield. "I tell you, my friend, there was something detestable about that man. I had the feeling he was deformed, although I couldn't see any actual deformity."

Mr. Utterson seemed to start at the name "Hyde," and his companion could see that he was upset in some way. So Mr. Enfield then proposed that they should continue their walk and not refer to the story again.

Mr. Utterson was indeed upset, for he had recognized the drab building as the laboratory of his good friend Dr. Jekyll, whose residence framed the opposite side of the courtyard. He had also recognized the name "Hyde." Could it possibly be, he asked himself as he parted from Mr. Enfield, the same Hyde whose name featured so mysteriously in Jekyll's most unsatisfactory will?

As soon as he returned home, he went to the safe in his study, pulled out the will, and re-read it. It stated clearly that Jekyll wished that all his possessions should go to his "friend and benefactor Edward Hyde," and that in the case of Dr. Jekyll's disappearance or unexplained absence for any period exceeding three calendar months, Edward Hyde should immediately inherit the doctor's house, money, and belongings.

Until now, the will had troubled Mr. Utterson, not only because of the clause about his friend's "unexplained absence," but also because he knew nothing whatsoever about this so-called "friend and benefactor." Now that he had learned what a monster this "friend" seemed to be, the lawyer was even more troubled.

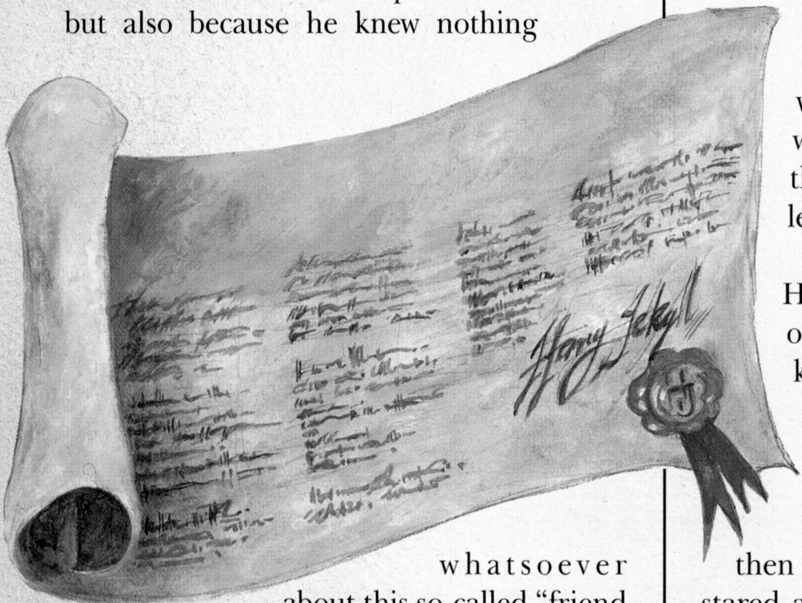

That night, his sleep was disturbed by two haunting images. The first was of the man and the child crashing into each other with the man trampling on the child's body; the second was of his friend, Dr. Jekyll, lying asleep with the same man standing over him, commanding him to get up and do his bidding. But in neither scene did the man have a face, and when Mr. Utterson awoke, he felt sure that if he could only see Edward Hyde's face then he might understand why his friend was in the power of this brute.

So whenever Mr. Utterson had a free moment, he went to the side street and kept watch opposite the door that led to Dr. Jekyll's laboratory, in the hope of catching a glimpse of Mr. Hyde. At last, one frosty night at about ten o'clock, he heard footsteps approaching. Then, from his hiding place, he saw a small man cross the road and head straight for the door. When Mr. Utterson saw the man pulling out a key, he walked up to him and tapped him on the shoulder, saying, "It's Mr. Hyde, isn't it?"

Mr. Hyde drew back like a startled weasel and then, keeping his face hidden, croaked, "Yes, that's my name. What do you want?"

Mr. Utterson explained that he was an old friend of Dr. Jekyll and was just passing when he saw him at the door and wondered if he might let him in.

"You won't find Dr. Jekyll here," Hyde snapped and, turning his back on Mr. Utterson, started to put the key in the lock. Then he added, "How did you know who I was?"

"I will tell you, if you show me your face," the lawyer replied.

Hyde hesitated for a moment and then turned around defiantly. Utterson stared at the pale face and narrow, mean-looking eyes. Then, to Utterson's surprise, Hyde told him he lived in Soho, gave him his address, and asked again how he had recognized him.

Utterson answered evasively, and Hyde's face flushed with anger. "You are nothing but a foul-mouthed liar," he snarled. And before the lawyer could say anything, Hyde turned the key, stepped into the house, and slammed the door behind him.

Mr. Utterson was shaken by this encounter, and as he walked away, he tried to figure out what made him loathe the man so much. He was ugly and dwarfish with a sneering smile and a grating voice, but there was

WORD POWER

illuminated—lit up

unrepentant—not sorry; showing no remorse or regret for one's actions

benefactor—a patron; a person who helps another person financially

evasively—in a manner that is not straightforward, or that tries to avoid difficulties

lavishly—richly; extravagantly

in the thrall of—being in the power of another person

something else about him—he couldn't quite put his finger on it—that both frightened and repulsed the lawyer.

He walked around the corner into a square and knocked on the front door of his friend Henry Jekyll's residence. The butler, Poole, showed him into the lavishly furnished hall and then announced that his master had gone out.

"I saw Mr. Hyde go into the laboratory by the side door, even though you say Dr. Jekyll is out," the lawyer remarked.

"Oh, that's all right, sir. Mr. Hyde has a key and comes and goes as he wishes. We all have orders to obey him."

Mr. Utterson took his leave and started for home, now even more worried.

"I know poor Henry was a bit wild in his youth," he said to himself, "but surely he does not deserve to be in the thrall of such a horrible monster."

Then another, even more appalling thought struck him. What if Hyde already knew that Jekyll had made a will in his favor? That would certainly explain his unexpected willingness to reveal his Soho address to an old friend of Jekyll's! And if that was the case, then Henry Jekyll could be in mortal danger!

Chapter 2

Some weeks later Mr. Utterson had dinner with his friend Jekyll and told the doctor that he had made some discoveries about Mr. Hyde that made him very uneasy about Jekyll's will. But Jekyll wouldn't discuss it with him, saying, "I know you mean well, my good Utterson, but this is a private matter. Let me assure you, though: I can get rid of Mr. Hyde any time I wish. And now, the subject is closed."

For many months, the lawyer heard no more about Mr. Hyde. But then, early one morning in October, there was a loud knock at the lawyer's door, and a messenger handed him a letter, panting, "There's been an 'orrible murder sir, and this envelope, wiv yer name on it, was in the dead man's pocket. Peeler said to tell you the body's been taken to Bow Street police station."

Mr. Utterson recognized the handwriting as that of his client, the distinguished Sir Danvers Carew. He dressed and hurried to the police station, where he was asked by a police officer to identify the blood-stained body of a white-haired gentleman. Mr. Utterson could only just recognize his client. Then the officer held up the splintered top half of a walking stick and said, "We believe that this might have been the murder weapon, sir."

Mr. Utterson felt a rush of fear; the stick was identical to one he had given to Dr. Jekyll. Trying to remain calm, he asked if anyone had witnessed the murder. The officer explained that a maid had seen a white-haired man walking toward a smaller man, then stop and ask directions from him. She recognized him as a certain Mr. Hyde who had once visited her master. Suddenly, as if he were possessed, this Mr. Hyde started to lash out at the gentleman with his walking stick, beating him so hard that it snapped in two. As the old man lay helpless on the ground, his assailant proceeded to stamp on him with such force that the maid swore she heard his bones cracking.

Mr. Utterson stopped the police officer's narration. "I do not need to hear any more. I will take you immediately to this man's lodgings."

The two men took a cab to a dingy street in central London, the address Hyde had given the lawyer. They knocked on the door, and a shifty-looking old woman answered. She told them that Mr. Hyde had come in late the night before, but had left his home a short while afterward.

They asked to be shown his rooms which, to Mr. Utterson's surprise, were tastefully furnished with paintings on the walls and silver on the dining table. Clearly the owner had left in a hurry because clothes were scattered about on the floor and drawers were left open. The inspector searched the room and found the bottom half of a walking stick behind the door.

Mr. Utterson knew that he must confront his friend Jekyll, for Hyde had to be caught immediately. So that afternoon he went to Jekyll's house and was shown into the laboratory by the butler, Poole. The windowless room was strewn with chemical equipment and straw-filled packing crates. The lawyer climbed the steps to the doctor's den where he found his friend, huddled by the fire, looking extremely pale and ill.

Utterson said, "I suppose you've heard the news? And I also suppose that you are not mad enough to hide this evil man?"

The doctor's normally calm manner deserted him. Instead, he rubbed his hands together feverishly and cried out, "I swear to God, Utterson, I will never set eyes on him again. He's gone for good, I can promise you that."

During the following months, there was not a single sighting of Hyde, even though a reward had been offered for his capture. As time wore on, the lawyer felt more relaxed. Dr. Jekyll was his old self again. He gave dinner parties, involved himself with charitable works again, saw old friends again. One of these was Dr. Lanyon, who had known Jekyll since college days.

On January 8, Utterson had spent a pleasant evening at Jekyll's house with Lanyon and a few others. A few days later, he stopped by to see Jekyll, but was told by Poole that the doctor did not want any visitors. The same thing happened on January 14 and 15. Worried about this change in Jekyll, Utterson went to talk to Dr. Lanyon. He was shown into the doctor's study and was startled to see how ill and frail the man was. His normally rosy-cheeked face was drained of color, and his eyes had a frightened look.

"My dear Lanyon! You don't seem well at all," he exclaimed.

"I have had a shock," said the doctor.

"Too great a shock. I fear I shall never recover."

Utterson, alarmed at how full of doom the doctor sounded, tried to change the subject.

"I think Jekyll must be ill, too. Have you seen him?"

At the mention of Jekyll's name, the doctor held up a trembling hand as if to stop Utterson and cried out, "I never wish to see or hear of Dr. Jekyll again."

Utterson left, deeply concerned about Lanyon and his obvious rift with Jekyll. Was Jekyll responsible for his frailty, his fears?

Two weeks later, a messenger brought the news that Dr. Lanyon was dead. After the funeral, Mr. Utterson sat down and opened an envelope addressed to him that had been found in Lanyon's study. Inside was a smaller envelope that read: "Not to be opened till the death or disappearance of Dr. Henry Jekyll." Here, once again, was the worrying idea that Dr. Jekyll might disappear for good.

A few days later, Utterson was sitting by his fire when he heard a hammering at his door. The servant showed in Jekyll's butler, Poole, who looked disheveled and was out of breath.

"Please sir, I beg you to come with me," he blurted out. "I think something terrible has happened to my master."

Utterson followed the butler straight to Jekyll's house where he found all the staff huddled together in the hall. Silently, Poole led him across the courtyard to the laboratory and signaled to him to stay at the bottom of the stairs while he knocked on the door of the doctor's den.

"Mr. Utterson to see you, sir," he cried.

"Tell him I can't see anyone," came the surly reply.

Poole descended the stairs and returned to the house, with Utterson following.

"Now, sir," he whispered. "Do you think that was my master's voice?"

Utterson reluctantly admitted that Dr. Jekyll's voice seemed to have changed a great deal. The butler grew very agitated and said, "That is not my master's voice. We heard the master cry aloud to God eight days ago, and, ever since, that thing in there has been moaning and crying, calling for medicine. Just as my master used to send me to deliver his prescriptions, this person has been ordering me to get him drugs. But each time I leave him a supply, he complains that the medicine is not pure, and I must try another pharmacist."

"Why else do you think that the man in there is not your master?"

Poole's voice dropped again and he said, "Because I've seen him. I came into the laboratory one day and found him digging about in the crates. He gave a cry when he saw me and ran up the stairs like a rat. It wasn't just that his face was different, the man I saw was like a dwarf. I think that my master's been murdered."

WORD POWER

Peeler—slang for policeman, named after Sir Robert Peel, who founded the London Metropolitan Police Force

assailant—attacker

narration—telling of an event

disheveled—in a mess

vial—a small container for liquids

Utterson stared at the butler's panic-stricken face. "It is my duty to break open the door," he announced solemnly.

Poole rushed away to fetch an ax, and together they climbed the stairs to the den.

"Jekyll!" shouted the lawyer. "If you don't open this door, we'll have to use force!"

"For God's sake have mercy, Utterson!" came the reply. This time there was no mistaking whose voice it was: both Poole and Utterson recognized it as Hyde's.

Poole swung the ax hard at the door and smashed the lock. The two men stepped in. A fire burned in the grate, the table was set neatly for afternoon tea, and jars full of chemicals stood in neat rows on the shelves. Sprawled out on the floor was the body of a man, his limbs faintly twitching, a crushed vial in one hand. Utterson rushed over, turned the man on his back, and found himself staring at the contorted face of Edward Hyde.

"He's dead," the lawyer announced, "and by his own hand, too. Now we must search for your master's body."

Chapter 3

Edward Hyde was dead. Now Utterson and Poole were looking for signs of Henry Jekyll, but had found nothing. Then Utterson spotted a large envelope addressed to him in Jekyll's handwriting. He ripped it open, and several documents fell out, including Jekyll's will. In it, Edward Hyde's name had been blotted out and replaced with Utterson's. The lawyer picked up a second piece of paper that was also in Jekyll's handwriting, and had been written that day. It told Utterson that by the time he read the note, he, Jekyll, would have disappeared. It also begged him to read the letter from Dr. Lanyon that was stored in his safe, then to look at the confession sealed in a separate packet.

Utterson picked up the packet that had fallen out of the envelope and told Poole that he was going home to find Lanyon's letter. "I shall return by midnight, and we will then send for the police."

As soon as he arrived home, Utterson retrieved Dr. Lanyon's letter from the safe and started to read. It revealed how Lanyon had received a letter from Henry Jekyll the night after they had dined at Jekyll's house, begging him to perform a life-saving favor for him. He was to go to Jekyll's house that night, where he would find Poole waiting with a locksmith who would force open the door to his den. Lanyon was to take some powders, a vial, and a notebook from a certain drawer and return to his home with them. There he should receive a man sent by Jekyll and hand over these items to him.

The tone of Dr. Jekyll's letter had been so desperate that even though he had thought his friend must be insane, Lanyon had done as he was asked. When he picked up the notebook, he had noticed that it was filled with what seemed to be records of experiments. Just after midnight, Lanyon had opened the door to a man who glanced furtively over his shoulder before coming in. Clutching at Dr. Lanyon, he had cried,

"Have you got them? Have you got them?"

Then, as Lanyon pointed to the items he had taken from Jekyll's den, the man let out a loud sigh of relief, picked up the vial, and started to mix together the salts with a red liquid. Lanyon had watched in amazement as the mixture changed to purple and then green. The man's eyes were bright with excitement, and he offered to let Lanyon see what would happen when he drank the potion. Horrified, yet fascinated, Lanyon had agreed to watch. The man seized the glass and gulped down the contents. Instantly he began to stagger, then, with a scream of agony, grabbed hold of the table, gasping for breath. His face had turned black, then his features had seemed to melt, so that Lanyon had not even been able to make out a nose or mouth. Lanyon had closed his eyes in terror. When he opened them again, Henry Jekyll was standing there, pale and shaken. When Lanyon had eventually spoken to Jekyll, the doctor admitted that the man who had mixed the potion before his very eyes went by the name of Hyde and was being sought for the murder of Sir Danvers Carew.

Utterson put down Lanyon's account and, with a heavy heart, picked up the confession of Henry Jekyll.

WORD POWER

furtively—in a secretive way

tincture—a liquid medicine

draft—a dose of medicine

flawless—without faults

consumed—obsessed

scaffold—a raised framework for hanging criminals

I was born into a wealthy family and knew from an early age that I was expected to lead a respectable and distinguished life. And, indeed, I myself passionately wished to be well respected and serious-minded. But I also had a wilder, more pleasure-seeking side to my character which, as I grew older, I felt I should hide from society. I came to realize that each man has two natures, not just one, and as I began to feel the battle between my two natures—the upright one and the reckless one—I told myself that if only I could separate the two, then I could ignore my dark side.

I started to experiment with scientific ways of arranging this separation, and even though I realized that this could end in my death, I was totally determined to succeed. So I prepared a tincture and then bought a large quantity of a special salt from a pharmacy. Then late one night, I boiled these ingredients in a glass beaker. When the bubbling mixture had cooled, I lifted it to my lips and drank the potion.

Instantly my body was racked with terrible pains, and it seemed as if my bones were being crushed by a powerful machine. But gradually these sensations faded, and I began to feel younger, lighter, freer, and ten times more wicked than my normal self. And I enjoyed these feelings. I stretched out my arms in delight and discovered that I was shorter, too. I crept across the courtyard and into my bedroom, where I saw the body of my other self in the mirror for the first time. I called it Edward Hyde, and even though it was ugly and deformed, I welcomed it.

As daylight was breaking, I knew that I had to hurry to attempt the second part of the experiment: to regain my old identity. I prepared another draft and drank. Having suffered the same horrors as before, I gradually resumed the body of Henry Jekyll.

The experiment should have stopped there, but I was so attracted to the irresponsible, carefree aspect of my Edward Hyde self that I was not able to resist returning to him. So I furnished a house in London for him, and told my servants that Mr. Hyde was to have full run of my own house. I also made out the will in favor of Hyde, so that if anything happened to the person of Dr. Jekyll, I could live as Hyde using Jekyll's money. So I started my new life, delighting in monstrous deeds when I was Edward Hyde, and remaining a man of good conscience as Henry Jekyll. I was nearly caught when I had to pay compensation to the family of a young girl I had hurt—I paid them with a check signed by Henry Jekyll. But after that I opened a separate bank account and devised a backward-sloping handwriting for Hyde.

One night I went to bed in my own home as Henry Jekyll. But when I woke next morning, the first thing I saw was the hairy, swollen-knuckled hand of Edward Hyde. To my horror, I had changed selves overnight, without the assistance of my drugs. I rushed across the courtyard to my den, swiftly mixed my potion, drank it, and resumed the body of Jekyll.

This new twist worried me, for I was spending more and more time as Hyde, and it was growing increasingly difficult to return to the person of Jekyll. I decided to abandon Hyde, and for two months led a flawless life as Jekyll. But one night I gave in to the strong temptation to be Hyde once more and, when I drank the potion, felt more evil and violent than ever before. I greatly enjoyed beating that innocent gentleman to death and ran through the streets devising more crimes. But when I drank the potion again and returned to Jekyll, I was so appalled at Hyde's deed that I resolved never to allow him out again. I locked the door of my den, and when I went out, it was as Henry Jekyll.

I kept myself busy with good deeds and visits to my friends. One day I was sitting on a park bench, when suddenly I felt horribly nauseous. My clothes seemed too large for me, and when I looked down at my hand on my knee, it was Hyde's, not Jekyll's. I then went to an inn and wrote to Lanyon, begging him to fetch the drugs from my den. The rest you know.

When I returned home, I realized that I no longer feared being caught and hanged for killing Carew; it was the horror of being Hyde that consumed me. I locked myself in my den and the days that followed were a living nightmare: I would go to sleep as Jekyll, but wake as Hyde, and needed double doses of the special potion to regain the person of Jekyll.

The final horror was when I started to run out of the salt and found that the supplies Poole brought back did not work. I realized that my first supply must have been an impure one, and it was this that had made the potion successful.

In half an hour from now, I shall become Hyde once more and have no more potion to help me regain Jekyll. Will Hyde die on the scaffold, or will he have the courage to end his own life? I do not know. What I do know is that this is the end of Henry Jekyll's very unhappy life.

THE END

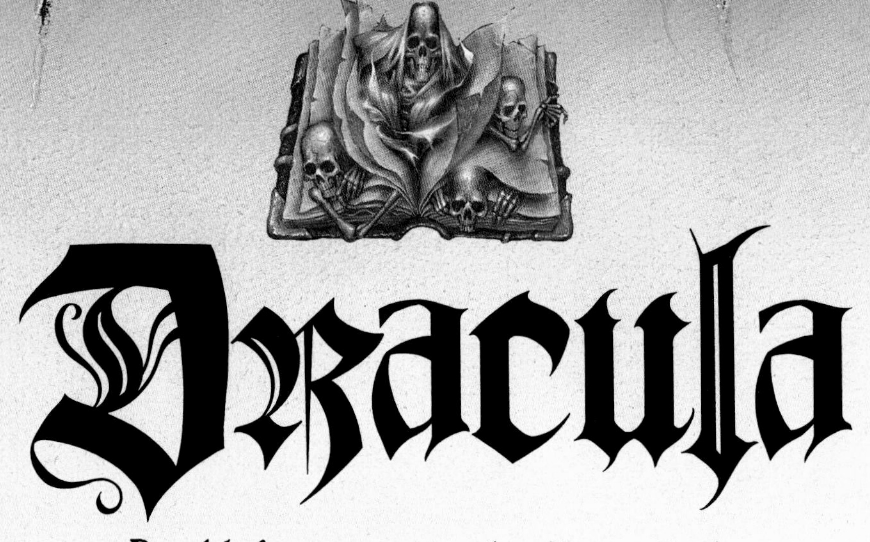

Dracula

Retold from a story by Bram Stoker

Jonathan Harker's Diary

Transylvania was unlike any place I, Jonathan Harker, had ever visited. The wild scenery was fascinating, the costumes of the people extremely strange. I had not wanted to leave Mina, my beloved bride-to-be, but my employer, Mr. Hawkins, had insisted that I go. My task was to advise a wealthy foreign aristocrat about a house we had found for him in England. I endured a long, uneventful journey before arriving in the town of Bistritz. This was the town nearest to Castle Dracula, home of Count Dracula, the gentleman I was to see.

When I asked my landlady whether she knew of the castle or the Count, she made the sign of the cross. This struck me as very strange, but I said nothing more. Then, just as I was leaving the inn, the woman rushed out to me and wailed, "Oh, young sir, must you really go there?" I explained that it was my job to do so. She then gave her crucifix to me and said I must wear it about my neck.

Following all of the instructions that the Count had sent me in a letter, I took a public coach to a place high in the mountains that was called the Borgo Pass. There I was to await the arrival of the Count's personal carriage. What strange people my fellow passengers were! When I mentioned my destination, they all shrank back in fear. Several made the sign of the cross, and one gave me a bulb of garlic. I did not wish to appear rude, so I accepted the puzzling gift with a smile.

The Count's coach came for me as arranged. The driver was a fierce-looking fellow, and he whipped the horses hard so that the carriage flew through the gloom of the night. Up and up, higher and higher into the mountains the carriage took me, until, with a jolt, the vehicle stopped and the old coachman gestured for me to alight. I looked around and spied a dark castle, its towers shrouded in a ghostly mist. Whether it was the sight of the castle or the distant howling of wolves I do not know, but I began to shiver.

The coach disappeared into the shadows, and I knocked on the dark castle door. There was a rattling of chains and a clanking of bolts before the door opened to reveal a tall man. He looked very distinguished and was dressed in black from head to toe. "Welcome to my house, young Mr. Harker," the man said, as he beckoned me to come inside.

I entered, then jumped a little as I shook the man's hand—it was as cold as ice. When the man withdrew his hand, with its long sharpened nails like cat's claws, he smiled. "So delighted to meet you in the flesh," he exclaimed, carefully closing and locking the door. Count Dracula led me through the silent, poorly lit castle and into the dining room. I noticed how deathly white his face looked and how two of his upper teeth stuck out from his cruel smile to rest on his bottom lip. But these thoughts were soon forgotten as I settled down to a most excellent dinner.

The Count stood by a grand stone fireplace as I ate and explained that he had feasted earlier. As he refilled my glass with a magnificent wine, I could not help recoiling from his terrible breath. It had about it the smell of death. The Count noticed my disgust and quickly stepped back. Then he appeared to listen hard to the howling of a pack of wolves outside the castle.

"Ah, the children of the night. What sweet music!" he cried, with a smile. I tried to smile back, but my face seemed frozen with the unease that I felt.

Next, Count Dracula explained that he would not be around until the evening on the following day. "Please make yourself at home and go anywhere in the castle," he said. But then he paused before adding mysteriously, "Except for the rooms that are locked. They are so for good reason."

The next day I rested, checked the papers relating to the house that the Count was buying, and awaited my host's return. It was late evening when he arrived. Again he refused to join me for dinner, insisting that he had eaten earlier.

The Count told me how he had longed to visit London for some time. "I dream of losing myself in its crowded streets, surrounded by its teeming millions. You see, everyone here knows me and who I am. I dream of being a stranger in a strange land. It's the only way for me to be free. Now Mr. Harker, tell me about Carfax, this lovely old house that you have for me. Both the name and the place intrigue me."

The Count quizzed me hard. He wanted to know every single detail. I was nervous.

Carfax was a mansion east of London. It had potential, but its lands included a church and graveyard, and its location next to a mental asylum would have discouraged many clients. Yet, as I told Count Dracula of these facts, he seemed pleased. "To be near the mad and the dead suits me, Mr. Harker," I can clearly remember him saying.

After dinner, we went to the Count's library and talked for many hours until the first pale hints of sunrise could be spied outside the window. Then Count Dracula quickly jumped up and said, "Ah, it's nearly morning. I have kept you up all night, Mr. Harker. Please forgive me and sleep as long as you want. I will be out until the evening."

WORD POWER

crucifix—a model of Christ on a cross, sometimes worn as a necklace

alight—descend from or leave a vehicle

distinguished—noble; aristocratic

recoiling—pulling back; withdrawing

potential—ability to become, but not yet being; latent

lair—an animal's den, often hidden or underground

predicament—an extremely difficult or dangerous situation

The Count left and I went to my room. I slept soundly through most of the next day and awoke in the early evening. I then decided to shave.

There was no mirror in my room, but I had brought along a tiny one that my dear Mina had given to me as a present. I had just started shaving when an icy hand touched me on the shoulder, and a voice said, "Good evening, Mr. Harker." The voice was unmistakable—it was the Count.

Amazingly, no reflection of my host appeared in the mirror. As I realized this, I jumped. My razor nicked my cheek, and I felt a tiny drop of blood trickle down it. Then I whirled around to spy the Count, who was now standing several paces away. He seemed his usual self until he

spotted the blood. Then his eyes blazed with an animal fury, and his arms sprung toward my neck.

As Count Dracula's pointed nails dug into my throat, his hands felt the landlady's cross that still hung there. At this, the Count drew back sharply and began to circle me warily, his eyes cleansed of the wildness that I had seen a moment earlier.

"Please try not to cut yourself. It is dangerous around here," he muttered as he grabbed my mirror and tossed it out of the castle window. Then he left my room without saying another word. A cold chill ran up and down my spine. Why had I not seen him in the mirror?

After another evening of questions, my work at Castle Dracula was complete. However, my peculiar host seemed unwilling to let me leave. Finally, he ordered me to write to my employer saying that I would be needed in Transylvania for a further 30 days. Another month! My heart sank as the Count uttered those words. I felt forced to stay with this strange man in his unpleasant lair, many miles from civilization.

During the days, when the Count was not around, I explored the castle at length. All the doors leading to the outside were locked. Several doors to rooms inside the castle were also barred. There appeared to be no way out. I was completely trapped, and when I realized this, I felt the rage of a madman overcome me. What did Count Dracula plan to do with me?

My mood improved when some gypsy workmen arrived one afternoon. The Count was nowhere to be seen as these men unloaded a stack of long wooden boxes from their horse-drawn carts. I tried to ask them to let me out of the castle. However, they did not speak English and could not understand, so simply smiled in response.

Then I decided on another course of action. I quickly wrote a note to Mina in shorthand and threw it down right in front of the men, together with some coins. The gypsies understood this desperate request and signaled that they would mail my letter. I was pleased, thinking that if Mina at least knew of my terrible predicament, she might be able to organize some help, perhaps even rescue me from my castle prison.

As night fell and Count Dracula did not appear, my feeling of helplessness returned. Looking around for a method of escape, I gazed out of my window and spied an incredible sight. It was the Count climbing up a steep castle wall with supernatural ease. Once inside, he made his way back down the wall as if he were some giant, bat-like creature. I was absolutely terrified. Was I imagining things? Had this awful place started to drive me mad? Or was the Count even stranger than I had suspected?

Chapter 2

Locked away in Castle Dracula, I now feared for my life. I vowed not to let the Count see my terror, and to do everything I could to leave this evil place.

I waited until the afternoon before building up the courage to break into one of the castle's locked rooms. When I had done so, I found that it had a pleasant atmosphere at odds with the rest of this foul place. I fingered the cross still hanging around my neck. It made me feel calm, and I explored further. I found nothing to aid my escape, but decided to linger in the room. I updated this diary and, feeling drowsy, lay back on a silk-cushioned couch.

When I awoke it was night, and I was not alone. Three young women of the greatest beauty were standing over me. Their teeth were a brilliant white and their full lips a vibrant red. I was mesmerized. The women whispered together, then started to laugh. The sounds of their mirth were like sweet music hanging in the midnight air. One of the three moved nearer. "He is young and strong," she said to the others. "There are kisses for all of us."

I was entranced by the loveliness of the woman who had spoken. But as she loomed closer, I saw that two of her teeth were fangs that curved down from her lips. They were aimed at my throat. Her breath stank of blood, and her eyes flashed with a crimson brilliance. Suddenly she was pulled away, and the Count stood in front of me.

"How dare you touch him," he roared. "This man is mine."

"There is plenty for everyone, for you and for us," one of the three females protested. But the Count ushered the women away and pursed his lips into an expression more like a grimace than a smile before closing the door.

I barely slept for the rest of the night. My mind was racing and my stomach was churning, as I had at last realized the terrible truth about the three women. Their strange teeth, their dreadful breath, the fact that they appeared only at night all pointed to one conclusion. All three were fiendish vampires. Worse, so was Count Dracula.

The next evening, the Count watched me dine as usual. I knew that he had no servants, so must have prepared my meal himself. I did not feel hungry and pushed the food away. Who could tell what devilish dinner lay on my plate?

"Write a letter to Mr. Hawkins, your boss," the Count insisted. "And make sure you do so in a regular, readable manner."

I was puzzled by Dracula's words until he produced my shorthand note to Mina, my bride-to-be. It had obviously never reached its destination.

"I do not care for this evil-looking writing, Mr. Harker," he said, and threw the note into the fire. "Tell Mr. Hawkins that you are well and are leaving the castle. Date your letter yesterday."

I nodded in agreement, but inside I felt my heart tear in two. I was doomed. If I stayed in the castle, I could not hope to escape death.

The next night, too, I lay awake trembling with fear. At one point, I heard the sound of voices just outside my door. It was the three female vampires crying out for me and Count Dracula's harsh tones saying that I would be theirs once he had left the next day. The news overwhelmed me. The Count was leaving me so that those female fiends could drink my blood.

As soon as dawn broke and I knew that all the vampires were at rest, I started to search feverishly for a way out. There had to be a key to the front door somewhere in this dreadful castle. The more I searched and found nothing, the more agitated I became, until I was rushing around like a madman.

I suddenly came across a narrow door that led down into the depths of the castle foundations. I half ran, half fell down the stairs until I found myself in a small, very dark chapel. The wooden boxes that I had seen being unloaded were there. I counted exactly fifty of them, all filled just with earth—or that is what I thought until I reached the final box, which was in a corner.

What I saw inside filled me with total horror.

Dracula lay on the earth, deep in sleep. His face was no longer old and pale. He looked thirty or more years younger. Blood ran from the corners of his mouth down his neck and onto his clothes. His appearance was of a wild animal fresh from killing its prey. The foul stench of raw flesh was overpowering, and I backed away. Yet as I did so, I saw Dracula's face change so that his expression was one of complete and utter hatred. I had never seen such evil before and knew I must do all that was in my power to rid the world of it.

I groped for a stone and prepared to hit the Count with it, but found myself quite unable to do so. I felt powerless against this supernatural creature. Then I heard horses arriving and quickly fled back upstairs.

I am writing these words back in my room. Below, I can hear the sounds of workmen collecting the long wooden boxes on their horse-drawn carts. I know now that the boxes are coffins and are bound for a distant sea port. I suspect that the coffin holding Dracula is among them.

I am alone and trapped here. I am sure that those female vampires will strike tonight. I plan to try to scale the walls of the castle after the workmen have left. I would rather fall to my death on the rocks than have those monsters drink my body dry. I will take this diary with me so that if I perish, someone may learn of the terrible secrets that lie in Castle Dracula. I just hope that I'll see my sweet Mina again.

Mina Harker's Story

I missed Jonathan so much while he was away, especially as the weeks turned into months. Only my friend Lucy Westenra was able to comfort me and ease my great worries. I stayed for a while with her family on the east coast near Whitby in Yorkshire, where we were occasionally joined by a dashing young doctor named John Seward.

During my stay, Lucy returned to her childhood habit of sleepwalking. I found her wandering around the house a dozen times. Then one night when there was a great storm, I could not find her at all. I roamed the clifftops searching for her, fearing the worst. When, in the full moon's light, I spotted a small figure sitting in the ruined abbey, I was relieved. Then I saw a dark shadow fall over her. I looked up at the moon—no clouds had obscured it. I looked again and called to Lucy. As I did so, the shadow moved, and I thought that I saw two small shafts of light.

By the time I had reached Lucy, the shadow had gone. But she was still completely in her trance. To warm her, I pinned my shawl around her shoulders. But I must have caught her not once but twice with the brooch pin, for her throat was pierced and several tiny drops of blood stood out on the fair skin of her neck.

I led Lucy back to bed and thought that would be the end of the matter. But the very next day, she was ill. I read in the newspaper that the storm had caused a shipwreck. There were no survivors, but some long wooden boxes had been picked up from the wreckage. Later, these strange boxes had mysteriously disappeared.

Lucy's illness continued. Every day she stayed in bed, but at night she would not sit still, let alone lie down. On the third night, I found her outside in the garden. As I walked over to her, I saw what looked like a giant black bird flutter out of sight. Lucy's exertions had re-opened the tiny wounds on her neck. Blood trickled down onto her nightgown, and she had grown paler and weaker than before. The next morning, I asked Dr. Seward to come to the house to see if he could help her.

Dr. Seward arrived and promised that he would attend to Lucy. I had to bid her a fond farewell because I had just received a worrying letter. It told me that Jonathan was in Budapest and very sick. He had left Castle Dracula and had been found some time later suffering from a terrible fever. I took the first train to be by his bedside. There, over a number of weeks, I helped nurse him back to health.

Jonathan refused to talk about his time at Castle Dracula. But he grew stronger, and soon he was well enough for us to return to England. We were married on September 1. As we made our way home through central London, I felt Jonathan's hand clutch my arm tightly. I looked up at him and saw that he had turned a ghostly gray. Sweat had broken out on his forehead.

"Oh, my God. It's him!" he cried.

I followed Jonathan's terrified gaze

across the street. He was looking at a tall, thin, well-dressed man, who was stepping into a horse-drawn carriage.

"Who, Jonathan? Who is it?" I asked.

"Count Dracula," Jonathan replied.

His voice was full of fear.

WORD POWER

at odds with—completely different from

mesmerized—in a trancelike state; spellbound

mirth—laughter; merriment

ushered—led; conducted

agitated—disturbed; unsettled

scale—climb

obscured—hidden; covered

exertions—activities; efforts

Chapter 3

After seeing the evil Count Dracula in London, Jonathan handed Mina the diary that he had written during his time in Castle Dracula. Mina was shocked by what she read. She could not bear to think that such a fiend as Count Dracula had nearly destroyed her young husband. When Mina and Jonathan arrived home, there was even worse news. Dr. Seward had arrived and announced that, despite his best efforts and the good work of a medical specialist, Lucy was dead.

Jonathan shared in Mina's grief and did his best to console her. But he could not stop his waking and sleeping nightmares, in which Count Dracula was alive and free, roaming the streets of London.

The grief-stricken couple welcomed a visit from the specialist who had tried to save Lucy. He was an energetic old man from Amsterdam called Professor Van Helsing, and Jonathan and Mina both warmed to him. He questioned Mina gently about Lucy's habit of sleep-walking outside the house. Finally, after he had learned a little about Jonathan's ordeal, Professor Van Helsing asked to read his diary.

Several weeks later, the professor burst into Dr. Seward's office and thrust a newspaper under his nose. One story was circled in red pen. It concerned a series of attacks on children in Hampstead, North London. The victims all had small wounds on their throats.

"It sounds just like what happened to poor Lucy," Dr. Seward muttered.

"It is worse than that, I fear," said the professor gravely. "Please don't think me mad when I tell you that those marks were probably made *by* Lucy."

Dr. Seward could hardly believe what Van Helsing had said to him. But he agreed to accompany the professor that night to the graveyard where Lucy's tomb lay. There the two men hoped to discover the truth.

Van Helsing and Seward conducted a long and patient vigil near Lucy's tomb until an hour before sunrise.

"My dear Professor, what are we waiting for... a ghost?" asked Dr. Seward.

"Something similar," replied the professor. "I suspect our wait will be over shortly and then you will see."

The professor was correct. Not ten minutes later, a figure appeared in the graveyard, moving stealthily between the headstones and tombs. As it came closer to them, Dr. Seward gulped.

"It is poor Lucy. But how her features have changed!"

Lucy's lips were crimson with blood, and her hair, wild and unkempt, flowed out like a cloak behind her. Both men crouched lower so as not to be seen. They watched in amazement as Lucy passed through a crack in the side of her tomb.

"I know it is deeply wrong to enter a sealed crypt, but we must. It is a matter of the very greatest importance," whispered Professor Van Helsing. Dumb with horror, Dr. Seward silently nodded his agreement.

The pair waited a short while before unlocking the tomb door and venturing inside. The air was thick with a foul-smelling odor, and Dr. Seward shivered.

"Keep your courage, Doctor," advised the professor, slowly opening Lucy's coffin. There she lay, her face contorted into a hideous snarl. Blood was dripping from the two fangs sticking out over her lips. Some had already stained her clothes.

"Now do you believe me?" asked the professor. "Lucy is a vampire, one of the undead. With those teeth she will quench her thirst for blood and will kill and kill again. You must drive a stake through her heart in the name of God. If you don't, she will never be at peace."

Dr. Seward took several deep breaths and tried to control his trembling hands. Meanwhile, the professor took a mallet and a wooden stake from his knapsack and explained exactly what to do. It took an age before the doctor was able to summon up enough courage. Then suddenly, wordlessly, he took a huge swing with the mallet. It came crashing down on the stake, which drove into Lucy's chest and on through her heart. She writhed and the most terrifying scream issued from her blood-stained lips. Then she gnashed her sharp teeth violently. Finally, all was quiet once more.

The two medical men stared at Lucy's motionless body. The change that had swept over her was dramatic. Her face was still pale, but now it looked peaceful and at rest. Professor Van Helsing closed her coffin and resealed her tomb. Then both he and Dr. Seward walked out of the graveyard in complete silence.

Two days later, Professor Van Helsing and Dr. Seward joined Jonathan and Mina at their home in London for a most serious meeting.

"Gentlemen and lady," said Van Helsing,

nodding toward Mina, "we have a duty to hunt down the monster who murdered Lucy and trapped Jonathan. We must share all that we know about vampires and together plot a way to defeat him."

Everyone agreed and vowed solemnly to do what they could. The meeting continued into the evening as the group talked. They discussed how vampires lived by feeding on human blood and how their powers only lasted from sunset to sunrise. Jonathan reminisced about how the inhabitants of Transylvania had made the sign of the cross whenever Count Dracula was mentioned. They had also given him a crucifix and garlic. Professor Van Helsing explained that these signs and objects warded off evil spirits, including vampires.

Jonathan then told them all some very important news. Despite the shipwreck, the 50 coffins from Castle Dracula had arrived at Carfax, the Count's new English home.

"And I have discovered an even more chilling fact," added the professor. "I do not know exactly where, but I believe that Count Dracula has bought another house in the center of London."

Mina and Jonathan both shivered. It was terrifying to think that the Count might be living so close to their own London home. Jonathan gazed out of the window.

"My god, there's a bat," he cried. But then he realized that it was no more than a blackbird swooping past the window.

"I'm sorry, my nerves are so on edge," he explained.

"That's all right, my dear Mr. Harker," soothed the professor kindly. "It's perfectly understandable. This is a very trying time." He then paused a while before continuing: "We know that Count Dracula's powers are strong during the hours of darkness and that he has the ability to turn into a bat or a wolf. So it is vital that we strike during the day when he is at rest. But first, the coffins at Carfax must be made safe."

Jonathan agreed to accompany Dr. Seward and Professor Van Helsing to Carfax to carry out the necessary work. But despite her protests, the men refused to let Mina join them on their mission.

The three vampire-hunters arrived at Carfax late one night. Jonathan had often visited the house before his Transylvania trip, but now it truly disturbed him for the first time. He tried to keep his nerve as he led the others to the chapel.

Professor Van Helsing insisted on entering first, his hands held high in the shape of a cross. The other two followed slowly and nervously. The stench of death was overwhelming. Even Van Helsing and Dr. Seward, hardened medical men, had to cover their noses and mouths with their handkerchiefs.

WORD POWER

unkempt—uncombed; tangled

crypt—an underground burial chamber

contorted—twisted out of its normal or usual shape

reminisced about—remembered and talked about

warded off—drove away; repelled

holy wafers—circles of flat bread used in Holy Communion services

sterilize—remove germs from to make spotlessly clean (sterile)

Inside, the three men counted the wooden coffins—there were just 29 of them. Then Professor Van Helsing reached into his knapsack and handed the others some holy wafers.

"With these sacred wafers," he explained in a whisper, "we can sterilize the earth in all the coffins. Once we have done this, these evil boxes can never be used as a place of rest for vampires."

The friends had started to place holy wafers in the soil when something made them look up. The room seemed to have grown lighter. The change was not caused by the approach of dawn or a lit candle, but by the red glow of hundreds of pairs of eyes. Legions of evil-looking rats were staring at them from all directions. The three brave men hurriedly finished their task and bolted out of the chapel.

"We still have much work to do—21 of the 50 coffins have yet to be found," noted Dr. Seward on their journey home.

"Yes, we will investigate tomorrow," Professor Van Helsing assured him.

But Jonathan Harker remained totally silent. He looked very unwell. The scene in the Carfax chapel and the terrible smell had brought back bad memories of his imprisonment in Castle Dracula, memories that he preferred to forget.

The three men returned in haste to the Harkers' home in London, and Jonathan went straight up to bed. Mina was already asleep. How pale and scared she looked, Jonathan thought, as he pulled up the bedcovers and snuggled down beside her. When he blew out the lantern on the bedside table, he did not notice the telltale pinpricks on poor Mina's neck. Streams of blood were trickling down from the holes and slowly beginning to dry.

Chapter 4

Professor Van Helsing, Dr. Seward, and Jonathan Harker left the house early the next morning, intent on finding Count Dracula's remaining coffins. They left Mina alone to rest, for she had awoken feeling very weak.

Many hours later, the three men entered a large house in a street just off Piccadilly in central London. They believed it to be the evil Count Dracula's new home. On the professor's instructions, they crept straight down into the cellar. They were not to be disappointed. The 21 wooden coffins that had been missing all seemed to be stacked up behind some pillars in its dank depths.

The three men quickly set to work and sterilized the coffins. As soon as they had finished, they hurried out of the cellar. But just as Dr. Seward reached out to open the front door, the dark figure of Count Dracula seemed to appear from nowhere.

Jonathan cried out and covered his face with his hands. Dr. Seward cursed. Their way out was completely barred, and Dracula was advancing toward them, snarling. But then the professor produced a crucifix from his pocket. He held it up in front of him, and Dracula stopped in his tracks. Dr. Seward, meanwhile, wrenched the door open. The three men rushed out and within seconds were in a cab bound for Mina and Jonathan's home.

On the journey home, Jonathan fingered the small wood cross that hung around his neck.

"Remember to use it when we next encounter that fiend," muttered the professor gravely.

"But there won't be a next time," replied Jonathan. "We have sterilized all the coffins. He has nowhere to sleep. When the sun rises, he will be destroyed..."

"I'm afraid that is not so," Dr. Seward interrupted. "I counted only 20 wooden coffins. There is still one missing."

"Oh, no," groaned Jonathan in horror, as the carriage pulled up at his house. It was dark inside, and there was no sign of life.

"Mina is probably asleep," whispered Jonathan, letting the others in with his key. But as Dr. Seward and Professor Van Helsing were going to their rooms, they heard a loud cry for help and rushed to see what had happened. Jonathan had found his bedroom door locked and could not get in.

The three men leaned their full weight against the solid oak door. It burst open with a crash. Inside, kneeling on the bed, was Mina. But she was not alone. Count Dracula was there, too, with his night-black cloak wrapped tightly around her.

When Dracula pulled away from Mina, the men saw that she had been gulping blood from an open wound on his chest! Jonathan roared with disgust and fury. Then Dracula turned around to face his enemies. An ugly snarl disfigured his whole face, his eyes flamed, and his mouth and chin were smeared with blood. He pushed Mina down on to the bed. She appeared to be in some sort of trance.

"It is too late. My revenge is complete. Your women are mine!" Dracula snarled. Then he sprang toward the group, his outstretched fingers like claws.

Professor Van Helsing immediately held out his crucifix, and Count Dracula stopped in his tracks. Then Jonathan followed suit with his wooden cross. Dracula started to back away into the far corner of the room, while the three men walked slowly forward. Suddenly, he leaped through the window and its panes shattered.

Jonathan, Dr. Seward, and the professor rushed to look out after him, but the evil vampire was nowhere to be seen. Instead, the three friends heard the flapping sound of some monstrous, birdlike creature.

Mina was now awake and crying.

"What happened?" cried Jonathan.

"It was like a dream," Mina said. Then she explained how Count Dracula had entered the locked room, torn at his own chest, and made her drink from the wound. Then he had said to her, "Now you have drunk my blood, we are of the same body and mind. You cannot escape."

Jonathan began to cry when he heard this, and Dr. Seward led him from the room.

"I had exactly the same dream the night before, but didn't think to tell my poor husband," Mina continued sadly. "He was already so troubled."

"Do not fear, my dear child," soothed Professor Van Helsing, reaching out for his pouch of sacred wafers. He pressed one to Mina's head in an attempt to cleanse her, but it burned a mark on her forehead. Poor Mina screamed in pain.

"I am so unclean, even the holy wafers cannot help me," she sobbed.

Professor Van Helsing held her tight as she wept. When Dr. Seward returned, the two men exchanged fearful glances. They had both noticed the puncture marks on Mina's white throat. Count Dracula had most definitely struck.

The following morning, they all ate breakfast in silence. Dr. Seward had left early and did not return until eleven. A heavy frown clouded his face as he sat down and told them the distressing news that he had learned.

"Count Dracula has now left England. This morning, after his visit here, a wooden coffin with him inside was loaded onto a ship. This ship was heading for Varna, a port in Europe."

"That's the nearest port to Castle Dracula," gasped Jonathan.

They had no choice. The three men and Mina set out immediately on a long journey. They crossed the English Channel on a steamship, then continued by carriage. Their aim was to meet the ship and its grim cargo at Varna. Throughout the journey, Mina grew weaker. Professor Van Helsing tried to comfort her husband, Jonathan, but told Dr. Seward of his fears.

"We have so little time," murmured the professor. "Only the death of the vampire whose blood she tasted can save Mina now."

When they reached Varna, the group found that Dracula had tricked them. The coffin had been unloaded at another port, Galatz. So they got into a carriage and headed toward Transylvania. When they reached the next village, they all left the carriage and hired four fast, strong horses to ride.

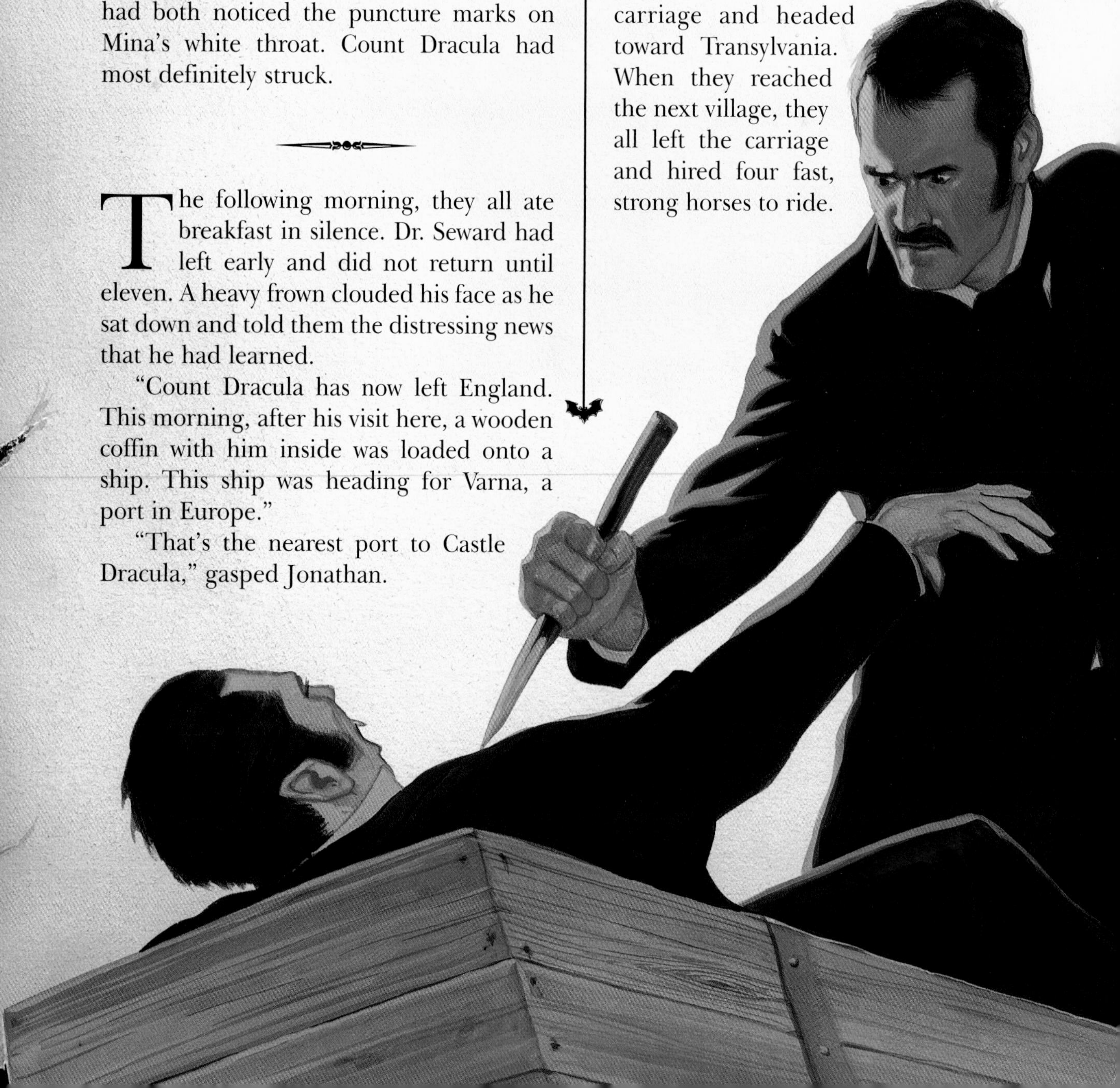

The villagers told them that a small group of gypsy workmen had been hired to transport a long wooden box through the Borgo Pass. No one would say where the box was going, but the terrified look in the locals' eyes told the party of vampire-hunters all that they needed to know.

With their mounts eating up the ground at high speed, it was not very long before the friends reached the Borgo Pass. The afternoon sun had started to descend, and a chilly fall evening was not far away.

"We have little time before nightfall," said the professor. He urged Jonathan and Dr. Seward to ride on ahead. Jonathan was by now so obsessed with catching Dracula that he had hardly noticed the fangs that were slowly growing over his wife's red lips.

Dr. Seward and Jonathan rode as fast as they could through the Borgo Pass. Professor Van Helsing followed on behind with Mina. Suddenly, Van Helsing heard a loud cry ahead and rode furiously to catch up. He saw a cart moving at great speed, with both Dr. Seward and Jonathan Harker in pursuit. The sky was gradually darkening. Van Helsing gasped in fear. There could be only a few short minutes left before sunset.

"Go on, my brave young friends. You must not, you dare not fail!" he muttered.

Dr. Seward and Jonathan Harker caught up with the cart and confronted the gypsy workmen. The last glimmer of the setting sun glinted on the sides of Dr. Seward's gun as he forced them to stop. Then, in a flash, Jonathan leaped up onto the cart and ripped off the wooden coffin lid. Staring up at him was Count Dracula. His eyes, his whole expression, were full of a deep and bitter hatred. As the sun finally dipped down below the horizon, a triumphant sneer swept over the vampire's hideous pale face.

Desperately, Jonathan reached inside his knapsack and took out a stake. Dracula tried to grab it from him, but the young lawyer was too quick. With a mighty swing of his mallet, Jonathan drove the stake through Count Dracula's wicked heart. For a moment, a look of disbelief swept across the vampire's face, but he made no sound.

Professor Van Helsing and Mina arrived just in time to see Dracula's body crumble into dust. At once, Mina snapped out of her trance and gasped weakly:

"Jonathan. My darling!"

Jonathan Harker turned to his wife as if seeing her for the first time. He was flushed from hunting down and destroying Dracula, and trembling violently. His eyes filled with tears as he stared at his beloved Mina. It was many moments before he was able to speak.

"Mina, my dear, your unnatural color has gone. So has the cursed mark on your forehead. You are well again."

"And we are all saved," said Professor Van Helsing, eyeing the empty coffin. "The nightmare is over."

THE END

WORD POWER

intent on—with the determined aim of

dank—unpleasantly cold and damp

disfigured—spoiled the appearance of

followed suit—did the same

mounts—horses

Dracula's Guest

Retold from a story by Bram Stoker

I stopped, for there was a sudden stillness. The storm had passed, and, perhaps in sympathy with nature's silence, my heart seemed to cease to beat. But this was only for a moment. Then, suddenly, the moonlight broke through the clouds, showing me that I was in a graveyard, and that the object looming in front of me was a massive tomb made of marble. It was as white as the blanket of snow that lay all around it.

With the moonlight there came a fierce sigh of the storm, which appeared to begin again with a long, low howl, as of many dogs or wolves. I was awed and shocked, and felt the cold grow upon me till it seemed to grip me by the heart. Then, while the flood of moonlight still fell on the marble tomb, the storm gave further evidence of renewing, as though it was returning on its track. Fascination made me approach the sepulcher to see what it was, and why such a thing stood alone in such a place. I walked around it, and read over the door:

Countess Dolingen of Gratz
In Styria
Sought and Found Death,
1801

On the top of the tomb, seemingly driven through the solid marble, was a great iron spike or stake. On going to the back I saw, graven in large letters:

The Dead Travel Fast

There was something so weird and uncanny about the whole thing that it made me feel quite faint... Here a thought struck me and gave me a terrible shock. This was the evening of May 1, Walpurgis Night! On this night, millions of people believed, the devil walked the Earth. On this night, too, the graves opened, the dead came forth and walked, and all the evil creatures of earth and air and water celebrated. This was where the countess who had killed herself lay. This was the place, too, where I was alone, shivering with cold in the snow, and with a wild storm gathering again upon me!

It took all my philosophy, all the religion I had been taught, all my courage, not to collapse in a fit of fright.

And now a perfect tornado burst upon me. The ground shook as though many thousands of horses were thundering across it. This time the storm bore on its icy wings not snow, but great hailstones which fell violently, beating down both leaves and branches. Underneath, the cypress trees offered no more shelter than stems of corn. At the first I had rushed to the nearest tree. But I was soon eager to leave it and seek the only spot that seemed to afford real refuge, the deep doorway of the marble tomb. There, crouching against the massive bronze door, I gained a certain amount of protection from the beating of the hailstones. Now they only drove against me as they ricocheted from the ground and the side of the marble.

As I leaned against the door, it moved slightly and opened inward. The shelter of even a tomb was welcome in that pitiless tempest. I was about to enter it when there came a flash of forked lightning that lit up the whole of the heavens. In the instant, as I am a living man, I saw a beautiful woman with rounded cheeks and red lips in the darkness of the tomb. She seemed to be sleeping on a bier. As the thunder broke overhead, I was grasped as by the hand of a giant and hurled out into the storm. The whole thing was so sudden that, before I could realize the shock, I found the hailstones beating me down. At the same time I had a strange and powerful feeling that I was not alone.

I looked toward the tomb. Just then, there came another blinding flash, which seemed to strike the iron stake on top and to pour through to the earth, blasting and crumbling the marble, as in a burst of flame. The dead woman rose for a moment of agony, while she was lapped in the flame, and her bitter scream of pain was drowned in the thundercrash. The last thing I heard was this mingling of dreadful sound, as again I was seized in the giant grasp

WORD POWER

awed—filled with fear and wonder

sepulcher—a tomb

ricocheted—bounced back and forth

bier—a platform on which a coffin is placed before burial

lethargy—lack of energy; fatigue

prudence—care; caution

acrid—sharp-smelling

in unison—together

and dragged away. Meanwhile the hailstones beat on me, and the air around was filled with the howling of wolves. The last sight that I remembered was a vague, white, moving mass. It was as if all the graves around me had sent out the phantoms of their dead, and they were closing in on me through the white cloudiness of the driving hail.

Afterward I gradually returned to consciousness. Then a dreadful sense of weariness came over me. For a time I remembered nothing. But slowly my senses returned. My feet seemed positively racked with pain, yet I could not move them. They seemed to be numbed. There was an icy feeling at the back of my neck and all down my spine, and my ears, like my feet, were dead, yet in torment. But there was in my breast a sense of warmth that was, by comparison, delicious. Yet it was as a nightmare, for some heavy weight on my chest made it difficult for me to breathe.

This period of semi-lethargy seemed to remain a long time, and as it faded away I must have slept or fainted. Then came a feeling rather like the first stage of seasickness, and a wild desire to be free from something—I knew not what. A vast stillness enveloped me, as though all the world were asleep or dead. It was only broken by the low panting as of some animal close to me. I felt warm, harsh breaths at my throat. Then came a consciousness of the awful truth. It chilled me to the heart and sent the blood surging up through my brain. Some great animal was lying on me and licking my throat. I feared to stir, for some instinct of prudence made me lie still. But the brute seemed to realize that there was now some change in me, for it raised its head. Through my eyelashes I saw above me the two great, flaming eyes of a gigantic wolf. Its sharp white teeth gleamed in the gaping red mouth, and I could feel its hot breath fierce and acrid upon me.

For another spell of time I remembered no more. Then I became conscious of a low growl, followed by a yelp, renewed again and again. Then, seemingly very far away, I heard a "Holloa! Holloa!" as of many voices calling in unison. Cautiously I raised my head and looked toward where the sound came from, but the cemetery blocked my view. The wolf continued to yelp, and a red glare began to move around the grove of cypresses, as though following the sound. As the voices drew closer, the wolf yelped faster and louder. I feared to make either sound or motion.

THE FACTS

Abraham, known as Bram, Stoker (1847-1912) was born in Dublin, Ireland. A sickly child, Bram was unable to walk until he was seven years old and was forced to spend most of his time in bed. To keep him amused, his mother read him horror stories. Later he made a full recovery and went on to become an outstandingly good athlete and scholar at Dublin University. But he never lost his childhood fascination for horror.

In 1897, after studying both Transylvania (a region of present-day Romania) and vampires, Stoker wrote the novel *Dracula*. It remains one of the bestselling horror stories of all time.

Dracula's Guest was first intended as a chapter in *Dracula*. But it was eventually published separately in 1914—two years after Bram Stoker's death—as a sequel. The story takes place in the mountains of southern Germany on Walpurgis Night, a holiday very much like Halloween.

Chapter 2

Nearer came the red glow, over the white pall that stretched into the darkness around me. Then, all at once from beyond the trees, there came at a trot a troop of horsemen bearing torches. The wolf rose from my breast and made for the cemetery. I saw one of the horsemen—from their hats and their long military cloaks, I could tell that they were soldiers—raise his carbine and take aim. A companion knocked his arm, and I heard the bullet whiz over my head. The firer had evidently thought that my body was the wolf's. Another soldier sighted the animal as it slunk away, and a shot followed. Then, at a gallop, the troop rode forward—some toward me, others following the wolf as it disappeared among the snow-clad cypress trees.

As the soldiers drew nearer, I tried to move. But I was powerless, although I could see and hear all that went on around me. Two or three of the soldiers jumped from their horses and knelt beside me. One of them raised my head and placed his hand over my heart.

"Good news, comrades!" he cried. "His heart still beats!" Then some brandy was poured down my throat. It put vigor into me, and I was able to open my eyes fully and look around. Lights and shadows were moving among the trees, and I heard men call to one another. They drew together, uttering frightened exclamations. The lights flashed as the others came pouring out of the cemetery pell-mell, like men possessed. When those who had been searching in the distance came closer, those who were already gathered around me asked them eagerly:

"Well, have you found him?"

The reply rang out hurriedly: "No! no! Come away quick—quick! This is no place to stay, and on this of all nights!"

"What was it?" was the question, asked in all manner of ways. The answer came in many different ways, too. It was as though the men were moved by some common impulse to speak, yet held back by some common fear from giving their thoughts.

"It indeed!" gibbered one, whose wits had plainly given out for the moment.

"A wolf—and yet not a wolf!" another put in quickly.

"No use trying to kill him without a special bullet," a third remarked.

"Serve us right for coming out on this night! Truly we have earned our money!" a fourth cried.

"There was blood on the broken marble," another said, after a pause. "The lightning never brought that there. And what about him—is he safe? Look at his throat! See, comrades, the wolf has been lying on him and keeping his blood warm."

A man looked at my throat and replied: "He is all right, the skin is not pierced. What does it all mean? We should not have found him but for the yelping of the wolf."

"What became of it?" asked the man who was holding up my head. He seemed the least panic-stricken of the party, for his hands were steady. There was the chevron of an officer on the sleeve of his uniform.

"It went to its home," answered the man, whose long face was pale, and who shook with terror as he glanced around him fearfully. "There are graves enough there in which it may lie. Come, comrades—come quickly! Let us leave this cursed spot."

The officer raised me so that I was sitting up. Then he uttered a word of command, at which several men placed me upon a horse. The officer then sprang into the saddle behind me, took me in his arms, and gave the word to advance. Turning our faces away from the cypresses, we rode away in swift, military order.

As yet my tongue would not move, so I had to remain silent. I must have fallen asleep, for the next thing I remembered was finding myself standing up, supported by a soldier on each side of me. It was almost broad daylight. To the north a red streak of sunlight was reflected, like a path of blood over the snow. The officer was telling the men to say nothing of what they had seen, except that they had found an English stranger, guarded by a large dog.

"Dog! That was no dog," cut in the man who had shown such fear. "I think I know a wolf when I see one."

The young officer answered calmly: "I said a dog."

"Dog!" repeated the other. It was evident that his courage was rising with the sun. Pointing to me, he said: "Look at his throat. Is that the work of a dog, master?"

Instinctively I raised my hand to my throat, and as I touched it I cried out in pain. The men crowded around to look, some stooping down from their saddles, and again there came the calm voice of the young officer:

"A dog, as I said. If anything else were said, we should only be laughed at."

I was then put onto a horse behind a trooper, and we rode on into the suburbs of a large city. Here I was lifted into a carriage, which was driven off to a large, elegant hotel. The young officer accompanied me, while a trooper followed with his horse and the others rode off to their barracks.

When we arrived, the maître d'hôtel rushed so quickly down the steps that it was apparent he had been watching from within. Taking me by both hands, he led me in. The officer saluted me and turned to leave. But I insisted that he come to my rooms. Over a glass of wine, I warmly thanked him and his brave comrades for saving me. He replied simply that he was more than glad, and that the manager had taken steps to make all the searching party pleased. These ambiguous words made the maître d'hôtel smile. The officer then left to carry out his duties.

"But how and why was it that the soldiers came to search for me?" I inquired.

The manager shrugged his shoulders and replied: "I was fortunate enough to obtain permission from the commander of my old regiment to ask for volunteers."

"But how did you know I was lost?" I asked, still curious.

"The driver arrived with the remains of your carriage, which had been upset when the horses ran away."

WORD POWER

pall—a dense haze

carbine—a type of light rifle

pell-mell—in a disorderly way

chevron—a badge in the shape of a V

barracks—a building where soldiers live and sleep

maître d'hôtel—(here) a hotel manager

ambiguous—having two or more possible meanings

Boyar—a type of Russian nobleman

"But surely you would not send out an entire search-party of soldiers merely for this reason?"

"Oh, no!" he answered, "but even before the coachman arrived, I had this telegram from the Boyar whose guest you are." Then he took from his pocket a telegram which he handed to me, and I read:

BISTRITZ

BE CAREFUL OF MY GUEST—HIS SAFETY IS MOST PRECIOUS TO ME. SHOULD ANYTHING HAPPEN TO HIM, OR IF HE BE MISSED, SPARE NOTHING TO FIND HIM AND ENSURE HIS SAFETY. HE IS ENGLISH AND THEREFORE ADVENTUROUS. THERE ARE OFTEN DANGERS FROM SNOW AND WOLVES AND NIGHT. LOSE NOT A MOMENT IF YOU SUSPECT HARM TO HIM. I WILL PAY YOU HANDSOMELY FOR YOUR EFFORTS.

DRACULA

As I held the telegram in my hand, the room seemed to whirl around me. If the attentive maître d'hôtel had not caught me, I think I should have fallen. There was something highly strange in all this, something impossible to imagine. There grew on me a sense that I was the object of a contest between opposite forces, good and evil. The idea seemed in a way to paralyze me. I was certainly under some form of mysterious protection. From a distant country had come, in the very nick of time, a message that took me out of the jaws of the wolf.

THE END

The Canterville Ghost

Retold from a story by Oscar Wilde

When Mr. Hiram B. Otis, the wealthy American minister, purchased the house known as Canterville Chase, everyone told him he was doing a very foolish thing, because there was no doubt the place was haunted. Indeed, Lord Canterville himself, an honorable man, had mentioned the fact to Mr. Otis.

"We have not cared to live in the place ourselves," said Lord Canterville, "since my great aunt, the Dowager Duchess of Bolton, was frightened into a fit, from which she never really recovered. This happened after two skeleton hands were placed on her shoulders. I must tell you, Mr. Otis, that the ghost has been seen by several other members of my family, as well as the rector of the parish. After the Duchess's awful experience, none of our younger servants would stay, and Lady Canterville often gets very little sleep during the night because of the mysterious noises that come from the corridor and library."

"My Lord," replied the minister, "I come from a modern country, where we have everything that money can buy. I reckon that if there were such a thing as a ghost in Europe, we'd have it at home in one of our museums, or on the road as a show."

"I fear the ghost really does exist," said Lord Canterville, smiling. "It has been well known since 1584, and always makes its appearance before the death of any member of our family."

"Well, so does the family doctor for that matter, Lord Canterville. But there is no such thing, sir, as a ghost."

"Well, remember that I warned you."

A few weeks after this conversation took place, the house purchase was completed, and the minister and his family went to Canterville Chase. Mrs. Otis, who had been a celebrated New York belle, was now a handsome, middle-aged woman. The Otises' eldest son, Washington, was a fair, good-looking young man, while their daughter, Virginia, was a lovely, blue-eyed girl of fifteen. The Duke of Cheshire had once proposed to her, but was sent back to Eton by his guardians. The Otises' two youngest children were delightful twin boys.

Because Canterville Chase is seven miles from Ascot, the nearest train station, Mr. Otis had arranged for a carriage to meet them. They started on their drive in high spirits. It was a lovely July evening, and the air was full of the scent of pine woods. But as the Otises entered the avenue of Canterville Chase, the sky became overcast, and the atmosphere grew still. Before they reached the house, rain had fallen.

An old woman wearing a black silk dress, with a white cap and apron, was standing on the steps to receive them. This was Mrs. Umney, the former housekeeper of the Cantervilles, whom Mrs. Otis had agreed to employ. She made them each a low curtsey as they alighted and said, "I bid you welcome to Canterville Chase."

Following her, the Otises passed through the hall into the library. At the end was a large stained-glass window, where they found afternoon tea laid out for them. After taking off their wraps, they sat and looked around, while Mrs. Umney waited on them.

Suddenly Mrs. Otis saw a red stain on the floor beside the fireplace and said to Mrs. Umney, "I am afraid something has been spilled there."

"Yes, indeed, madam," replied the old housekeeper in a very low voice. "Blood has been spilled on that spot."

"How horrid," cried Mrs. Otis. "I don't at all care for bloodstains in a living room. It must be removed at once."

The old woman smiled and said, "It is the blood of Lady Eleanor de Canterville, who was murdered on that very spot by her husband, Sir Simon de Canterville, in 1575. Sir Simon survived her nine years, then mysteriously disappeared. His body has never been discovered, but his guilty spirit still haunts Canterville Chase. The stain cannot be removed."

"That is nonsense," cried Washington Otis. "Pinkerton's Champion Stain Remover will clean it up in no time," and before the housekeeper could interfere, he had begun scouring the floor with a black stick. In just a few moments, absolutely no trace of the blood could be seen.

"I knew Pinkerton would do it," he exclaimed triumphantly, as he looked around at his admiring family. But then a terrible flash of lightning lit up the somber room, a fearful peal of thunder made everyone jump to their feet, and Mrs. Umney fainted.

"What a monstrous climate!" said the American minister calmly. "I guess England is so overpopulated they don't have enough decent weather for everybody. Emigration is the only solution."

In a few moments, Mrs. Umney came to. She was extremely upset, and sternly warned Mr. Otis to beware of trouble coming to the house.

"I have seen things, sir," she said, "that would terrify any Christian, and many a night I have not slept because of the awful things that have been done here."

THE FACTS

Oscar Wilde (1854-1900) was born in Dublin, Ireland. As a young man, he studied first at Trinity College in that city, then at Magdalen College, Oxford. In the early 1880s, Wilde started to publish his writings. They included poetry, fairy tales such as *The Happy Prince* (1888), his only novel, *The Picture of Dorian Gray* (1891), and humorous plays such as *The Importance of Being Earnest* (1895). In 1897, Wilde went to live in France, where he died just three years later. He is buried in Paris.

But Mr. Otis and his wife assured the woman that they were not in the least afraid of ghosts. Then the old housekeeper slowly tottered off to her room.

The storm raged fiercely all night, but nothing of particular note occurred. However, the next morning, when the Otises came down to breakfast, they found the terrible bloodstain on the floor once again. "I don't think it can really be the fault of Pinkerton's Stain Remover," said Washington, "because it has never failed before. It must be the ghost."

Washington then rubbed out the stain a second time, but the next morning it appeared again. A third time he cleaned it, but the following morning it was there, too, though Mr. Otis had locked the library the night before and carried the key upstairs.

The whole family was now interested. Mr. Otis began to suspect that he had perhaps denied the existence of ghosts too firmly, while Mrs. Otis expressed her intention of joining the Psychical Society. Then, that very night, all doubts that there was a house ghost were removed forever.

The day had been warm and sunny. In the cool of the evening, the family went out for a drive. They did not return home until nine o'clock, when they had a light supper. The conversation was varied and lively. But no mention was made of the supernatural, or of Sir Simon de Canterville.

At eleven o'clock the Otises went to bed, and by half past all the lights were out. Some time after, Mr. Otis was awakened by a curious noise in the corridor, outside his room. It sounded like the clank of metal, and seemed to be coming nearer. He got up at once, struck a match, and looked at the time. It was exactly one o'clock.

The strange noise continued, and with it Mr. Otis heard the sound of footsteps. So he put on his slippers, picked up a small vial, and opened the door. He

saw an old man standing right in front of him in the moonlight. The man looked terrible. His eyes were as red as burning coals, and long, gray hair fell over his shoulders in matted coils. His garments, which were extremely old-fashioned, were dirty and ragged. Heavy manacles hung from his wrists and ankles.

"My dear sir," said Mr. Otis, "I really must insist on your stopping those chains from making that awful noise. I have brought you for that purpose a small bottle of Tammany Rising Sun Oil. It is said to work after just one application. I shall leave it here for you by the bedroom candles, and will be happy to supply you with more should you require it." With these words, the minister laid the bottle on a nearby table and went back to bed.

For a moment, the Canterville Ghost stood motionless with anger. Then he threw the bottle on the floor and fled down the corridor, emitting a ghastly green light. But as he reached the top of the stairs, a door opened behind him. Then two little figures appeared, and a pillow whizzed past his head! At once, the shocked ghost vanished through the wooden wainscoting.

When he reached his secret chamber, the confused ghost leaned against a moonbeam and began to think. In his entire 300-year career he had never been so insulted. He thought of the Dowager Duchess, whom he had frightened into a fit. He thought of the housemaids, who had become hysterical when he had merely grinned at them through the curtains. He remembered, too, old Lord Canterville with the jack of diamonds playing card stuck in his throat. Just before he choked to death, the lord had confessed that he had cheated a man out of £50,000 with that card. He also swore that it was the Canterville Ghost who had made him swallow it as a punishment.

In his mind, the ghost relived all his best haunting performances. He could not believe that after all his great achievements, some modern Americans had tried to clean away the ancient Canterville bloodstain, offered him Rising Sun Oil for his noisy chains, and even thrown a pillow at his head! It was absolutely unbearable. No ghost in history had ever been treated in this appalling way. He decided on revenge.

WORD POWER

dowager—a "dowager duchess" is a duke's widow. The title is used to distinguish her from the wife of the new duke, known simply as "duchess"

belle—a beautiful young woman

overcast—full of clouds

psychical—dealing with the supernatural

matted—tangled into a single mass

manacles—metal cuffs; shackles

wainscoting—(here) wall paneling

Chapter 2

The next morning when the Otis family met at breakfast, they discussed the ghost at some length. The American minister was naturally a little annoyed to find that his present of oil had not been accepted.

"I have no wish," he said, "to do the ghost any personal injury, and I must say that, considering the length of time he has been in the house, I don't think it is at all polite to throw pillows at him."

This was a very just remark, at which, I am sorry to say, the twins burst into shouts of laughter.

"Upon the other hand," Mr. Otis continued, "if he really declines to use the Rising Sun Oil, we shall have to take his chains from him. It would be impossible to sleep with such a noise going on outside the bedrooms."

For the rest of the week, however, the Otises were undisturbed, although the bloodstain on the library floor was continually renewed, in many different colors. Some mornings it was red, others it was purple, and once a bright emerald-green. These changes amused the party very much. But Virginia did not enter into the joke. She was always distressed at the sight of the blood, and nearly cried the morning it was green.

The second appearance of the ghost was on Sunday night. Shortly after the Otises had gone to bed, they were alarmed by a crash in the hall. Rushing downstairs, they found that a suit of armor had fallen from its stand onto the stone floor. Nearby, seated in a chair, was the Canterville Ghost. He was rubbing his knees with an expression of agony on his face.

The twins at once fired two pellets at him with their peashooters.

The ghost started up with a shriek of rage and swept through them. He extinguished Washington Otis's candle as he passed, leaving them all in total darkness. At the top of the staircase, he recovered himself and gave a peal of evil laughter. But hardly had the echo died away when a door opened, and Mrs. Otis came out. "I am afraid you are far from well," she said, "so I have brought you a bottle of Dr. Dobell's tincture. If it is indigestion, you will find it a most excellent remedy."

The ghost glared at her in fury and began to make preparations for turning himself into a black dog. But the sound of approaching footsteps made him hesitate, so he just glowed strangely. Then, just as the twins came up to him, he vanished with a deep groan.

On reaching his room, the ghost broke down in sobs. The actions of the twins and Mrs. Otis had been annoying. But he was distressed above all because he had been unable to wear the suit of armor.

He had hoped that even modern Americans would be thrilled by the sight of a specter in armor. Besides, it was the suit that he had worn while still alive. Yet when he had put it on, he had been overpowered by its great weight and fallen on the stone floor, grazing his knees and bruising his right hand.

For some days after this, the ghost was ill and hardly stirred from his room, except to renew the bloodstain. However, he recovered and resolved to make a third attempt to frighten the Otises. He spent almost a day looking over his wardrobe to find the ideal outfit. In the end, he chose a large hat with a red feather, a winding-sheet, and a rusty dagger.

Toward evening, a violent storm came on. It was the type of weather that the ghost loved. He planned to make his way to Washington's room, gibber at him from the foot of the bed, then stab himself three times in the throat to the sound of slow music. He bore Washington a special grudge, because he had removed the famous Canterville bloodstain.

The ghost planned to visit the room of the minister and his wife next. He would place a clammy hand on Mrs. Otis's forehead, while hissing terrifying secrets into her husband's ear. He had not made up his mind about Virginia. She had never insulted him and was pretty and gentle. A few groans from the closet, he thought, would be enough.

As for the twins, he was determined to teach them a lesson. First, he would sit on their chests to produce a stifling sensation. Then he would stand between their beds in the form of a green, icy-cold corpse, till they became paralyzed with fear. Finally, he would throw off the winding-sheet and crawl around, with white bones and one rolling eyeball on show.

At half-past ten, the ghost heard the family going to bed. By a quarter past eleven, all was still, and as midnight sounded, he went on his way. The wind wandered moaning around the house. But the Otis family slept, unaware of their doom. High above the rain and storm, he could hear the steady snoring of the American minister.

The ghost stepped stealthily out of the wall with a wicked smile on his cruel mouth. On and on he glided, like an evil shadow. Finally, he reached the corner of the passage that led to Washington's room. For a moment he paused there, the wind blowing his long gray locks about his head. Then the clock struck quarter past midnight, and he decided the time had come.

The ghost chuckled and turned the corner. But then, with a wail of terror, he fell back and hid his pale face in his hands. Right in front of him was a monstrous specter! Its head was bald, its face round and white. Hideous laughter stretched its features into a grin. From the eyes streamed rays of scarlet light, its mouth was a wide well of fire, and a hideous garment covered its huge form. On its breast was a placard covered in old-fashioned writing. With its right hand it held up a steel sword.

Never having seen another phantom before, the Canterville Ghost was frightened and fled back to his room. Once in his own apartment, he flung himself down on the bed. After a time, however, he decided to go and speak to the other ghost as soon as it was daylight. So as dawn was breaking, he returned to the spot where he had seen the phantom. He felt that, with his new friend, he might even be able to deal with the twins.

On reaching the place, however, a terrible sight met his gaze. The light had faded from the specter's eyes, the sword had fallen from its hand, and it was leaning against the wall in a peculiar position. The Canterville Ghost seized the figure in his arms. To his horror, the head slipped off and rolled on the floor, the body fell over, and he found himself clasping a white curtain, with a sweeping brush, a kitchen cleaver, and a hollow turnip at his feet! Then he grabbed the placard and read these words:

YE OTIS GHOSTE.
Ye Onlie True and Originale Spook.
Beware of Ye Imitationes.
All Others are Counterfeite.

He had been tricked by the twins! He ground his toothless gums together and swore that, after the cock crew twice, he would commit murder.

Hardly had he finished this awful oath when the cock crew. He laughed and waited. Hour after hour he waited, but the cock did not crow again. At half past seven, the arrival of the housemaids made him give up his vigil, and he stalked back to his room. He cursed the cock for its failure to crow once more, then retired to a coffin, and stayed there till evening.

The next day the ghost was weak and tired. For five days he stayed in his room, and at last made up his mind not to renew the bloodstain. If the Otis family did not want it, they did not deserve it. But he felt that it remained his solemn duty to appear in the corridor once a week, and to gibber from the large window on the first and third Wednesday of every month.

For the next three Saturdays, he walked along the corridor between midnight and three o'clock as usual, but now tried not to be heard or seen. He removed his boots, trod as lightly as possible, wore a black velvet cloak, and was even careful to smear his chains with the Rising Sun Oil, which he had stolen from Mr. Otis's bedroom.

But the twins still played tricks on him. He tripped over strings that they had

stretched across the corridor and once fell after treading on a butter-slide that they had constructed. This last insult so enraged him that he resolved to make one final effort to assert his dignity. He decided to visit the young men the next night in the form of a headless earl.

WORD POWER

winding-sheet—a sheet used to wrap a corpse

gibber—utter streams of meaningless sounds

stealthily—acting with stealth; in a secret or furtive manner

cleaver—a large, heavy knife

cock crew—the rooster crowed

vigil—a watch, especially during the night

Chapter 3

It took the Canterville Ghost three hours to prepare for his appearance as the headless earl. He was very satisfied with the result, and at a quarter past one crept down the corridor.

On reaching the twins' room, he found the door ajar. When he flung it open, a jug of water fell down on him, wetting him to the skin. At the same moment, he heard shrieks of laughter. The shock was so great that he fled back to his room, and by the next day he had a severe cold. He was very glad that he had not taken his head with him to catch a cold, too.

He now gave up all hope of ever frightening this rude American family, and contented himself with creeping about the passages in slippers. Then he received the final blow to his pride. He had gone downstairs to the hall. It was a quarter past two in the morning, and no one was stirring. As he was strolling toward the library, however, two figures leaped out. They waved their arms wildly, then shrieked "BOO!" in his ear.

Seized with panic, the ghost rushed for the staircase, but found Washington Otis waiting for him there. Hemmed in by enemies on every side, he vanished into the stove and made his way home through the flues, arriving at his room in a state of despair.

After this disaster, the Canterville Ghost was not seen again on any nocturnal expedition. The twins lay in wait for him on several occasions, but it was pointless. The family assumed that he had gone away.

Then one day, Virginia went riding with the Duke of Cheshire. She tore her dress so badly that, on her return home, she went up by the back staircase so as not to be seen. As she ran past the Tapestry Chamber, she saw someone inside. She looked in and discovered the ghost! He was sitting by the window. His head was leaning on his hand, and he looked depressed. Virginia was filled with pity, and decided to comfort him.

"I am so sorry for you," she said, "but my brothers are going back to school tomorrow. Then, if you behave yourself, no one will annoy you."

"It is absurd to ask me to behave myself," he answered. "I must rattle my chains and walk about at night. It is my only reason for existing."

"It is no reason at all for existing, and you know you have been wicked. You killed your wife."

"Well, I admit it," said the ghost, "but it was very much a family matter, and concerned no one else."

"It is very wrong to kill anyone, family or not," said Virginia.

"But my wife was plain, never had my ruffs properly starched, and knew nothing about cookery. Anyway, it is all over now, and it wasn't very nice of her brothers to starve me to death, even though I did kill her."

"Starve you to death? Oh, are you still hungry? I have a sandwich in my case. Would you like it?"

"No, thank you, I never eat now. But it is very nice of you to offer, and you are much nicer than the rest of your horrid, dishonest family."

"Stop!" cried Virginia. "It is you who is horrid, and as for dishonesty, you know you stole the paints from my box to renew the bloodstain in the library. First you took all my reds, then you took the emerald-green. I never told on you, though I was very annoyed. It was ridiculous, too, for who ever heard of emerald-green blood?"

"Well, really," said the ghost, "what was I to do? It is difficult to get real blood now, and as your brother began it all with his stain remover, I saw no reason why I should not have your paints. As for color, that is a matter of taste. The Cantervilles have blue blood, for example."

"Don't be ridiculous," said Virginia and stood up to leave.

"Please don't go, Virginia," the ghost cried. "I am so unhappy. I want to sleep and I cannot."

"That's absurd. You just go to bed and blow out the candle."

"I have not slept for three hundred years," the ghost said sadly, "and I am so tired."

Virginia grew serious. She came toward him and looked into his ancient face.

"Poor Ghost," she murmured, "is there nowhere you can sleep?"

"Far away beyond the pine woods," he answered, "there is a garden. There the grass grows long, the nightingale sings all night, the crystal moon looks down, and the yew tree spreads its long arms over the sleepers."

Virginia's eyes filled with tears, and she hid her face in her hands.

"You mean the Garden of Death," she whispered.

"Yes, death. Death must be so beautiful. To lie in the earth and listen to silence. To have no yesterday, and no tomorrow. To forget time, to forgive life, to be at peace. You can open the doors of death's house for me, for Love is always with you, and Love is stronger than Death."

Virginia trembled, and for a few moments there was silence. Then the ghost spoke again.

"Have you read the old prophecy on the library window?"

"Oh, often," cried the girl. "There are only six lines:

When a golden girl can win
Prayer from out the lips of sin
When the barren almond bears,
And a little child gives away its tears,
Then shall all the house be still
And peace come to Canterville.

"But I don't know what they mean."

"They mean," the ghost said, "that you must weep for my sins, as I have no tears, and pray with me for my soul, as I have no faith. Then the Angel of Death will have mercy on me. You will see fearful shapes, and wicked voices will whisper in your ear, but they will not harm you, for Hell cannot prevail against a child's purity."

Virginia gave no answer. Then she stood up. "I am not afraid," she said, "and I will ask the Angel to have mercy on you."

The ghost rose from his seat with a cry of joy and led Virginia across the room. Huntsmen, embroidered on the wall tapestry, blew their horns and said, "Go back, Virginia." But the ghost clutched her hand, and she shut her eyes against them. Evil-looking animals blinked at her from the carved chimney-piece and murmured, "Beware, little Virginia! We may never see you again," but the ghost glided on and Virginia did not listen.

When they reached the end of the room, the ghost stopped and muttered some strange words. Virginia opened her eyes to see the wall fading away and a black cavern in front of her. "Quick," cried the ghost, "or it will be too late." In a moment, the wainscoting closed behind them.

About ten minutes later, the bell rang for tea. As Virginia did not come down, Mrs. Otis sent one of the servants to get her. However, he could not find the young girl. Mrs. Otis was not alarmed at first, but when six o'clock struck and Virginia did not appear, she became agitated and sent the boys to look for her. She and Mr. Otis, meanwhile, searched every room in the house. At half-past six, the boys came back without their sister.

Then Mr. Otis remembered that, some days before, he had given a band of gypsies permission to camp in the park. He at once set off for Blackfell Hollow where they were, accompanied by his eldest son and two servants. But on arriving at the spot, they found that the gypsies had gone.

WORD POWER

flues—pipes that carry smoke from an inside fire to the outside

nocturnal—taking place at night

ruffs—high, pleated collars worn in the 16th and 17th centuries

prevail against—overcome; master

Mr. Otis then asked Washington and the two servants to search the district, while he ran home and sent telegrams to the police, telling them to look out for Virginia. When he had finished, he rode off on his horse to join the search. He had hardly gone a couple of miles when he heard somebody galloping after him, and saw the Duke of Cheshire on his pony.

"I'm awfully sorry, Mr. Otis," gasped out the young man, "but I can't rest as long as Virginia is lost. Please, don't be angry with me. You won't send me back, will you?"

The Minister smiled at the young man and replied, "Well, Cecil, I suppose you must come with me." Then the two of them galloped on to the train station. There Mr. Otis asked the station master if Virginia had been seen on the platform, but could get no news of her. The station master, however, assured him that a strict watch would be kept.

Mr. Otis and the Duke then rode to Bexley, a nearby village that was a well-known gypsy haunt. Here they roused the policeman, but could get no information from him. So they turned their horses homeward and reached Canterville Chase at about eleven o'clock. Not the slightest trace of Virginia had been discovered there. The gypsies had been caught, but she was not with them. The pond had been dragged, and the whole Chase searched, but with no result. For that night, Virginia was lost to them.

Chapter 4

Mr. Otis and the boys had failed to find Virginia. They walked up to the house in a state of depression. In the library they found poor Mrs. Otis, almost out of her mind with worry. Mr. Otis at once ordered supper for the whole party. It was a melancholy meal, as hardly anyone spoke. Afterward, Mr. Otis sent them all to bed, saying that nothing more could be done that night.

Just as they were leaving the dining-room, midnight boomed from the clock tower. Then there was a sudden shrill cry, a peal of thunder shook the house, and unearthly music floated through the air. Next, a panel at the top of the staircase flew back, and Virginia stepped out, carrying a little casket. In a moment they had all rushed up to her. Mrs. Otis clasped her in her arms, the Duke smothered her with kisses, and the twins did a wild war dance around the group.

"Good heavens, child, where have you been?" said Mr. Otis, rather angrily, thinking that she had been playing some foolish trick on them. "Cecil and I have been riding all over the country looking for you, and your mother has been frightened to death. You must never play these thoughtless practical jokes any more."

"My own darling, thank God you are found. You must never leave my side again," murmured Mrs. Otis, as she kissed the trembling child. "Papa," said Virginia quietly, "I have been with the ghost. He is dead, and you must come and see him. He had been very wicked, but he was really sorry, and he gave me this box of jewels before he died."

The whole family gazed at her in amazement, but she was quite serious. Turning around, she led them through the opening in the wainscoting down a secret corridor. Washington followed with a lighted candle. Finally, they came to a great oak door. When Virginia touched it, it swung back on its hinges, and they found themselves in a low room with one tiny grated window. In the wall was a huge iron ring, and chained to it was a skeleton. It was stretched out on the stone floor, and seemed to be trying to grasp an old-fashioned trencher and ewer, that were just out of its reach. This was where Sir Simon had once starved to death.

Virginia knelt down beside the skeleton and began to pray silently. The rest of the party looked on in wonder.

"Hello!" exclaimed one of the twins, who had been looking out of the window to try to discover where in the house they were. "The withered almond tree has blossomed. I can see the flowers in the moonlight."

"God has forgiven him," said Virginia gravely as she rose to her feet, and a beautiful light illuminated her face.

"What an angel you are!" cried the young Duke, and kissed her.

Four days after these curious incidents, a funeral started from Canterville Chase at about eleven o'clock at night. The hearse was drawn by eight black horses with ostrich plumes on their heads. The coffin was covered by a purple pall, on which the Canterville coat-of-arms was embroidered in gold. By the side of the hearse and the coaches walked the servants with lighted torches. Lord Canterville was the chief mourner and sat in the first carriage along with Virginia. Then came the American minister and his wife, then Washington and the three boys, and in the last carriage was Mrs. Umney. A grave had been dug in the corner of the churchyard, under the old yew tree, and the service was read by the Reverend Augustus Dampier.

When the ceremony was over, the servants extinguished their torches. Then, as the coffin was being lowered into the grave, Virginia stepped forward and laid on it a large cross made of white and pink almond blossoms. As she did so, the moon came out from behind a cloud and flooded the churchyard with silver light. From a distant copse a nightingale began to sing. Virginia thought about the prophecy on the library window and about the ghost's description of the Garden of Death. Her eyes filled with tears, and she hardly spoke during the drive home.

The next morning, Mr. Otis spoke to Lord Canterville about the jewels that the ghost had given to Virginia. They were magnificent, especially a 16th-century ruby necklace, and their value was so great that Mr. Otis felt unsure about allowing his daughter to accept them.

"My Lord," he said, "I know that in this country mortmain applies to trinkets as well as to land, and it is clear to me that these jewels are heirlooms in your family. I must beg you, accordingly, to take them, and to regard them simply as a portion of your property. My daughter is merely a child, and has as yet little interest in such luxury items. I am also informed by Mrs. Otis, who knows a great deal about art, that these gems are very valuable. Under these circumstances, Lord Canterville, I feel sure that you will recognize how impossible it is for my family to keep them. Indeed, all such vain toys, however necessary to the dignity of the British aristocracy, would be out of place among those who believe in American simplicity.

"Perhaps I should also mention that Virginia is very anxious that you should allow her to keep the box as a memento of your unfortunate ancestor. As it is extremely old, and so a good deal out of repair, you may perhaps think fit to agree."

Lord Canterville listened gravely to the Minister's speech, pulling his moustache now and then to hide a smile. When Mr. Otis had finished, he shook him by the hand and said, "My dear sir, your charming daughter provided a very important service to my unlucky ancestor, Sir Simon, and I and my family owe her a great deal. The jewels are clearly hers, and I believe that if I were heartless enough to take them, the wicked old fellow would be out of his grave in a fortnight, making my life a misery.

"What is more, the jewels are not heirlooms, because nothing is an heirloom that is not mentioned in a will or legal document. As the jewels' existence was unknown until now, they are accordingly not mentioned anywhere. I assure you I have no claim on them, and when Miss Virginia grows up, I dare say she will be pleased to have such pretty things to wear."

Mr. Otis was greatly distressed at Lord Canterville's refusal, and begged him to reconsider. But the good-natured lord was quite firm and persuaded the Minister to allow his daughter to keep the ghost's present.

Virginia married the young Duke of Cheshire as soon as he came of age. They were both so charming, and they loved each other so much, that everyone was delighted at the match—except Mr. Otis. He was extremely fond of the young Duke personally, but he objected to titles, and was afraid that a pleasure-loving aristocrat would make his daughter forget the principles of American simplicity. But his objections were overruled, and when he walked up the aisle of St. George's Church in Hanover Square in London with his daughter on his arm, there was not a prouder man in England.

After the honeymoon was over, the Duke and Duchess went down to Canterville Chase. The day after their arrival, they walked over to the churchyard by the pine woods. It had been difficult to decide what to engrave on Sir Simon's tombstone, but finally they had put simply the initials of his name, and the verse from the library window.

The Duchess had brought with her some roses, which she scattered on the grave, and after she and the Duke had stood by it for some time, they strolled into the ruined abbey. There the Duchess sat down on a fallen pillar, while her husband lay at her feet, looking up at her beautiful eyes. Then he took her hand and said, "Virginia, a wife should have no secrets from her husband."

WORD POWER

melancholy—sorrowful; sad

trencher—a wooden board used as a plate

ewer—a large pitcher

pall—a heavy cloth

mortmain—a legal term for permanent ownership

memento—an object that acts as a reminder of a person, occasion or place

fortnight—a period of two weeks

came of age—reached the legal age of adulthood (then 21)

"My dear Cecil! I have no secrets from you."

"Yes, you have," he answered, smiling. "You have never actually told me what happened to you when you were locked up with the ghost."

"I have never told anyone, Cecil," said Virginia gravely.

"I know that, but you might tell me."

"Please don't ask me, Cecil, I cannot tell you. Poor Sir Simon! I owe him a great deal. He made me see what Life is, and what Death signifies, and why Love is stronger than both."

The Duke rose and kissed his wife.

"Have your secret as long as I have your heart," he murmured.

"You have always had that, Cecil."

"And you will tell our children, won't you?" said the Duke.

Virginia blushed.

THE END

The Phantom of the Opera

Retold from a story by Gaston Leroux

"We've seen the ghost!" screamed a young dancer, bursting into the dressing room of the star ballerina, La Sorelli. "He came through the wall in the passage!"

"He looks like a walking skeleton—and his eyes...!" cried another.

La Sorelli tried to calm the young girls, but she was uneasy. Over the last few months, people had talked about nothing but the opera ghost. Joseph, a scene shifter, had met the ghost coming up the staircase from the cellars. He described the ghost's face as a death's head with eyes glowing deep in their black sockets. The ghost's yellow skin was stretched tightly over his bones as over a drum, and three or four locks of hair hung limply across his forehead.

Others spoke of him stalking the many underground storerooms and the warren of gas-lit passages backstage, appearing, then disappearing into thin air. He always wore evening clothes that hung loosely on his thin body. No one but Joseph was able to describe his face, which seemed to be hidden by a mask—but they all remembered his glowing eyes.

"Mother says Joseph should not have said anything about the ghost—he doesn't like to be talked about," said Meg Giry, one of the young dancers. Meg's mother was the concierge who unlocked the private boxes on the Grand Tier. The girls gathered around Meg, asking questions about the ghost. "Mother says he has his own box. She has often heard him in there, but she has never seen him," Meg told them.

"What nonsense you talk!" La Sorelli interrupted the gossiping dancers. "Come on, pull yourselves together, it's time for our performance." The ballerina led the young dancers up to the stage for their part in the evening's celebration gala.

When their dance was over, they waited in the wings to listen to Christine Daae, a new young opera singer who was making her debut. On this special night she seemed to be inspired and sang so beautifully that the audience went mad, rising to their feet, clapping and cheering. Christine was so overcome, she fainted and had to be carried to her dressing room.

A young man had been watching Christine intently from his box. His name was Count Raoul de Chagny. When he saw her collapse, he became very pale. Leaving his box, he rushed backstage to her dressing room. There, he ordered everyone out of the room except the doctor. Then he fell to his knees beside the unconscious singer and watched her as she slowly came to.

"Are you feeling better?" he asked her.

"Who are you?" whispered the girl.

"We used to play together when we were young and lived in the country. I have been coming every night to hear you sing," replied the count. "Could I speak to you in private?"

Christine looked troubled. "Another time," she said, then added, "I feel much better now, but I need to be alone. Please go, both of you." The doctor and young man left the room. Raoul lingered outside, hoping to speak to her when she came out. Suddenly, from the passageway, he became aware of voices inside the room.

"Christine," said a man's voice. "You must love me."

"How can you talk like that?" the girl said sadly. "I sing only for you, and tonight I gave you my soul."

Raoul's heart beat so loud, he feared they would hear it! He hid in the shadows, hoping to catch a glimpse of the man. But when eventually the door opened, it was Christine leaving alone. Raoul went into the room. He struck a match and looked about—but the room was completely empty!

In the director's office of the opera house, the retiring managers were handing over the keys to their two successors, Moncharmin and Richards. They also gave them a strange book.

"These are the terms of your employment, and we have to draw your attention to the final two clauses." At the end of the book, in red ink, was written: "The manager will pay the opera ghost the sum of 20,000 francs a month. Box 5 in the Grand Tier will be at the disposal of the opera ghost for every performance."

"Why should we agree to this?" cried Richards. "We don't even believe in the opera ghost!"

"You soon will if you do not keep to his conditions," answered the retiring managers. "Because if you don't, something disastrous will happen."

At that moment, the door burst open, and the stage manager rushed in. "Joseph has been found hanging in the cellar under the stage! " he gasped. "I went for help to cut him down, and when we returned, the body was no longer hanging from the rope. It was lying on the ground, and the rope had disappeared!"

"Now you see what happens when the ghost is angry," said one of the retiring managers, nervously.

"If the ghost really does exist, why didn't you have him arrested when he came to his box?" asked Moncharmin.

"How could we?" the retiring manager replied. "We have never seen him in the box."

The two new managers looked at each other and burst out laughing. "We'll see about that," they said. "No ghost will stop us making some money by selling Box 5!"

A few days after Moncharmin and Richards had taken over the running of the opera house, they received a letter written in red ink.

"I am disagreeably surprised to find that, on arriving at the opera house to hear that charming singer, Christine Daae, my box had been sold. I understood you knew my terms, and if you wish to live in peace, you must not take away my private box. Your obedient servant, Opera Ghost."

"No ghost is going to dictate to us," the two men agreed. However, at the very next opera performance, they were sent for because of a disturbance in Box 5. Some people were complaining that they had been turned out of the box by a strange ghostly voice that said that the box was occupied, although there was nobody there!

WORD POWER

death's head—another name for a skull

concierge—French doorkeeper, usually a woman

gala—a special performance

debut—the first performance by a person or group of people

aria—a song sung by one person in an opera

petrified—terrified, unable to move

chandelier—light fixture, usually made of glass, that hangs from the ceiling

The managers summoned Madame Giry, the concierge, but all she would say was that every time the ghost's box had been sold, bad luck followed. The managers questioned her closely.

"I've never seen the ghost myself," she said, "but once he asked me for a footstool. And he always leaves me money after a performance." When Madame Giry had left, the managers agreed that the poor old dear was probably crazy and gave instructions that she should be fired. They also decided to use the box themselves the following Saturday to watch a performance of the opera *Faust*.

Before Saturday arrived, the managers found a letter from the opera ghost telling them to reinstate Madame Giry and to let Christine take the main part on Saturday night. Carlotta, the leading singer, also received a note. It warned her that if she appeared in the opera on Saturday, a misfortune worse than death would occur when she tried to sing.

They ignored the notes, and on the evening of the performance, the managers took their seats in Box 5. "Do you see that woman in the center of the orchestra?" Moncharmin said, pointing to a large lady in black. "That's our new concierge for the Grand Tier. I've given her free tickets for the opera tonight."

The curtain rose, and Carlotta began to sing. She was in excellent form, and the audience applauded loudly. In the intermission, Richards said, "You see, everything's going well."

The curtain rose again and Carlotta entered to thunderous applause. It was her big moment—the grand aria in the second act. Her first note was thrilling, and then—CROAK! The audience gasped, and Carlotta turned pale. She tried again, but all she could produce was an horrendous CROAK! Poor, despairing Carlotta. The uproar in the house was indescribable, and in Box 5, the two new managers were petrified. They both felt there was someone in the box, someone standing behind them, breathing over them. Sweat poured down their faces. Too frightened to move or turn around, they heard a voice whisper, "She's singing tonight to bring the chandelier down." As they looked up, the two uttered an awful cry. The huge chandelier in the center of the ceiling creaked and suddenly plunged downward. Amid shouts of fear, it smashed into the center of the orchestra—killing the new concierge of Box 5!

Chapter 2

Despite her triumph, the singer Christine Daae did not appear at the opera house in the next few weeks. Count Raoul sent messages to her lodgings, but there was no reply. Then one morning she sent him a note. "I have not forgotten our happy childhood together," she wrote to him. "I am travelling to Brittany today to lay some flowers on my father's grave."

The count threw some clothes into a bag and consulted the train timetable. There was just time to catch the afternoon train. He traveled in a state of great excitement. Christine must want him to follow her. Why else would she have written that note? He went over in his mind the little he knew of her background. Her father had been a Swedish violinist, traveling around Europe playing Scandinavian folk melodies while Christine sang to his music. Every summer they went to Brittany. It was there as a young boy that Count Raoul had first met Christine and heard the wonderful tales her father told. The ones about the Angel of Music had particularly caught his fancy. This Muse was said to visit every great musician, and Christine's father had told Raoul that his daughter must have been visited in her cradle.

"The Angel is never seen, but he is heard, whispering in the ear of those who are meant to hear him," said the old fiddler. "I will send him to you when I die and go to heaven," he told his daughter.

Three years later, when Raoul was a young man, he met Christine and her father in Brittany again. They spent many happy days together and when he left, Raoul promised Christine that he would never forget her. Years later, when Raoul saw Christine singing at the opera, he fell in love with her all over again.

Raoul arrived at the village and went with Christine to the churchyard to visit her father's grave.

As she placed some red roses on the grave, she asked, "Do you remember the legend of the Angel of Music? Well, I have been visited by the Angel—he comes to my dressing room and gives me lessons. It was he whom you heard talking to me that evening."

The young man laughed in disbelief, and Christine took offense.

"It's true!" she cried. Then she turned and ran back to the inn where they were staying. Before he left the graveyard, Raoul noticed a macabre pile of skulls and bones lying by the wall of the church. The villagers must have dug up the ancient graves to make room in the graveyard for the recently dead.

That night Raoul was woken by a sound outside his window. Looking out, he saw Christine leaving the inn. Putting on a cloak, he followed her as she made her way to the church. He saw her kneel down by the heap of whitened skulls and bones piled against the wall. As he drew closer, Raoul could hear heavenly music.

"Someone is skulking behind the bones," he thought, but as he came closer, the skulls started to move. Raoul froze to the spot as one by one they started to roll down the slope toward him. More and more bones fell and, as they did so, a shadow in a cloak slipped past the young man. Raoul grabbed at the cloak, and the figure stopped. A terrible death's head with scorching eyes stared at him, turning his soul to ice, and he fainted. When he came to, Raoul found himself in his room at the inn. He discovered that Christine had left without a word.

Two weeks after he had returned to Paris, Raoul received another note from Christine. It read: "Go to the masked ball at the opera tomorrow night. Wear a white cloak and mask to disguise yourself and stand by the door leading to the great hall. Do not tell anyone where you are going."

The ball was a popular, noisy affair. As Raoul waited by the door, a figure in black passed him and squeezed the tips of his fingers. It was Christine. As he followed her through the crush, Raoul spotted a guest dressed all in red. His disguise was so gruesome, it was causing a sensation. Everyone had turned around to look at him. As Raoul passed him, Red Death turned and Raoul gasped—it was the death's head from the graveyard in Brittany! With no time to think, and fearful of losing Christine's black-robed figure, Raoul pressed on through the crowds and up two staircases. Finally Christine stopped at a door and slipped through. Raoul followed.

"Keep in the shadows," whispered Christine, putting her ear to the door. She reopened the door a crack and Raoul, glancing through the opening, glimpsed the frightening costume of Red Death turning into the corridor just as Christine slammed the door.

"You must stop loving me," Christine whispered. "I wanted to tell you that I may never sing again at the opera, and you must forget me." As she spoke, Raoul studied Christine's face and was overwhelmed by the harrowing change in her. She looked deathly pale with dark shadows under her eyes, and her lips seemed bloodless. Before Raoul had time to speak, she gave a gesture of farewell and slipped away.

WORD POWER

Scandinavian—from Scandinavia, the peninsula divided into Norway and Sweden

Brittany—a region in northwestern France

Muse—a spirit that inspires great musicians, poets, and artists

macabre—gruesome, morbid, grisly, frightening

skulking—lurking or lying in wait for something

harrowing—very distressing or disturbing, heart-rending

When Raoul returned to the party, he asked if anyone had seen Red Death. Everyone had seen the figure, but no one knew where he had gone. Raoul wandered the empty corridors of the opera house in search of the mystery guest and eventually found himself outside Christine's dressing room. On an impulse he went inside, but the gas-lit room was empty. Hearing footsteps outside, Raoul slipped behind a curtain just as Christine entered, looking weary and sad. She sat at her dressing table with her head in her hands, and a few moments later, the sound of singing could be heard, very soft and faint, through the walls of the dressing room. The song became louder until it seemed as if it was in the very room.

Christine rose. "Here I am," she said, a smile of happiness appearing on her pale face. The voice without a body went on singing, and Raoul had never heard anything so glorious and triumphant. As the final words, "Fate links thee to me forever and a day..." faded away, Christine walked toward her reflection in the full-length mirror. Raoul stretched out to catch her in his arms, but an icy blast flung him backward, and for a moment, he saw two, four, eight images of Christine spinning before him. When everything stopped moving, he found himself in front of the mirror, staring at his own reflection—but Christine had totally disappeared!

THE FACTS

Gaston Leroux (1868-1927) was a French writer whose zest for life and passion for writing and travel kept him in the public eye. As a journalist, he wrote for newspapers about the trials of the day. Later, he covered the early days of the Russian Revolution. He loved to explore the more remote parts of Africa or Scandinavia, and was happy to disguise himself if he needed to. His daring sense of adventure was always getting him in—and out—of trouble. This exciting life inspired Leroux to write some brilliant popular novels, and his detective stories rivaled those about Sherlock Holmes. *The Phantom of the Opera* is his most famous novel.

Chapter 3

Following Christine's disappearance through the mirror of her dressing room, Raoul went to her lodgings. To his amazement he found her in the garden.

"You are under some sort of spell," Raoul said to her bitterly. "I saw your face while you listened to the song that came from your dressing room walls. And then you disappeared. Where did you go?"

Christine looked scared. "You must not spy on me," she whispered. "Do you want to get yourself killed?"

"I have come to tell you that I have to go away," Raoul told Christine. "I want us to spend as much time as possible together before I go." She seemed upset at his news, but the only place she would agree to meet him was at the opera house. Over the next few days, they spent many happy hours wandering through the corridors and exploring behind the scenes of the empty stage. Once, when they were passing one of the open trapdoors in the stage floor, it closed with a swift gliding movement.

"Shall we explore down there?" suggested Raoul, but Christine looked terrified and pulled him away.

"Everything that is underground belongs to him!" she cried.

"Who is he? I have to know," asked Raoul. "Tell me, please, Christine!"

Christine did not answer, but taking him by the arm, she dragged him up the stairs, going ever higher until they were under the very roof of the opera house. Despite looking behind her at every turn, Christine failed to see the dark shadow that followed them, stopping whenever they stopped and moving on when they did. And Raoul, who only had eyes for Christine, never once thought to look behind him.

WORD POWER

parapet—a low wall running along the edge of a roof

abductor—a person who kidnaps, or abducts, someone

sublime—awakening feelings of awe; exalted, supreme

intently—earnestly, diligently, intensely

ventriloquist—a person who can speak to give the illusion that the sound is coming from somewhere else

impregnable—fortress that cannot be taken; withstands attack

snuffing—extinguishing; putting a candle out with snuffers or by blowing on it

Out on the roof by the parapet, overlooking Paris, the air was clear and the sun shone. Christine began to tell Raoul the story of the voice; how it had started to sing to her, and how she had imagined it to be the Angel of Music sent by her father. It had given her lessons in her dressing room every day, which is how she had started to sing so gloriously.

It was only when Christine had seen Raoul, night after night at the opera, that the voice had become angry and jealous. With the croaking singer and the falling chandelier, Christine had realized that this was not an angel, but a terrible presence who had taken over her life.

"And that evening, when you completely disappeared from the dressing room through the mirror?" asked Raoul. "Whatever happened then?"

"I cannot explain it," she replied. "It first happened on my return from Brittany. Suddenly there was no mirror, and I was in a dark passage. A cold, bony hand grabbed

my wrist, led me away, and put me on a horse. We rode in darkness to the edge of a lake and then took a boat to a house. Finally, I was led into a room filled with dazzling light, and when my eyes became used to it, I saw it was filled with flowers. I turned to look at my abductor and saw a man whose face was covered by a mask, but whose voice I recognized as my Angel. It was the Phantom of the Opera, who lives deep below the opera house."

"How did you get away?" asked Raoul.

"The Phantom told me I should stay with him for five days, and then I could return. For the next few days, he showed me around his domain, and every day he sang to me in his wonderful voice. On the fourth day, while we were singing a duet, I had an uncontrollable urge to see the face beneath the mask and I tore it from his face. Oh! It was so horrible..." Christine's voice trailed off, as she shuddered into silence.

"I will kill him for what he has done to you!" Raoul cried out. At this, the black shadow on the roof behind stirred a little, but neither Christine nor Raoul noticed his presence. Christine continued.

"Listen to me, Raoul! The Phantom's face is so terrible that I knew that because I had seen it, he would never let me go. For the next few days, I listened to his sublime singing, and I told him that if I appeared to shiver when I saw his face, then it was because I was so thrilled to witness his genius. I lied for the price of my freedom, and little by little, he believed me when I said I wanted to leave, but that I would come back. When he finally let me go, I sent you the note to meet me at the masked ball.

"So, Raoul, I made a promise to return to him," Christine sighed, in despair. "But these past weeks with you have been so happy that I can't bear the thought of going to live with him. Yet if I don't go, something terrible will happen!"

"Why must you go?" demanded Raoul.

"His voice will make me," she replied. "He will go on his knees with his terrible face staring at mine. He will tell me he loves me and he'll weep. Raoul, you cannot imagine how ghastly it is to see that skull cry!"

"We must run away together, tomorrow night!" said Raoul. Then, as he kissed Christine tenderly, there was a great clap of thunder, followed by a lightning flash that rent the evening sky. Looking up, they saw two dreadful, blazing eyes, watching them intently. The couple fled from the roof.

Raoul and Christine raced down the stairs and along corridors—anything to get away from the piercing, glowing eyes of the watcher in the shadows. Without looking where they were going, they came to a part of the opera house they did not know and were startled by a figure wearing a colorful robe, who stepped out of an alcove.

"Go that way and you will be safe!" he said, pointing down some nearby stairs. Soon they found themselves outside Christine's dressing room.

"Who was that strange man?" asked Raoul. "I've not seen him before."

"He's called the Persian," Christine replied. "He knows everything about the opera house, and it is rumored that he even lives here."

"You know, the Phantom is everywhere. He's bound to know what we are planning. We must leave together, immediately!" Raoul pleaded.

But Christine shook her head, sadly.

"I cannot do that. I have promised to sing in the performance tomorrow night," she explained. "But as soon as it ends, please arrange for a coach and horses to wait for us at the stage door and we will run away together."

The Persian watched the pair of them as they disappeared. He sighed as he remembered the terrible crimes the Phantom had committed at the Shah's court in Persia. As chief of police, the Persian had been outwitted time and again, but once he had saved the Phantom's life. He had followed him to Paris to try and discover the Phantom's secrets, and now he feared for the safety of the young opera star.

Over the years, the Persian had watched and waited, learning the tricks the Phantom had devised while living deep beneath the opera house. He had found the trapdoors through which the Phantom appeared and disappeared, like a ghost. He had listened to the Phantom throwing his voice like a ventriloquist, fooling people such as the two managers into believing that he was standing right behind them, whispering in their ears, even though no one was there.

Investigating the strange death of Joseph, the scene shifter, the Persian found a secret passage leading to a subterranean world under the theater, where the Phantom had made his home. A strange world of dimly lit passages, it had an underground lake and an impregnable fortress.

It was to the fortress that the Phantom had taken Christine to try to persuade her to be his bride. Now that Christine and Count Raoul were plotting to run away together, they were in terrible danger. The Persian could only watch and wait to see what the Phantom would do.

That night, Raoul could not sleep. It was clear that the Phantom had heard the plans they'd made on the roof. Suddenly, he saw two glowing eyes staring at him from the foot of his bed. Was there nowhere safe from the Phantom? Raoul struck a match to light the candle beside his bed. The flame created shadows on his bedroom walls, but there was no one there.

"Just a nightmare," he thought, snuffing the candle. Yet there were those eyes again. Reaching for a pistol he kept near his bed, he took aim and fired between the dreadful eyes. With a scream, they disappeared. The gunshot brought his servant running.

"What happened?" he asked Raoul, who was examining the window. It had been pierced by the single bullet. Outside on the balcony, he could see drops of blood.

"No ghost bleeds like that," Raoul said to himself, feeling a little relieved. "So the Phantom is flesh and blood after all."

Chapter 4

Raoul spent the next day preparing for their journey, but he was at the opera house to hear Christine sing for the last time. The performance was a triumph. But as she came to the very last line of her part, the star of the show simply disappeared!

An immediate search was ordered, the police were called, and, along with everyone else, Raoul was questioned. However, he wisely refrained from mentioning the Phantom.

As he left the managers' office, he was stopped by the Persian.

"Christine is in great danger, and only I can help you find her," he told Raoul. "I know many of the Phantom's tricks."

"We must go through the mirror in Christine's dressing room," advised the Persian. "It is the way to the Phantom's house." The mirror was, in reality, a revolving door. "We just need to find the mechanism that turns it," he said, touching a raised part of the patterned wallpaper. The mirror swung around, and the two men walked into a dark passage.

Raoul crept along through a maze of passages under the stage of the great opera house, but they gradually left these familiar areas behind them.

The dark passages grew damp, and Raoul remembered Christine speaking of crossing an underground lake.

"That is the way the Phantom will expect us to come," said the Persian. "But my route leads *behind* the lake." The Persian stopped at a paved area and pressed a spring between two stones; a slab slid sideways to reveal a dimly lit room below. "I will drop down first," he said. As Raoul landed, the slab in the ceiling closed, shutting off their means of escape.

They were in a room with six walls, all made of mirrors! In one corner was a huge metal tree whose reflection bounced off the mirrored walls, giving the appearance of a forest. Every way he turned, Raoul saw an infinity of reflections of himself and his companion!

"We are in his torture chamber," said the Persian. "One wall is a door to his house;

somewhere there must be a spring release."

They heard voices. It was the Phantom talking to Christine. "Choose, my dear. Wedding march or funeral march? If you refuse me, I shall destroy everyone. You have until midnight to decide!"

Then the Phantom left. Raoul called to Christine through the wall: "The Persian and I are here to rescue you. Tap on the wall where the door is, and we will find the secret spring."

"I cannot move," wailed Christine. "He has tied me up because I tried to kill myself, but I will try to get him to untie me." Later, they heard Christine pleading to be freed. Finally, the Phantom agreed.

"I shall be in the next room," he told her, "composing the final part of my wedding march." Christine crept into the room and slipped the key into her pocket, but when the Phantom returned, he noticed that the key had vanished.

"Aha! So you want to see who is in my torture chamber!" he screamed. "Shall I take a look? Or shall I let you see?"

Christine begged to look for herself. "There is no one there," she lied.

While the Persian looked for the hidden spring, their prison was suddenly getting hotter. A bright, merciless light shone, and Raoul began to hallucinate. He screamed for water as the Persian pressed a tiny nail head between two floorboards. Part of the floor opened, and cool, damp air flooded in. Stone stairs led down to a vast dungeon, with huge wine barrels along the wall. The two men pulled out one of the corks, but when at last it was free, gunpowder—not wine—trickled out!

"So *this* is how the Phantom plans to kill everyone, by blowing up the opera house and all its inhabitants!" said the Persian.

The two men climbed back into the now-darkened torture chamber. "Phantom!" screamed the Persian. "Remember how I once saved *your* life?"

Christine called through the wall, "In five minutes it will be midnight, and I must give The Phantom my answer. I must choose between two handles. One is a scorpion, the other a grasshopper..." She was interrupted by the Phantom's return.

"So you are still in there," he called to the trapped men. "Christine must now choose between the scorpion that stings and the grasshopper that jumps sky high." His dreadful laugh froze the listeners' bones to the very marrow.

Raoul entreated, "Christine! Don't turn the grasshopper handle!" for he was thinking of the gunpowder, which could indeed blow them all sky high! On the stroke of midnight Christine called out, "I have turned the scorpion."

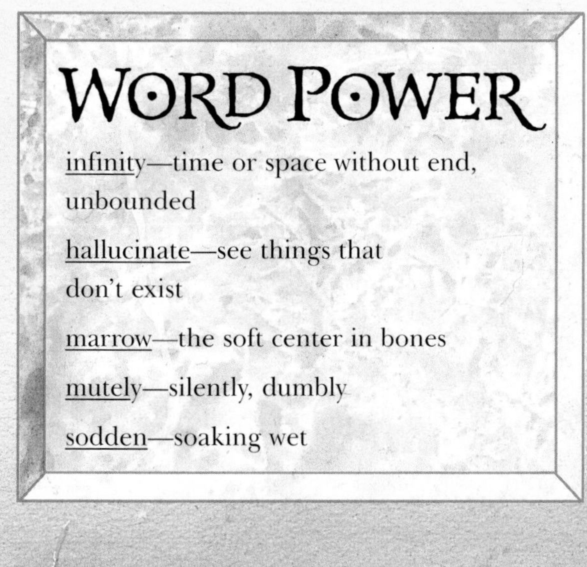

WORD POWER

infinity—time or space without end, unbounded

hallucinate—see things that don't exist

marrow—the soft center in bones

mutely—silently, dumbly

sodden—soaking wet

The two men waited mutely in the chamber—but then a hissing sound made them turn. Water was welling up from the dungeon, and they saw barrels of sodden gunpowder floating up.

Raoul and the Persian scrabbled against the slippery walls and reached the branches of the iron tree, where they hung on desperately.

"Christine… Christine!" was Raoul's last, pleading cry before he lost consciousness.

When the Persian awoke, he was back in his own bedroom. "You were found asleep, propped up near the door of the main entrance to the house," his servant told him.

Once he had recovered, the Persian went to look for Count Raoul and Christine, but no one had seen them. Returning home, he found an "unusual" visitor waiting. There, leaning against the mantelpiece, was the Phantom himself. But he was a changed man. His terrible face was covered by a mask of white wax, and his voice was weak and shaky.

"I must tell you that I am dying," he told the Persian. "Dying of love. I have kissed Christine—she looked so beautiful."

"For pity's sake! Tell me if she and Count Raoul are alive or dead!" cried the Persian.

"When I kissed her, she was alive," answered the Phantom. "And she has saved your lives. She pleaded with me to spare you both. Only then would she consent to be my wife. Then, when I agreed—and despite my terrible face—she gave me a kiss. Even my own mother could never bring herself to do that. I felt Christine's warm tears flow onto my face, but she did not run away. Then I realized how great her love must be for that young man. I could do nothing other than release her to him. They have left France to be married in Christine's own country."

The Phantom staggered and nearly fell over. "I was shot recently, and I feel that my end is near. I must go now, my friend, but I will let you know when I die."

Three weeks later, the Persian opened his newspaper to read the fateful announcement: "The Phantom is dead."

THE END